Second To Nun

Second To Nun

A GIULIA DRISCOLL MYSTERY

Alice Loweecey

HENERY PRESS

SECOND TO NUN
A Giulia Driscoll Mystery
Part of the Henery Press Mystery Collection

First Edition
Trade paperback edition | September 2015

Henery Press
www.henerypress.com

ISBN-13: 978-1-941962-93-0

Printed in the United States of America

To my family, who are still waiting to be killed off in a heart-wrenching scene in one of my books. Not this time, guys.

ACKNOWLEDGMENTS

As always, thanks to my Awesome Agent, Kent D. Wolf; and my terrific editor, Rachel Jackson. To Natalie Case, for sharing her Tarot expertise. To my fellow Hens for their continual support and encouragement. And to everyone whose phobias include clowns and creepy dolls, my apologies.

One

Hot, tired, and triumphant, Giulia Driscoll pushed open Driscoll Investigations' frosted glass door.

"Nobody talk to me until I rip these nylon torture devices off my legs."

She hung her purse on the coat rack and headed straight for the narrow bathroom. Seconds later, she stuffed her pantyhose into the pocket of her navy blue suit jacket and wiggled blissfully free toes. She opened the door again, carrying her low-heeled shoes in her left hand.

"A few years back, I thought pretending to be a nun again was the worst undercover job I'd ever have. Wrong. If that company calls me for a follow-up interview, I'm wearing pants."

Zane, her all-but-genius admin, looked at her with that expression men get when women are the most inscrutable creatures on the planet. Sidney, her perky, all-natural assistant, fist-bumped Giulia as she went past.

"If I ever try to institute a formal dress code here," Giulia said, "you have permission to pour cold water over my head until I come to my senses."

"Did they fall for it?" Zane said.

"Did you catch the cheating scumbag harassing the receptionist?" Sidney said.

"To answer Zane's question: Possibly. I gave the HR person ideal canned answers as much as I could. That's one reason I used my maiden name. You never know if someone's heard of Driscoll Investigations."

She pulled out a chair at the worktable under the single window and stretched her spine, dangling her head over the back of the chair and dropping the shoes in the same motion.

The position gave her an upside-down view of the stores across the street: The pizza place that filled the air with the aroma of frying sausage every morning, the celebrity tanning studio, the combination New Age/Tarot Reading shop, and the cell phone store on the corner. The pre-lunch rush had started. Several people headed into the cell phone store. The pizza delivery Honda pulled into traffic after a taxi and a city bus zoomed past. The tanning salon looked deserted, as always. A tall, white-haired woman in flowered capris and a blue camp shirt came out of the Tarot shop.

Zane said, "How soon did they ask you about your greatest weakness?"

Giulia sat up again and laughed. "It's one of the questions on the intake form."

Zane leaned forward, his white-blond hair falling over his eyes. "Do they think anyone answers that question honestly?"

"Maybe it's their inside joke. Sidney, the cheating scumbag did indeed harass the receptionist. He's so good at it—you know what I mean—that if I hadn't been looking for inappropriate touching I wouldn't have noticed anything out of the ordinary."

Zane mirrored Sidney's frown so well they looked like the positive and negative prints of a photograph. "Seriously, why is that receptionist putting up with his crap? This isn't the 1950s. The company's employee handbook has to have a section on sexual harassment."

"It's not that straightforward. The CEO and the scumbag are golf and drinking buddies. He's done this before and gotten away with it. He targets a low-level employee who can't afford to make trouble at the job. The receptionist's disabled father lives with her and her income pays the rent. She needs the job for that and the health insurance."

Sidney made a noise that sounded like an angry bear. "We've got giant hogweed in the fields behind our alpaca pasture. Let's toss him into it naked."

Giulia said, "Is it similar to poison ivy?"

"Not even close. Hogweed gets like ten feet tall and causes blisters and burns that can hang on for years."

"That's much better than my idea of dumping him into the koi fountain in the company's lobby." Giulia stood, still barefoot. "Did I miss anything around here?"

The door burst open. The white-haired woman from the Tarot shop strode in and looked at all three of them in turn.

"I need the owner, right now."

Giulia stepped forward. "I'm Giulia Driscoll. How may I help you?"

The woman grabbed Giulia's hand and dragged her toward the door. "I have to take you to Lady Rowan."

Giulia dug her heels into the just-buffed wood floor. "Release my hand, please."

The woman tugged harder. Giulia braced against her and kept herself in the same spot.

"Please release my hand."

"All right." The woman complied. "I'm sorry, but this is urgent. Lady Rowan told me that I must seek the Veiled Woman immediately."

Giulia glanced at Sidney and Zane, who both shrugged.

"She's the Tarot reader, of course." The woman pointed out the window with her left hand and reached into her straw purse with her right. "Here." She slapped a checkbook with a lighthouse cover on Zane's desk. "Private detectives get a retainer, right? They always do in the movies. You hold my checkbook while I take your boss to consult with Rowan. When we return I'll pay for this appointment."

Giulia slipped bare feet into her shoes. This promised to be much better than spying on a cheating husband. "Let's go."

Giulia and her new client walked side by side downstairs and out onto the sidewalk. Both women dodged a score of hurrying pedestrians.

"Those stairs are an accident waiting to happen. I'm MacAllister Stone. Everyone calls me Mac. Here's a gap in this insane traffic. Ready to run for it?"

They dashed across the street to the music of honking taxi horns and at least one physically impossible suggestion. Giulia figured Mac to be in her early seventies, but her fitness level shaved off a good twenty years.

"People these days have no manners." Mac led Giulia past the tanning salon's wide glass windows and under the New Age shop's deep purple awning.

The restrained storefront showcased different styles of Tarot decks for sale. A black velvet picture frame enclosed a rate sheet for various types of readings. The awning blocked the June sun, creating a pool of twilight for them to stand in. Mac opened the door and ushered Giulia inside. A bell chimed a single high note.

Opposite them, a huge vase filled with stargazer lilies sat on the floor between two flowered armchairs. The scent of violets hung in the air, but didn't overpower it. The dark floral carpet and mauve wallpaper completed the color scheme.

"Jasper, you're a lifesaver," Mac said to the ponytailed young man behind the counter.

"I can do more than blow stuff up, Aunt Mac." He held out a prosthetic hand to Giulia. "I'm Jasper Fortin, Lady Rowan's nephew."

Giulia shook hands. "I seem to be missing an essential clue here."

Jasper smiled. "Sorry. Hazard of the profession." He stepped over to a violet jacquard tapestry hanging in a doorway. "They're back."

A fluting voice answered, "Send them in, please."

He held aside the tapestry, still smiling. "Lady Rowan will see you now."

Mac led the way into a square, dim room with the same carpeting and wallpaper. A circular table and three Mission-style chairs took up seventy percent of the space.

A dark-haired woman faced them. "Ms. Driscoll, I'm relieved you agreed to come with Mac. Take the right-hand chair, please. Mac, the other is the chair you sat in earlier."

She pressed a remote control and recessed ceiling lights brightened, banishing the spooky atmosphere. "Much better. Let's get down to business."

Giulia sat in the indicated chair, trying to decide whether Lady Rowan was emulating Maria Ouspenskaya in *The Wolf Man* or going for cliché New Age Summer Fashion.

Rowan winked at her. "Certain customers expect the mysterious Hollywood getup, Ms. Driscoll. Mac here likes the whole cosplay treatment. If it were just you and me, I'd wear a business suit. You don't need the ambiance."

Giulia gave her points for reading all the nuances of the newcomer's body language.

"Rowan and I were sorority sisters," Mac said. "I think she looks adorable in all those scarves and shawls."

"I'm too old to qualify for adorable. Only because this place has excellent air-conditioning am I sporting the layered look today." She placed her hands on either side of the complex pattern of Tarot cards on the table. "This isn't your reading, Ms. Driscoll, so

I won't unpack everything. That would take another half-hour. The reason I sent Mac for you is this combination of the High Priestess, the Hanged Man, and the Moon."

The many bracelets on her arms jingled as she indicated the cards. "The High Priestess guards the veil of knowledge. When she combines with The Hanged Man in relation to Mac's situation, the meaning started to become plain to me. When I turned over the Moon card, everything settled into its proper place."

Giulia turned her polite smile on both of them. "I don't quite see what's been settled in relation to Driscoll Investigations."

Rowan cackled. "That was a beautifully subtle mood-killer. In brief, I told Mac that she was to do nothing without consulting she who uncovers the truth. I called Jasper in here. He's clairvoyant but needs more practice. He knew right away to whom the cards referred."

"You see?" Mac said. "The cards and Jasper directed me to you, the former nun. The Veiled Woman. You're meant to help me."

Giulia didn't have Rowan's people-reading skills, but she knew how to take control of a situation. Step one was to get back on her own turf. "I appreciate your confidence in me. If Lady Rowan will excuse us, we can discuss in my office the possibility of Driscoll Investigations taking you on as a client."

Rowan smacked the table with one multi-ringed hand. "See, Mac? Ms. Driscoll is already in charge. Go, go. Come back here afterward."

Mac popped up. "Of course. Ms. Driscoll, I should warn you that I have a wall covered with framed sales awards, and I haven't lost my touch."

Giulia stood and smoothed her suit skirt. "It was a pleasure meeting you, Lady Rowan."

In the outer room, Jasper was marking sale prices on essential oils. Three teenage girls entered the shop, giggling and whispering. Giulia led the way this time and Mac followed.

Three

Giulia closed the door to her private office.

"Mac, what exactly do you hope we can do for you?"

Mac settled in the client chair, a whole head taller than Giulia, even sitting down. "I think my family ghost is trying to evict me."

Giulia groped for words.

Mac smiled. "You think I'm batty. I know that look. Is it the Tarot or the ghost or both?"

Giulia put an answering smile on her face. "Not at all. I know several people who are skilled in Tarot reading. I was thinking that removing a ghost requires a different type of investigator."

"Nope." Mac shook her head with decision. "Rowan and I have been friends since we were seventeen years old. Her skills are the real thing. If she says I need you, I'm not arguing."

A client referred by Tarot was a first for DI. Giulia wanted to take her on, if only to watch Sidney's practical head explode. But ghost-hunting?

"Mac, in all seriousness, our usual caseload involves insurance fraud, background checks, and deadbeat parents. Tangible things."

Mac snorted. "Please. Who should I contact? That ghost chaser who buys infomercial space on late-night TV? The husband and wife team who advertise on Craigslist? No. I need a real private investigator and I want you. Give me ten more minutes of your time to convince you."

Giulia liked her enough to give her the chance. "Go ahead."

Mac leaned forward.

"My great-grandfather built Stone's Throw on Conneaut Lake as his family's home when he married my great-grandmother. He always wanted to live in a lighthouse. It was never a working one because the lake isn't deep enough or long enough for real shipping, but that didn't bother him. He and his wife had eleven children and twenty-seven grandchildren. They scattered all over North America and none of them wanted to take over the old place. It sat empty for two decades before I bought it."

She brought out an Android phone. "When I retired, I'd been regional manager for a hotel chain for thirty years. I knew I could turn Great-Grandpa's white elephant into a working bed and breakfast. I had plenty of real-world experience, enough money saved, and excellent credit. I sank everything into the renovations. I've been breaking even for seven years, but something's changed. Please look at these pictures."

Giulia came around the desk.

Mac held up the phone. "This is the inside of the lighthouse. See the scratches on the stairwell walls? They're higher than anyone can reach. I'm six foot one and they're a foot above my fingertips." She swiped to the next picture and enlarged it. "This is the living room. See behind the drapes? Those aren't my sheer white curtains." She swiped again. "This is the attic. I keep all my decorating supplies up here. I have the only key to the attic door. Now look at those cracks in the window facing the lake. Do you see anything?"

Giulia studied the random damage to the glass. All at once a pattern emerged. "It says 'Mine.'"

"Oh, good. You do see it." She returned the phone to her straw purse. "I bet you're going to tell me there are simple, logical explanations for everything I just showed you. Perhaps the scratches are cracks in the old plaster or bird claw marks. Maybe the white curtain is really fog or sea mist. By chance an unseen flaw in manufacture appeared in the glass as it got old. Am I right?"

"I'd want to see everything in person before making that call."

Mac's wrinkles all scrunched together from her huge grin. "I was hoping you'd say that. Okay, look. There's a lot more to this: We have a family tradition of a lost hoard of gold coins that might be involved, plus a psychic I've hired to do weekly séances and who's convinced one of my ancestors has turned into a Woman in White."

Giulia took a legal pad and a pen out of her center drawer. "We need to start at the beginning."

"Not here. On the premises is best. I want you to stay at Stone's Throw. Are you married?"

"Yes."

"Good. That wasn't meant to be rude. Stone's Throw is all about the romantic getaway. If the Veiled Woman comes to me, I know you'll fix my ghost problem." She reached into her purse, but came up empty.

Giulia buzzed Zane. "Would you bring Ms. Stone her checkbook, please?"

After Zane closed them in again, Mac gestured for Giulia's pen. "What are your rates?"

Giulia told her the usual retainer amount and the per-diem fees while Mac wrote a check.

"Here you go, plus your time today. Now." She pulled Giulia's legal pad toward her, wrote a dollar figure, and reversed the pad. "This is my offer for you and your husband to evict whoever or whatever is trying to ruin my business."

Frank would've whistled. Giulia restrained herself. "That's serious money."

"Nobody alive or dead is going to force me into a retirement home to crochet afghans until my brain atrophies. Today's Thursday. I have a free room starting tomorrow night. I'll keep it open for you and your husband. I don't want my obituary to read 'Death by Ghost.'"

Four

Giulia went straight to the window after her new client left. Mac crossed the street and headed directly for the Tarot shop.

"Giulia." Sidney's plaintive voice reached out to her. "You are a cruel boss to leave us in suspense. You have to tell us what the Tarot client said."

Giulia turned to face the room. Zane and Sidney weren't even pretending to work. They turned their chairs to her and leaned forward in tandem.

"She thinks her house is haunted."

Sidney snorted. "You're kidding. There's no such things as ghosts."

"She's quite serious."

Sidney's suspicion eyebrow went up. "She looked pretty happy when she left. Did she hire us?"

"She did. I will be heading to Stone's Throw Bed and Breakfast, possibly tomorrow, to thwart either a cranky ghost or a phony psychic."

For half a second Giulia thought Sidney's head really was going to explode.

"Zane, tell her there's no such things as ghosts. You're the computer brain in a human shell."

Zane didn't answer for a moment. "I'm not prepared to give a definitive answer on the subject."

Giulia cut off Sidney's reply. "Why not?"

"I've never experienced anything supernatural, but my grandmother told us a lot of stories. Half of them could've been made up to scare us on a summer night. But if the others were even partially true, there's some weird shit out there. I beg your pardon."

"That's okay. Mac mentioned something called a Woman in White."

Zane nodded. "*La Llorona.*"

"Who?" Sidney said.

"It's a spirit legend in dozens of countries. Sometimes it's considered an omen of death."

"If she hired the psychic to conjure up this death omen once a week to entertain the guests, it was an extra good marketing choice on her part," Giulia said. "Anyway, now she's found what she thinks are evidences of an actual haunting."

Zane frowned. "If she has a poltergeist, why is she talking to us? Oh, right. The Tarot reader across the street told her to. Do you know her? Him?"

"No, but our reputation preceded us. When the Tarot reader told Mac to do nothing until she consulted the veiled woman, the reader's nephew pointed her over here." Giulia snagged one of Zane's retro pink "While You Were Out" notepads and wrote two names. "Can you check Rowan Fortin for fraud and otherwise bilking the gullible, and can you find out if Jasper has a war record? He has a prosthetic hand and dropped a casual remark about explosions, but that means nothing."

Sidney dragged a hand over her face. "We don't hunt ghosts. Right? Please say I'm right."

Giulia tried not to enjoy Sidney's theatrics, without success. "Correct. But we do hunt humans who commit clever acts of vandalism with the goal of perhaps getting their hands on prime waterfront property. Mac's place is on Conneaut Lake."

As he typed, Zane said, "I've been there. It's a typical quaint tourist trap, but all the hotels and bars were packed every night."

"I suppose the psychic is her drawing card. Movie night isn't enough entertainment for the price of a bed and breakfast."

A strangled squeak from Sidney. "What are we going to do out there? Get an EMF meter to whirr and beep as we wave it at dark corners in the basement?"

"Wait a minute, Ms. Skeptic," Giulia said. "How do you know about EMF detectors?"

"Olivier watches those ghost hunter shows. He says it relaxes him." She made a gagging face.

"*We* are not going to do this. I am," Giulia said. "You know I don't take on extra work only to dump it in your laps. I'll go up to Conneaut Lake tomorrow. Hopefully Frank will be able to get the next few days off and join me. Stone's Throw is a non-working lighthouse. Our new client carried out massive renovations when she bought the place. I'm confident I'll find a bunch of creaking boards and settling foundations as the cause of her haunting."

"Why the overnight stay, then?" Zane's voice was distant as he read his screen.

"It's not the ghost I'm concerned about; it's the psychic. Mac might be cutthroat in sales, but her weakness for psychics is like a bright red target painted on her back."

More typing from Zane. "Speaking as one with a mortgage and utility bills every month, a steady gig is a good thing. Why would her psychic mess with it?"

"Mac also mentioned a family legend of buried gold."

Sidney said, "Greed. People suck. Now that I'm running my own house I'm suspicious of anything that remotely smells like a scam. You remember that driveway repair guy who tried to fast-talk Mom and Dad into putting gunk all over the store's parking lot?"

"Didn't he just get arrested?" Zane said.

"You bet, and I was one of the ones who blew him in. It cost the old folks at the next farm four thousand dollars to repair the damage he did to their place." She sat up straighter. "So, my lesson for the day is: Don't trust anybody."

"It's getting so I can't argue with that advice," Giulia said.

"Ms. D., preliminary sleuthing results in good news and bad news," Zane said. "The bad news is Rowan Fortin, born Matilda

Jane but changed her name legally on her eighteenth birthday, has never been indicted for fraud. Her last business tanked in 2002 and she filed for bankruptcy. She fell off the radar until 2010, when she opened a Tarot reading shop in Wilkes-Barre. The local newspaper ran a series of articles in 2013 on a mall developer's land grab in which many small businesses were forced to relocate because of massive rent hikes. She moved to Cottonwood last summer and opened up the place across the street. Nothing since."

Giulia frowned. "My hunches can't be right all the time. What's the good news?"

"Jasper Fortin is a decorated war veteran who saved the lives of five fellow soldiers when he lost his hand. Uh...much technical jargon and...summarizing it with war hero, great guy, women everywhere want to marry him. Worst thing I can find? Facebook pics of a tattoo on an R-rated body part."

Giulia made an "eh" gesture. "Just once I'd like an easy suspect. At least my hunches are redeemed. I got a good vibe from him."

Sidney spoke through her cupped hands, creating a hollow voice. "Maybe he hypnotized you."

"Or his prosthetic hand implanted a control chip in mine when we shook hands." She shook her head. "I have to stop watching so many late-night sci-fi movies."

Five

Giulia walked the few steps into her office and came back with a fresh legal pad out of the filing cabinet.

"Zane, you're my expert today. What do you know about the type of ghost called the Woman in White?"

Zane got a faraway look for several seconds before he refocused on Giulia and Sidney.

"A friend of my grandmother married a widower whose first wife died in childbirth and who lost the baby as well. My grandmother's friend had four children with her new husband. Soon after each birth, she woke up in the night to see a ghostly woman hovering over the crib and heard a faint voice singing a lullaby."

Giulia said, "Did the ghost ever harm the mother or the children?"

"Giulia," Sidney said.

"No," Zane said.

"That makes the Stone's Throw ghost a different type," Giulia said. "Sidney, don't wail at me again. It's unprofessional to rule out any possibility before examining the evidence."

"At least something today makes logical sense," Sidney said.

Giulia pretended not to hear. "Zane, do you have any stories of angry ghosts?"

"One, but it's way out there. My grandmother also told us about her oldest son, one of my uncles. He was a party animal in college. Liked to get drunk four nights out of seven. His grades tanked and he was about to get kicked out of school. One night he stumbled up the stairs to his frat house and the door wouldn't open. He fished out his key and scraped it on the door until he found the lock, and it still wouldn't budge. He banged and shouted and suddenly, bam! The door flew wide open, knocking him flat on his back. He looked up and saw his dead father looming over him. His father's hair was undulating in all directions, his face was chalk-white, and his eyes were sunken, but my uncle could see pupils burning with red flames. The ghost didn't say anything out loud, but my uncle swore he heard its voice in his head, threatening to make his life a living hell if he didn't shape up."

He took a breath. Sidney stirred in her chair, restlessness in every movement.

Zane spoke more to Giulia now. "Here's the thing: Our family moved to America twenty years before this story happened and worked hard to assimilate. My uncle knew maybe a dozen words in Estonian, most of them scatological. He taught them to us when our grandmother wasn't around. He told us this story when my brothers and sisters and I were between eight and twelve. He swore up and down that his father's ghost spoke right inside his head in Estonian and he understood every word. He said as soon as the ghost vanished he crawled to the edge of the porch and puked all over the bushes. Later on, when it was just the boys of the family, he confided that he also ruined his boxers, if you get me."

"Zane, no offense," Sidney said, "but that story sounds like something deliberately manufactured to make you kids stay away from alcohol."

"We thought so at first. We were cynical little brats. My oldest sister and I researched ghost legends and cornered our uncle a week later with our findings. He vowed on the heads of the gods the story was true. He went through the legends we showed him and described the ways his experience differed." Zane shrugged. "He didn't change from a party guy into a monk or anything extreme like that, but he did graduate with a 3.1 GPA and two job offers."

"Speaking as devil's advocate," Giulia said, "perhaps your grandmother planned it to get her son back on track and convinced one of her other sons to play ghost?"

"We thought of that too. My uncle said his father's ghost hovered over him like that angry mom ghost in *Ju-On*. Have you seen that movie?"

"No way," Sidney said. "I like to sleep at night."

"Wuss," Giulia said. "I saw it in a double feature with *Ringu*. Zane, your uncle's ghost story occurred before those movies came out, right?"

"Decades before. He said that hovering ghost in *Ju-On* scared him almost as much as the actual ghost that night on the porch." Zane spread his hands. "That's all I got."

Giulia stood. "So despite my personal lack of experience, ghosts possibly exist. In the opposite corner, because of Sidney's lack of personal experience, ghosts do not exist. Neither choice negates the possibility that a live human could be playing poltergeist in that lighthouse. I'm still going in with a hypothesis of greedy psychic is greedy. Thanks for the crash course in hauntings. Can you carve out an hour to dig a little deeper into those two?"

Zane checked his onscreen schedule. "I can between four and five. I think tonight's group game night will include Call of Duty: Ghosts. For some reason, I'm in the mood."

Sidney shivered. "I'm going home and playing with Jessamine for two hours straight as soon as Jane gets here."

Giulia snapped her fingers. "Jane. I knew there was something else on my to-do list. If she shows up, don't let her into my office until I open the door."

She sat in her desk chair and soaked in the atmosphere of the room. The linen-lookalike curtains rippled in the breeze. The soft lemon walls evoked morning sunshine. She loved the design of this space, a combination of restful colors and business efficiency. Her focus shifted away from ghosts and psychics and Tarot cards. Now that Sidney was back part-time from maternity leave, Jane's temporary employment as Sidney's replacement would end in two weeks. Giulia knew an excellent full-time job fit for Jane, and had the power to all but make it happen.

She picked up the phone and called the Ninth Precinct, but not to talk to her husband.

"Captain Reilly, please...Jimmy? It's Giulia. You know how you're always trying to lure me into working for you? Let me tell you about my temp."

Six

Giulia finished explaining to Jimmy what an asset Jane would be to the Ninth Precinct. It wasn't even one thirty and her "Must Complete Now" task list had quadrupled. Well, complaining wouldn't get anything done. Lunch would. She got up for probably the last time today and opened her door.

"Anyone going—Hi, Jane."

Sidney was eating something natural on whole wheat at her desk. Zane was gone. Jane had a brown bag in hand.

"Bad timing. Not you, Jane. My multitasking. What's up?"

"Developments on the insurance fraud case."

Giulia waved her through the open doorway. "My office? I just need to get some lunch up here."

Jane followed Giulia in and closed the door. Giulia called downstairs to Common Grounds, the coffee and lunch shop, and ordered the special with a Coke.

"I'm all yours, Jane. Go ahead and eat."

This Jane was slightly mellower than the Jane of three months ago who'd bristled at any perceived slight and plastered makeup over her tattoos. She stood taller and smiled now and then. Giulia attributed that to steady employment and Jane's discovery of an unexpected talent at shadowing people.

Today emerald streaks embellished her black hair. Her green sleeveless shirt picked up the highlights. She pulled a four-by-six spiral-bound notebook out of her backpack.

"I won't eat until I report, Ms. D. I need my notes to summarize. Our middle-aged husband went to his stockbroker job as usual. His charming wife entertained guests, relaxed in her garden, and otherwise was an ornament to the neighborhood."

Giulia frowned. "That's no help to us."

"It gets better. Tonight they're invited to a political fundraiser. Three hundred bucks a plate. If she's going to wear her supposedly stolen diamonds, it'll be then."

"We need pictures."

"Already on it. I borrowed a swanky party dress from my sister. You should see the updo wig I found. I look positively middle class in it."

"Make sure you keep track of your hours. I'm sure you've worked more than twenty this week."

"You bet." Jane hesitated. "Would you write a reference letter for me? When we finish this insurance fraud business I've got to start job hunting again."

"Of course. You've been terrific. I'm going to miss you."

Jane smiled. "Zane gave me an open-ended invitation to join his gamer crowd. You'll still hear my name once in a while."

Sidney knocked and opened. "Nine bucks with tip, please." She set a Coke and a plastic container with a sandwich and salad on Giulia's desk.

Giulia handed her the money.

"I'm out of here," Sidney said. "Jessamine has a checkup tomorrow morning, so I'll be in after that."

"Sounds good," Giulia said to her, then to Jane: "Go eat. Shoo. Excellent work. I've got a thousand items to plow through and no time for fun things like conversation." As Jane opened the door, Giulia called her back. "I'm going out of town early tomorrow afternoon. Can you be in here by ten to let me know what happened at the fundraiser?"

Jane wilted, but rallied a moment later. "I'll set two alarms."

Giulia ripped several pages from the legal pad and spread them out on her desk. One she labeled "Cheating Husband," the next "Insurance Fraud," the third "Diocesan Retainer," and the fourth "Haunted Lighthouse."

She stabbed a plastic fork into the Caesar salad. "I need to clone myself."

Since that wasn't about to happen in the near or far future, she turned her usual business methods upside down and started out of order with the Diocesan Retainer.

Okay, she'd lied about not getting out of her chair. To take care of that item, she needed the file from Sidney's desk. Chewing on a bite of ham and pepper jack on wheat, she found the fluorescent green folder in the middle slot of Sidney's inbox.

Back at her own desk, she read the two-page contract twice. Ever since she and Frank had quietly taken care of a massive drug-dealing scandal at Giulia's old convent, the Diocese of Pittsburgh had made DI their preferred digger of dirt. It made perfect sense to convince the Diocese to agree to a monthly retainer.

Zane returned. Giulia called him in. He put on an innocent expression when he saw the open green folder.

"Say it," Giulia said.

"You've been spinning your wheels on the final retainer version for days," he said. "You don't usually take this long to make a decision."

"I don't trust the Diocese's lawyer. He was in the first senior class I taught thirteen years ago. He was underhanded at age seventeen and he didn't seem to have changed much at our retainer negotiation meetings."

"You trust our lawyer, don't you?"

"I have to. He's one of my brothers-in-law." Giulia sat back in her chair. "Besides, Mom Driscoll would never raise a dishonest son."

"You married into a useful family." Zane crossed his arms. "It resolves to one question: Do you have any reason not to sign this retainer?"

Giulia hesitated only a fraction of a second. "No." She signed all three copies of the last page and jogged all the pages together.

"This is as good as we can make it. The church might think it's getting the better part of this deal, but they don't have to make a budget stretch to cover rent, salaries, and health insurance every month. A guaranteed monthly income is like having a birthday present every thirty days." She handed the folder to Zane. "Please write a cover letter and courier this to the Bishop's office for their countersignatures."

"Your hardworking staff agrees about the monthly birthday present." Zane patted the folder and headed to his computer.

Next ball in her juggling performance: The cheating scumbag, also known as Flynt. She connected her phone to her computer and uploaded the surreptitious photos she'd taken after her phony job interview.

Flynt leaning on the receptionist's desk as Giulia crossed the lobby. Her own fingers as she palmed the phone for a better angle. Flynt handing the receptionist a cup of tea. She'd tried to refuse it but he pushed it into her hand, prolonging the contact of his fingers on top of hers.

Giulia repeatedly held down the button to take several pictures in rapid succession. Her targets shifted in and out of frame as she'd pretended to search for her car keys. Flynt then pulled his own undercover stunt. He appeared to walk away, but as he passed behind the receptionist he trailed his fingers up her arm and rested his hand on the back of her neck.

"Thank you, Saint Veronica." Giulia enlarged one beautiful, slightly off-kilter picture of Flynt's middle finger stroking up into the receptionist's hairline.

She opened the ongoing report for her client, Flynt's wife, and inserted that photo uncropped.

Not enough.

She checked the spreadsheet she'd created of Flynt's usual weekly schedule. Bingo. Golf every Friday morning. If Flynt didn't change his pattern, she could wrap up this case tomorrow afternoon. The pantyhose-and-suit torture would not be squandered.

Her fingers pounded the keys as she summarized five weeks of work, inserting placeholders on the last two pages for tomorrow's coup de grâce photos.

Zane poked his head around the doorframe. "Ready for DI's version of *The Scoop*?"

Seven

Giulia held her pen ready to write. "Let's see. What would make that slimy TMZ-wannabe local TV show sit up and beg? Rowan is an undercover Homeland Security agent and Jasper's prosthetic hand secretly records every Tarot reading for code words?"

Zane stared at her, unblinking, for a long second.

For the umpteenth time, Giulia reminded herself that Zane was still adjusting to working in a casual atmosphere with humans, not in telemarketing hell micromanaged by angry demons recently passed over for promotion.

"You have to admit *The Scoop* would kill during sweeps week with that story. What did you discover?"

After one more second, Zane said, "Rowan's been married four times. Number three is the real reason the mall developer hiked the rent to force all those small businesses to shut down. The developer claimed Rowan stole her husband, so she convinced her company to locate the mall right on top of Rowan's business."

Giulia held up a finger, finished a sentence, and said, "A little tame for *The Scoop*."

"That was Act One. In Act Two, Rowan's husband divorces her and remarries the developer."

"This is where I say that perhaps a good Tarot reader might have seen this coming if she ever did a reading for herself." Giulia made a wry face. "But that would be judgmental."

Zane winked. Giulia considered that a sign of hope.

"Rowan moved to Cottonwood after the divorce," he continued, "and opened the shop across the street with her nephew, Jasper."

"Wait. You said four husbands."

"I did. Rowan's fourth is one of Jasper's fellow explosive experts who now runs an Army-Navy surplus store unhindered by his artificial legs, plural. Before you ask, he's ten years older than Jasper. Rowan is seventy-four. Jasper is thirty."

"True love?"

"More like true beef bourguignon. I compared his photo in the newspaper at his store's grand opening with one of his Memorial Day TV commercials. He's at least forty pounds heavier now."

"Zane, you made a joke. No, no, stop looking guilty. I'm always pleased when you get a little more comfortable working here."

The blush stuck on Zane's cheeks. "So anyway, Rowan's still paying off three separate divorce lawyer debts. The mortgage on their house is in her husband's name, but the payments are on time."

"I disagree with your earlier assessment." Giulia smiled up at him. "*The Scoop* likes dirt. This skirts the edges of heartwarming."

He shook his head. "On the surface. He drinks. She's got a bunch of rich women on the hook."

Giulia reread the last paragraph. "As con artists go, I've seen worse."

Zane's eyebrows rose. "If this really was an episode of *The Scoop*, everything I've described would turn out to be the front of Rowan and Jasper's two-man operation to bleed those rich women."

Giulia did not let one centimeter of her internal grin appear. "Does your assessment arise from a new film noir game on Steam or too many late nights of *CSI* reruns?"

He ducked his head, hiding his eyes beneath his hair. "Binge-watching *Columbo* on Netflix."

Giulia did chuckle at that. Zane's throaty baritone could double for Columbo as well as Sam Spade.

"Okay, then. Whether Rowan is a gifted Tarot reader or a fraud is irrelevant for our purpose. She has enough financial reasons to be frightening her old sorority sister into abandoning her waterfront property. What about the nephew? Is he parlaying his war hero status into a charming and sympathetic lure for rich women and Mac as well?"

Zane rocked one hand back and forth. "Still working on him. He's for real, though: Has a Purple Heart. His debt is minimal. His degree is in engineering, but he's never used it. No significant other. He hunts in season and knows a lot about single malts. Sees a VA shrink for PTSD."

Giulia frowned. "Good-looking, heroic, eligible male with minimal flaws. No wonder his aunt's shop has giggling teenage girl clientele." She tapped her pen on the yellow paper. "I'm not cynical enough to believe a war hero is running a con with his eccentric elderly aunt. But I might have to be."

"Let me dig some more," Zane said. "How long will you be here tomorrow?"

"At least through lunch. The stars need to align for me to catch Flynt with his current mistress tomorrow morning, so I can finish that report, add pictures, and call in Flynt's wife. Plus Jane's insurance fraud case, plus anything else that may walk through the door."

"At least it's never boring," Zane said.

Eight

In the backyard after supper, Giulia told Frank about her new client and the impending road trip.

"A bed and breakfast?" Frank set two beers on a small square table between two lawn chairs. "Those places are crawling with snowbirds and tourists."

"Snowbirds go to bed early. Tourists go out drinking." Giulia unreeled the hose and started watering her tomato plants.

"True, but it'll be crammed with atmosphere and kitsch." He started on his beer. "Like candles and doilies and antimacassars, whatever they are."

Giulia laughed. "B&Bs are not old ladies' retirement homes." She tugged on the hose. "Could you unkink for me?"

Frank leaned over as far as possible without leaving his chair, tilting it on two legs, and snagged the bent hose with three fingers. He whipped it around itself as his chair *thunked* back onto the grass. "There you go."

"That was either quite clever or quite lazy." She turned the water onto the peppers. "Thank you."

"Clever, of course."

The three preschool-aged boys next door splashed in an inflatable pool. In the long backyard behind both houses, two Boston Terriers yipped at the hose, and the boys streaked back and forth along the chain link fence, chased each other, and began the cycle over again.

Giulia looked in the bushes for fireflies, but it wasn't dark enough yet.

"The peppers are too small to be any use," Frank said as she finished watering the rest of the garden and sat in the other chair.

"It's only June. Wait a few weeks. Full-grown peppers don't appear in the grocery store by magic."

They drank beer in silence as the neighborhood's evening rituals progressed. At seven fifteen the terriers zipped into their front yard and commenced their nightly barking trash-talk with the Rottweiler from the end of the block as his owner walked him. The rolls and clacks of a street hockey game interspersed with tapped car horns and the players booing the drivers, followed by laughter and more clacks and rolls.

Any leftover tension slipped from Giulia's shoulders.

"Scheduling everything is my real concern about three or four or five days at Stone's Throw," she said. "Can Zane and Sidney handle it with Sidney and Jane still both at part-time? When we need to connect, how good is the Wi-Fi out by the lake? People don't come to a pricey vacation house to check Facebook."

"They'd Instagram."

"True. Good publicity for the B&B. Which reminds me." She went back inside and returned with her iPad. "Let's see what Trip Advisor has to say."

Frank sighed. "Woman, you're off the clock."

"We are researching a vacation spot." She arched her brows at him.

"At least I knew you were a workaholic when I married you."

"And I knew you were a sports fiend. They cancel each other out." She typed in the name. "Whoa. There're a whole bunch of places named 'Stone's Throw.' Want to spend a week at a jewelry store or a recording studio or any one of a dozen bar and grill joints? Don't answer that."

"That name is cute." His face expressed the opposite opinion.

"Agreed. Here's our Stone's Throw on Trip Advisor from Halloween of last year: 'Loved the haunted lighthouse tour and the antique decorations. The themed activities were fun without being cutesy.'" She scrolled down. "Another one, same week: 'The decorations and activities were corny but the owner gets points for enthusiasm. Would not return that week, but would any other week.'"

"Why book Halloween week if you're not going to get into the spirit of the thing?"

"Perhaps they expected something quaint and Victorian with period costumes and a taffy pull. A third review says: 'I lost a year of my life between the haunted tour and whatever was rigged up in the attic. Didn't sleep a wink on October 31. Loved it and will return next year.'"

Frank stopped at the last swallow of his beer. "Why do you have that look?"

"She's added a weekly séance to the amenities. All season, not just at Halloween."

"Someone wants to make sure the regulars aren't bored."

"Someone is hooked on psychics." Giulia sipped her beer. "Ugh. It's getting warm." She finished the last two inches. "Can't let a Murphy's Irish Red go to waste."

The terriers ran into their backyard, woofing and nipping each other. The mother next door stood up from her chair next to the pool. The kids splashed onto the grass, whining but obedient.

The foghorn-on-steroids noise of a vuvuzela echoed up and down the street.

"It must be eight o'clock," Frank said. "The younger Templeton brat is right on time. Next on the program: Mama Templeton."

A woman's high-pitched voice: "Time to come in, Rupert!"

Frank said, "Three. Two. One."

A young boy's voice: "Five more minutes, Ma!"

Giulia said, "Cue the next vuvuzela blast."

The horn shattered the evening again.

"I'll get you, Roland."

The boy's voice again. "All right, Ma."

"Life imitates *Mary Poppins*," Giulia said.

"Heaven forbid. Can you picture that little monster with a cannon?"

"Not if I want to sleep at night." She leaned forward with her elbows on her knees. "Coming back to the scheduling. I plan to wrap up two separate cases tomorrow, assuming cooperation from thieves and scumbags. We've got three other active cases, with Sidney and Jane both part-time for two more weeks. Sidney hasn't taken on this level of responsibility before."

"Are you saying that closing the office last year for our honeymoon was short-sighted?"

"No, because I would've obsessed for the entire week, and so would you. But I can't stay at a B&B by myself. They're a couples thing. Remember how you've been saying you need more time with your wife?"

"I'm still saying it."

"Can you get time off on such short notice? If you can't, a whole chunk of wife-time will be delayed by several days." When Frank didn't reply, she added, "Did I mention the large fee she offered?"

"You did, and a very nice number it was, too. Then again—"

Giulia put a finger on his lips. "I already thought it. The very size of the fee makes it suspicious."

Frank sucked on the tip of her finger. Giulia lost her train of thought. He released her finger, grinning, and stood.

"I'll check the schedule tomorrow morning with Jimmy and see if I can get away. Several days of wife-time is worth encountering a few antimacassars."

Nine

Because the bright copper Nunmobile might be a little too memorable, Giulia waited near Flynt's house in Frank's maroon Camry Friday morning. Clouds threatened Flynt's weekly golf outing, but she had no doubt a true adherent of the Religion of Golf wouldn't cancel for anything less than nuclear war.

At six forty-five, Flynt came out the side door of his two-story Colonial carrying a golf bag and pressed something in his hand. The garage door swung up and open.

As Flynt tossed the bag into the back of his SUV, twin girls about six years old in identical Hello Kitty dresses ran out of the house. Giulia rolled down her window an inch.

"You didn't kiss us goodbye, Daddy!"

Flynt scooped up one in each arm. "Daddy thought you were sleeping." He kissed them and set them down. "You help your mommy while I'm gone, okay?"

"We will." They ran back inside and waved from the door as Flynt backed out.

Giulia didn't have to see through the SUV's windows to be certain he turned his charming smile on his daughters.

"You give pond scum a bad name, Flynt." Giulia started the Camry and pulled out into the street before the SUV turned the corner. She followed it for a mile and a quarter. They passed the golf course entrance and turned into the exclusive housing development adjacent to the back nine. The SUV parked in the driveway of a three-story mansion complete with pillared porch in the front and tennis court out back.

Giulia parked at the end of the empty street. In these places, even though every house possessed an attached garage, the Camry could still pass muster. If anyone bothered to look out their window, it could be taken as a real estate agent's car or even someone scoping out the neighborhood with an eye to moving in.

Giulia slipped her camera in her right jacket pocket and her telephoto lens in the left and zipped everything closed. Then she stood next to the car in her warm-up suit and went through her pre-run stretch routine. Two minutes of that and she power walked down one side of the long block and up the other. Beads of sweat formed at her hairline and in the small of her back. The motionless air promised lots of rain. She'd have to improvise a shield for her camera lens.

Without breaking stride, she left the street and walked between the blind sides of the pillared house and the gabled one next to it.

The development had been around long enough to rate real-sized trees in the backyards. Climbable trees, she'd discovered when she'd checked out the development last week. When she left the security of the houses, she hid behind a spruce, dashed over to another, avoided three birches because their trunks wouldn't conceal a supermodel, and finished up at an oak three times her height.

She climbed onto a branch so sturdy her weight barely rustled the leaves. Her butt complained at the rough seat, but she ignored it and put her camera together. The view wasn't quite what she wanted, so she squirmed around and stretched prone on the branch, wriggling farther along until two smaller branches supported her elbows.

This position gave her an unobstructed view across the backyard, over the tennis court, and one story above the ginormous gas grill, straight into the master bedroom. Several prior visits to this little stretch of woods confirmed that Flynt's mistress seldom closed her bedroom curtains. Squirrels and birds were her only back neighbors, for which Giulia thanked the development's landscapers.

A Biblical storm chose that moment to break. Giulia never cursed, ever, but this downpour tested her resolve. Of course it couldn't be a light summer shower. She pulled her jacket over her head and the camera. Water pummeled her back and poured into her pants.

Fortunately, Giulia had plenty to distract her. The mistress hadn't wasted time while Giulia played dedicated athlete up and down the street.

She envied the mistress' hourglass figure and how well she filled out her glittery push-up bra and matching panties. The mistress was already on her knees and Flynt's knickers were on the floor. Knickers. Did the man think he was Bobby Jones? Did Bobby Jones play golf commando style? Did golf historians have access to such details?

Her attempt at distracting herself failed. Giulia's face heated with embarrassment as she took a stream of salacious pictures.

During those first months out of the convent four years ago, she'd eaten at her friend's soup kitchen because her minimum wage job couldn't cover food and rent. Of all the better-paying jobs she was now qualified for, she could say with confidence that hiding in a tree taking close-ups of a nearly naked woman performing fellatio on a cheating husband was never a planned part of that list.

She wiped stray spatters off the lens to get a clearer shot of Flynt's face. When his mistress led him to bed, Giulia adjusted her position again to capture both of them in the frame.

Oh, joy.

But for Giulia's purposes, the mistress couldn't have picked a better morning to cowgirl Flynt. Giulia finished her Friday morning voyeurism with a telephoto series of damning pictures.

When the volume of their shouts got loud enough to cover any noise Giulia might make, she slid down the drenched tree and squelched between the houses back to the street.

Even if anyone had seen her power walk earlier, the still-pouring rain gave her an obvious reason to skip her usual set of cool down exercises.

The illusion of a nondescript adult varying her morning workout routine complete, Giulia squished into the driver's seat and drove away. Good thing she'd planned to go home and change out of her stalking clothes.

The XXX peep show she'd documented kept playing in her head. Maybe 7-Eleven sold eye bleach.

She let herself into the house, left her shoes on the mat by the door between the garage and kitchen, and took off her socks before she left a trail of wet footprints.

"I'm back," she said as she opened the bathroom door.

Frank stuck his head around the shower curtain. "You're wet."

"Taking pictures of a cheating husband during a downpour will do that." Giulia peeled off her jeans and shirt. "Even my underwear is soaked." She dropped her bra and panties on the pile of clothes.

Frank's hand grasped her bare arm and pulled her toward the shower. "Come get warm."

Giulia stepped into the tub. "There's shampoo in your hair." She backed her husband under the water and sluiced away white foam until his head was ginger again.

"Want me to wash your back?" He pulled her against his chest.

"Yes, please."

Ten

At nine fifteen, Giulia stood in line at Common Grounds in wet hair, dry clothes, and perfect contentment. Neither she nor Frank had time to make coffee at home after that shower.

"Giulia! You've been neglecting our croissants." The barista poured Giulia a large French roast without asking.

"I've been keeping weird hours, Mingmei. Caramel syrup, please."

"You don't want that. We've got mint chocolate brownie now." The petite black-haired woman wagged the syrup bottle in Giulia's face.

"You've won me over. Inject my coffee with that and tell me when you got the ear helix piercing."

"A couple of weeks ago. Hurt worse than the belly button one, remember? Tell me how much you like my dragon cuff." She put a lid on the coffee.

"It's beautiful. His sapphire eyes go with your hair." Giulia stepped back and studied the pastry shelves.

"Don't bother." Mingmei reached into the lower shelf and brought out a fresh croissant filled with apples and cinnamon.

"You know me too well." Giulia paid for breakfast. "Girls' night out soon?"

"Vacation next week, but maybe at the end of the month. I'll call you. Have to get your drinking in before Frank knocks you up."

Giulia blushed. Mingmei pounced.

"What's that face mean? Are you pregnant and didn't tell me?"

Giulia glanced around her at the full tables and the five people in line behind her. Everyone not focused on their cell phones was smiling. She glared at Mingmei, who was laughing now.

"No, I'm not pregnant. We're too busy for that. We're planning a family eventually, and thank you for discussing my reproductive capabilities in a public place. I'll find out the patron saint of inappropriate questions and pray to her for you." She tried to keep the glare through this speech, but lost it halfway through.

Mingmei laughed even harder. "Take your breakfast and get out of here before the boss catches me having fun."

"It would serve you right." Giulia stuck out her tongue at her friend and left.

Giulia tried the coffee on her way upstairs and decided it was delicious but more suited to a cold winter day. Probably the mint.

From his desk, Zane said, "Good morning, boss. Why do I suddenly want Girl Scout Thin Mint cookies?"

Giulia wafted the steam from her coffee toward him.

He inhaled. "I don't do flavored coffee, but I might make an exception for that."

"Downstairs. They cater to your every sugary need." She flipped the light switch in her separate office.

The door opened again. Giulia turned and saw a member of the local courier service Driscoll Investigations always used.

"Morning. Delivery from the Bishop's office."

Giulia signed the carbonless slip and took possession of the nine-by-twelve envelope. She listened for the sound of the downstairs door closing behind the courier before she tore the envelope open. When she saw the countersigned retainer agreement she whooped and kissed the top copy.

"Steady income for the next twelve months. Today is a very good day."

Zane opened the window. "We can expect year-end bonuses, right?" After a deep inhale, he said, "Now I want Thin Mints and pizza."

"For breakfast?" Giulia said from behind her desk.

"As a responsible adult, I have the freedom to eat cookies and pizza for breakfast if I choose."

Sidney's voice in the doorway groaned in response. "Do you have any idea of the amount of chemicals in processed baked goods? I won't even mention the hormones added to pig feed that end up in the sausages."

"Good morning, Sidney," Giulia and Zane said.

"I won't lie and say that sausage and pepperoni on a pizza don't smell really good." The beeps and clicks of Sidney's computer starting up punctuated her words. "But I'd never, ever put those poisons in my body or in Jessamine's."

"I'm still kind of disappointed you didn't name her mini-Sidney," Giulia said.

"Olivier liked Sidney but I didn't want two people with the same name in the same house. I wanted something really unusual, like a Celtic word for the moon or the sun. We compromised on a flower name. Now we have jessamine planted all around the cottage. They're beautiful."

Giulia said, "I will hide behind my monitor and eat my delicious processed baked good while I upload the latest photos of the charming Mr. Flynt."

"I'll pretend not to see you," Sidney said.

Giulia hooked the camera up to her computer. The croissant tasted so good she even neglected the coffee for several minutes. When the download completed, she wiped her hands and opened the file.

"You, sir, are going down in flames."

"You're talking to yourself again," Sidney called from the other room.

"Give me credit for decreasing the habit since I got married."

"We do. Olivier says it's an indication that you no longer think you have only yourself to rely on."

Giulia made a face. "It's weird knowing your husband spends part of his spare time examining the inside of my head."

"He's good at his job. That's why he's only six months away from leaving that three-psychologist office and opening up his very own place."

"With enough extra money to move out of the cottage surrounded by alpacas that use him for spitting target practice?"

"He may have mentioned that a few dozen times."

Giulia squared off against her monitor and opened the folder uploaded from her camera. Hooray. Every single picture she'd taken from the tree perch was crisp and detailed. She chose five that captured the affair in its explicit glory and added them to her Flynt document. Then she downed the rest of the brownie coffee in one long swallow.

Not enough. She grabbed her wallet and headed past Zane and Sidney without speaking.

When she returned with a fresh cup, Zane said in his old scared-rabbit voice, "Are you okay? Your face is all red."

Giulia touched the back of her free hand to her cheeks. "Courtesy of Mr. Flynt. I trailed him to his mistress' house this morning and took pictures of them doing things he should only be doing with his wife."

Zane's mouth dropped open. "I won't ask to see. Is that why the second coffee?"

"Not only the second. This one is double-strength and black."

Sidney's head popped up over her monitor. "You're drinking black coffee? Did aliens abduct you and flip-flop your brain?"

"I'm desperate. Flynt and his sexual antics require extreme coffee measures."

Sidney's eyes got big. "Do I want to know?"

"You do not."

She gave Giulia a thumbs-up. "Way to take one for the team."

"That's why I make the big bucks."

Eleven

Jane Pierce walked in waving her camera as Sidney and Zane hooted with laughter.

"I have pictures!"

Giulia fist-pumped. "Yes. Come plug in and show me this magically restored jewelry."

"Our Congressman brought his ex-underwear model wife to the fundraiser," Jane said while the pictures uploaded. "Fanboys and fangirls crowded around her to get selfies. Nobody looked twice at me."

Giulia unhooked the USB cable from her tower. "You'll make me very happy if our insurance fraud couple fought for one of the selfies."

Jane snorted. "Not a chance, but something better. They were so conscious of their image their posing pretty much did my job for me."

Giulia opened the folder of pictures. "Forty-seven?"

"It's not as bad as it looks. Can I drive?"

Giulia relinquished her chair. Jane opened the photo viewer and clicked through the pictures too fast for Giulia to tell who was in them.

"Here." Giulia enlarged an image of their targets talking with a young couple in expensive-looking evening wear. "Mrs. Insurance Fraud's nose got wicked out of joint when she priced that woman's dress. Look at her eyes. She can paste that social smile on but she can't control her baby blues." She clicked to the next picture. "I heard *The Scoop* talking in the background and then a camera click. It wasn't mine; I put mine on silent. Both of them posed facing right at me. I got like six in a row. Here's the diamond necklace and earrings they claimed were stolen. Look at that sparkle. Those trinkets could pay my rent for three years. Four."

"You're terrific." Giulia watched the photos speed past again. "You'll be twice as terrific if you caught him wearing the Rolex."

"You can put 'terrific' on my letter of recommendation, because here..." *click, click* "...it is."

In the picture now on the screen, the Congressman was shaking hands with Mr. Insurance Fraud, the latter's sleeve pulled back just far enough to reveal the miraculously restored stolen Rolex.

"Rhetorical question," Giulia said. "Was our Congressman impressed by said Rolex?"

"Nah. He had one eye on his wife's cleavage all night and the other eye on all the men checking out his wife's cleavage. Her dress covered her naughty bits only by the grace of God and double-sided tape."

"I bet *The Scoop* didn't thank God for an evening without a wardrobe malfunction. Their viewers will be so disappointed." Giulia dragged her client chair next to Jane. "*The Scoop* and our corrupt politicians are blights on the county. I can't decide which is the bigger blight. Scroll through all the pictures again, please. I want to select some of Mr. and Mrs. Fraud together and separately for the insurance company."

Giulia and Jane sorted the pictures into Yes, No, and Maybe folders.

In less than half an hour, Giulia found three clean photographs of the one hundred fifty thousand dollar diamond earrings and necklace from different angles, and two of the husband with the Rolex peeking out from his sleeve.

"Excellent job, Jane. Thank you." Giulia rubbed her temples. "Stress headache. I may have reached my multitasking limit."

"I can write up this report in about an hour, then I have a job interview." Jane somehow looked both excited and terrified. "Could you write that recommendation letter before I go? I don't want to blow this."

With a perfectly straight face, Giulia composed a generic letter praising Jane's intelligence, work ethic, adaptability, and quick learning curve. Jimmy would see all this and remember everything Giulia had told him yesterday about Jane. With what Giulia knew about both the precinct and its captain, Jane would return here with a job offer in hand. One more monkey kicked successfully off Giulia's back.

Jane ran out to the printer and walked back, reading the letter. "You make me sound like I could work at a real-life *CSI*."

"You could, with some more training and experience. Don't be modest at your interview. Make your potential boss afraid to let some other company snap you up."

Jane looked down at her. "I'll try."

"Don't make me quote Yoda at you."

Jane smiled at that. "Yes, ma'am."

Giulia's face scrunched. "Please, no 'ma'am.' It makes me sound like an old woman."

Her cell phone rang and Frank's picture appeared on the screen. Jane went into the main office and closed the door. Giulia hit the FaceTime button.

"Hey, babe," Frank said. Behind him, she caught glimpses of people crossing the room.

"Good news?" Giulia said. "Or have I fallen from the pedestal upon which Jimmy placed me three years ago?"

Two different phones rang in the crowded detectives' space. Frank raised his voice. "Where is the innocent, simple ex-nun I married?"

Giulia stuck out the tip of her tongue at him. "Are you implying I would tread on Jimmy's high opinion of me?"

Frank moved the phone far enough away so she could see him hold up one hand in surrender. "Let's move on. If the combined expertise of myself and my partner plays out as expected, I should be able to get away tomorrow afternoon." A pause as his desk phone rang. "Nash, can you get that? Thanks." To Giulia: "Don't make that face. It squinches up your lips. The last time our expertise failed us was more than a year ago, so expect me there tomorrow to defend you from snowbirds and kitsch."

"I'll give you a cover story to explain why I'm there a day ahead of you." Scenarios started to play in her head.

"Hello?"

She blinked. "Sorry. Already brainstorming. I'll call you tonight from the B&B."

"Yes, ma'am." An evil laugh. "I know you hate that word."

"Everyone is conspiring against me this morning. Stop laughing, you. The plan is to wrap up everything possible, pack, and head up to the lake before rush hour."

Frank's partner photobombed the call. "Hey, Giulia. Frank, the bartender says he wants to talk."

"Gotta go, hon. See you tomorrow night." He ended the call.

Zane knocked five minutes later.

"Mrs. Flynt to see you."

Giulia nodded. He ushered a statuesque woman with hip-length black hair into Giulia's office and closed the door.

"Please have a seat, Mrs. Flynt." Giulia didn't smile as she handed her a dark green pocket folder with DI's logo embossed in the lower right corner.

The woman opened it and read the summary page in the left-hand pocket.

Her face paled under her discreet makeup. She raised her eyes to Giulia's.

"I was certain he had one woman on the side, but I had no idea he'd already picked out the next one." Her voice maintained the coolness Giulia had heard in their first meeting.

"If you'll open the bound report in the other pocket, I'll run through our findings with you."

Mrs. Flynt spread the report flat on the desk.

"The pictures from this morning are somewhat extreme," Giulia said.

The perfect upper lip rose with the hint of a sneer. "You were able to capture him being serviced by his fancy piece."

"Yes."

The lips compressed. "Go on."

Giulia turned the page for her. The telephoto pictures on the two-page spread told their own complete story, from foreplay to mutual orgasm.

Mrs. Flynt dug into her Coach bag. Giulia brought out a box of tissues from her bottom drawer and passed it across the desk. Her client snatched one and blew her nose.

"He treats women like we're his personal dessert cart." Her eyes never left the pictures as she groped for another tissue. "So much for his seven fifteen 'tee time.'" With an abrupt movement she yanked the diamond eternity band from her ring finger and slammed it on the desk. "Do you know anyone who wants some useless jewelry?"

Giulia gave her a slight smile. "Perhaps it could help with the legal fees?"

Mrs. Flynt's lips smiled, but the smile didn't reach her eyes. "The money in this family is mine. He married up."

"A college starter fund for your children, then."

Mrs. Flynt considered the idea. "I like it." She stashed the ring in her purse. "My former life partner will have to pawn his wedding ring to survive this divorce. I'll see to it that Melissa has her last few tax returns investigated as well." Her smile widened. "Oh, yes, I know his mistress. She's Franklin's ex-wife."

"Franklin?" Giulia ought to sell the rights to this story to a soap opera.

"The owner of Glacier Business Solutions. They've both been to our house for Christmas parties." The smile vanished. "I feel sorry for that receptionist. My husband mentioned how she'd just completed her GED. She dropped out of high school to get a job to help pay for her father's health expenses. I gather she's afraid my husband will get her fired if she protests. She and I are going to have a talk."

She read through the invoice behind the summary in the right-hand pocket, nodded, and wrote Giulia a check. Giulia sent a receipt to the printer. Zane brought it in and slipped out again. Mrs. Flynt checked it over and slid it behind the invoice.

"I don't know if you're familiar with old black-and-white horror movies, Ms. Driscoll, but my husband liked to call me Vampira. I have what used to be termed a wasp waist. When you put that together with my long hair and the right Halloween costume, I have a passing resemblance to the actress with that stage name. He thought the resemblance was such a good joke. Since I intend to bleed him dry financially and professionally, I wonder if he'll still consider his joke so amusing."

She closed the folder and stood. Giulia came around the desk to shake her hand.

"Thank you for an excellent and within-budget investigation. Your reputation is not exaggerated. I'll make certain this doesn't reach the divorce courts, so we won't be seeing each other again."

"You're welcome," Giulia said, keeping her voice and face neutral. "If your attorney needs clarification on any item in the report, our contact information is on the inside folder pocket."

Giulia waited until the downstairs street door closed behind Mrs. Flynt before she let loose an impressed whistle.

Twelve

"Dear God, it's after one." Giulia grabbed her wallet. Jane and Sidney were already gone.

Zane said, "I'm taking a late lunch. I'll mind the store."

"I'm only going downstairs. Be right back."

The lunch line at Common Grounds was worse than the breakfast line that morning. At a table near the counter, a man drank espresso and shouted a one-sided argument into his cell phone. Two businesswomen threatened to call the owner because of slow service. A total of three people were ahead of Giulia and four behind her. The smell of burnt toast clashed with grilled cheese and hazelnut coffee.

Gary, the other daytime barista, steamed whole milk, wrapped two croissant sandwiches, and created a latte and a cappuccino to satisfy the businesswomen. The young man directly in front of Giulia read his order from his phone: Two large dark roasts with shots of almond, four bacon and egg white crumpets, two with turkey bacon, two with tofu bacon, one fat-free iced chai, one Earl Gray with lemon.

Gary stood in place for a long moment. Then the door opened and two children's voices discussing Mario Kart strategy cut through the other conversations.

Mingmei appeared out of the chaos, ducked under the open part of the counter, and magicked a Common Grounds coffee-colored apron over her shorts and t-shirt.

"I've got the crumpets."

Gary, energized, snatched four paper cups and transformed into a movie bartender. He popped a lemon wedge and tea bag in one, chai concentrate in another, and measured almond syrup into the remaining two.

He gave Giulia a puppy dog look when her turn at the counter arrived.

"Ms. Driscoll, I was just about to beg you to come behind the counter and help because you used to work here." He switched the puppy dog eyes to Mingmei. "Coworkers shouldn't be allowed a break on days like this."

Mingmei finished making change for the complex phone order. "Elaine would've handed you your ass on a plate if you did that." She smiled at the flunky as he trapped a bag of specialized muffin sandwiches under his chin. "Thank you; come again." When the door chimes tinkled his exit, she whispered to Giulia, "People with complex hipster orders belong in Starbucks." Without skipping a beat, she said to the woman behind Giulia, "Italian on cheese coming up." She sliced a cheese croissant and layered prosciutto and provolone inside. To Giulia she said, "You, on the other hand, are choosing the honey-wheat muffin with Virginia ham, cucumbers, and Gouda."

Giulia had no desire to disagree. "Yes, I am."

Gary said, "Large French roast with vanilla?"

"I think so; so it won't clash with the ham."

"The customer is always right." Gary poured and measured and handed her the coffee with a bow.

"Especially when she appreciates our service." Mingmei blew Giulia a kiss. "Go away now. We're busy."

Giulia laughed and escaped. Twenty minutes later, as she savored the last of her coffee, footsteps pounded up the stairs. Jane skidded to a halt in the middle of the main office.

"I got a job, I got a job, I got a job!"

She ran into Giulia's office and squeezed all the breath out of her. Zane came in and rescued Giulia's lungs by high-fiving Jane.

This was a new Jane: Neither the bristly woman-against-the-world nor the shy, semi-confident Jane who'd been appearing more often toward the end of her tenure at DI. Giulia almost didn't recognize happy Jane.

"Personal assistant to Captain James Reilly, your husband's boss, Ms. D. Captain Reilly is a lot stricter than you are, but it's a whole different atmosphere at the police station. He said he completely trusted your letter of recommendation and I start in two weeks right after I'm done here, and oh my God, a full-time job with a real salary so I can finally get out of the shithole I've been living in because my asshole ex left me with nothing." She took a breath. "Oops. Sorry about the language, but I have a job!"

Giulia applauded. "I'm thrilled for you. Can you stop floating for a group meeting?"

"Oh, yeah. Sure. What's up?" She sat on Sidney's desk.

"Zane, can you get Sidney on the phone?"

When Sidney joined them on speaker, Giulia said, "I'm heading out to Stone's Throw this afternoon to earn Mac—Ms. Stone's—beautiful chunk of money. She has either an angry ghost, a sabotaging guest, or an underhanded psychic."

"I vote sabotaging guest," Sidney's echoey voice said.

"Frankly, so do I," Giulia said. "Guest or psychic, that is. Thus my ongoing self-defense lessons and gun range practice."

"The well-dressed PI never leaves home without her Glock," Zane said. "But have you considered the one in one thousand chance the troubles are supernatural rather than mundane?"

Giulia overrode the spluttering noises coming from the speakerphone. "Sidney, do not rant. You'll upset Jessamine. Zane, I have. If that's the case, I know how to cleanse a house with sage and salt."

Zane shook his head with emphasis. "Don't cleanse without trying to communicate first. Even if the spirit appears to be attacking at random, it will have a reason."

A cross between a growl and a moan came from the speaker. "Zane, if my head explodes, you're responsible."

Jane spoke up. "I'm riding the fence on this one. My tattoo artist has some wild stories about ghosts, and not all of them involve magic mushrooms."

Giulia held up her iPad. "Ghosts or not, I'm going to be out of town for several days. May I have the specifics of everyone's caseload?"

Zane said, "I've got the preliminary research for the twins looking for their birth mother."

Sidney said, "A deadbeat dad and sussing out the possible humongous evangelical church embezzlement."

Jane said, "I'm helping both of them, and they're also walking me through the bride and groom prenup life histories for the Van Alstyne wedding."

Giulia typed everything in. "The Flynt case is finished, but I've still got two background checks for the Diocese. Jane, it's a good thing you're here for two more weeks. Can you and Sidney split the background checks?"

"No problem," Sidney said. "Are you going there as an investigator or as a paying guest?"

"As a guest. Frank's coming to give me a perfect cover as a couple on vacation. I'll try to get back here at least once, especially if the Wi-Fi out there isn't powerful enough."

"Take lots of ghost pictures," Sidney said. "*The Scoop* will be all over you like a rash. They'll probably give you your very own half-hour guest spot."

Giulia aimed a completely fake smile at the phone. "If I fire you for cursing me with *The Scoop*, how will you be able to keep Jessamine in all-natural baby food?"

The only answer from the phone was the theme from *Ghostbusters*.

Thirteen

At ten after six, finally free of rush-hour traffic, the Nunmobile exited I-79 at 285 West. As Giulia circled the off-ramp, she could just see the top of the lighthouse. At the end of the ramp she saw water and turned left on Water Street. Cute.

Giulia presumed the Conneaut Lake beach possessed a wide strip of accessible sand, but she couldn't see much of it. Kids running and shrieking, old couples walking, and young ones kissing covered ninety percent of the space she glimpsed from the car. A volleyball game off to one side revealed the largest patch of actual sand visible for a quarter mile.

"It should be right up here somewhere—" Her words cut off in a gasp as she slammed on the brakes.

A beach ball bounced off the hood. A little boy chased it into the street and stopped a whisker away from the car's hood. An adult male dashed after the boy and scooped him up.

"Thanks." He nodded at Giulia.

Cars going in the opposite direction also stopped. The man kicked the ball onto the far sidewalk and followed it out of danger to the boy and himself.

Giulia blew out a breath. "Adrenaline is more effective than espresso."

The street rose at a gentle angle as she neared the lighthouse. Giulia had thought it would be on its own point of land. Instead, a lighthouse-shaped sign directed her to an open wrought-iron gate.

It arched six feet above the Nunmobile, a pattern of four-petaled flowers along its upward curve. The wide driveway beyond split in two around a grassy island. She drove around the left-hand side of the oval toward a carriage house larger than her and Frank's little Cape Cod. The carriage house concealed an eight-car parking lot on the side away from the entrance drive.

Giulia removed her suitcase from the trunk and took in the view: The lake beyond, lined with pine trees and shimmering in the afternoon sun, framed a brick three-story house with a white porch. Behind and to the left rose a lighthouse built out of the same deep red bricks as the house, its gallery visible two stories above the house's roof.

With the picturesque buildings shielding her from the noises of Sea-Doos on the lake and people on the beach, Stone's Throw couldn't have looked less like a haunted lighthouse.

Giulia walked up the porch steps and petted a calico cat sitting in a regal pose on a white wicker chair. A beagle lying next to the chair opened one eye when Giulia stroked the cat, didn't appear to consider Giulia a threat, and closed it again.

Giulia knocked on the screen door frame and opened the door, walking into an antique kitchen complete with trestle table, coal-fired stove, vintage high chair, and deep enamel sink with attached water pump. Mac entered from a doorway to the left, holding a can of spray polish and a dustcloth.

"Welcome to Stone's Throw. I'm MacAllister Stone, the owner. Please call me Mac. Everyone does. You must be Giulia Driscoll." She stage-winked at Giulia as they shook hands.

Laughter came from down a hallway opposite the screen door.

"Pleased to meet you," Giulia said. "My husband had a work emergency, but he'll arrive tomorrow."

"That's no way to start a vacation." Mac moved toward the hallway. "Let me show you up to your room. Breakfast is at nine a.m. every day including weekends. We have a bonfire on the beach Sunday, Wednesday, and Friday. Eight o'clock. S'mores fixings are provided." She stopped at the second floor landing. "What's a vacation on the beach without a bit of your childhood thrown in, right?" She continued toward the lake side of the house. "I've put you in the Sand Dollar room, across the hall from the library."

She opened a door painted the color of real beach sand, not the pale kind sold in plastic bags at the toy store. "Our beach is semi-private with only a low fence, so you can easily access the public beach from it without going all the way around by the street. We have croquet and bocce ball set up on either side of the patio. Boat and Sea-Doo rentals are available a quarter-mile east along the beach, near the shopping district." She opened the windows and stood by another door like Vanna White showing off a new puzzle on *Wheel of Fortune*. "The bathroom is in here. You'll find locally crafted soap and hand lotion in the basket on the sink."

A door opened behind Mac and a woman's voice said, "The first martini of the night is calling me. Let's go."

"Thank you," Giulia said to Mac. "I'll certainly call on you if I need anything."

Mac stage-winked again and left. Giulia closed the door behind her. More voices and footsteps in the hall. Everyone appeared to be headed out to supper. Perfect.

She appropriated the right-hand sides of the two dresser drawers and unpacked. The weather for the next several days promised to be a bit of everything, so she'd packed for everything. Capris, sneakers, and casual shirts, plus jeans and a sweatshirt. The downside: None of those items could conceal her Glock.

The room had a classic Entrance to Narnia wardrobe. She opened it hoping for fur coats, but no luck with that in June. No snow fell on her hands, either, when she reached to touch the back panel.

Adulthood had its disappointments.

She kept her gun and its ammunition in her suitcase, which she locked and set against the back of the wardrobe. The key she dropped into her travel jewelry box at the back of the top dresser drawer. She didn't anticipate using the gun on this case, but she wasn't naïve enough to assume.

The nightgown she'd purchased on her way out of Cottonwood rolled into a surprisingly small tube. It looked like another pair of socks, if one didn't inspect it too closely No laundry for either of them on vacation, so no danger of Frank noticing her odd silky "socks." Giulia smiled to herself in anticipation of his reaction when she put it on tomorrow night.

Silence greeted her when she opened the bedroom door. Excellent.

First order of business: How many haunting gadgets had Mac installed for Halloween week? Ancillary business: How many hidden gadgets had the psychic installed, and could Giulia tell them apart?

Giulia walked softly downstairs, making no assumptions about the inn's deserted state, and started with the cellar. Cement walls and floors. Laundry room, storage room, chest freezer, fruit cellar. Everything on open shelves. Phone ready to take incriminating pictures, she moved and replaced tools and canned goods, inspected boxes of dishes and paint supplies and soap. Not a suspicious gizmo anywhere. Eh. She hadn't expected it to be that easy.

Back to the first floor. The main hallway connected the kitchen to a music room, a living room, and next to that, a screened-in porch facing the lake. Back in the antique kitchen area, a square archway on the right past the vintage stove opened onto a formal dining room. A narrow doorway to her left, behind the trestle table, led to an L-shaped modern working kitchen. Near the water pump, another door, locked.

She started with the trestle table. No hidden speakers or wires under the table or benches, or in the vase holding freesia and daisies. Nothing remotely modern in the stove or the deep sink and attached water pump.

On to the dining room. No hidden wires in the drapes. No switches or miniature speakers under the intricately carved table and chairs. The piano and bench in the music room: Clean. Also the wall art and throw rug. The living room drapes and coffee table:

Clean as well. The cumbersome 1930s-style radio complete with speakers resembling a cathedral window hid a modern receiver and CD player. She didn't see any overt signs of tampering. Neither Mac nor her psychic were following the huckster's rulebook.

A china doll lay in a baby carriage at the foot of the stairs, both carriage and doll from the turn of the last century. If Mac had claimed this doll floated in the air or performed an *Exorcist*-style head spin, Giulia might've believed her.

The stairs were narrow by today's standards. This time up she touched one of the worn Oriental carpet runners in the hope of feeling the real thing, but her fingers informed her it was polyester. A pedal-operated sewing machine was the second floor's antique of choice. The stained glass window was the true prize of the hall. The setting sun through its panes created ribbons of jewel-colored light on the oak floor.

She went into the library first, starting at the walls lined with bookshelves. Two overstuffed armchairs sat at right angles to each other on a different oriental rug. The white curtains let in diffused sunlight, making the room cool and inviting.

Giulia checked the curtains and the small side tables next to the chairs. Clean. Maybe the psychic used portable tricks because he or she only came here once a week. That would explain the lack of gadgets, but it would also make this case difficult.

Carpet runners in a third pattern lined the next flight of stairs. A narrow table in this hall supported a lamp with red-edged fringe, eight scooped side panels in different lace patterns, and eight glass panels in different floral patterns angling to a point at the top. A brass pineapple finial crowned it. Giulia couldn't wait for Frank's reaction to it tomorrow when she showed him around.

Two of the three bedrooms on this floor showed signs of occupation. Giulia gave all three the same inspection, adding a check under the beds and in the wardrobes. The edges around one windowsill let in a whiff of breeze, but nothing extreme. Mac must have spent a fortune restoring this place. It showed. But she found no haunting equipment anywhere on the third floor.

Returning to the second floor, she checked out the other two bedrooms, then her own. Her bathroom boasted a Victorian shower and a pull chain toilet. Frank's reaction to this might surpass his opinion of the fringed lamp. That and the lace canopy over their bed.

All of it proclaimed its innocence of any motive other than to make a guest's stay comfortable and relaxed.

Well, she wasn't licked yet.

Fourteen

Twilight fell as she returned to the first floor and the glass-eyed doll. At the foot of the stairs she turned left instead of to the right, back into the living room. She entered some kind of history and souvenir room crowded with small tables, an intricate dollhouse, and a bookshelf of kitsch.

She passed through this room into a vestibule with an oak door to her right leading to the patio. Yet another door faced her. She opened it and stepped back. A complete suit of armor guarded the lighthouse stairs. If she'd come upon it in the dark, her heart would've leaped out of her chest through the door, taking any attempt at stealth with it. The darn thing looked as though it could come to life if needed to protect the house against intruders.

Giulia climbed the narrow spiral stairs up into the lighthouse proper. The wooden steps, firm under her feet, emitted hardly a creak. When she reached the first deep-set window she sat on a step and examined the treads and the railing. New and sturdy construction, all of it.

The stairs ended at a catwalk running around the inside of the tower. A five-rung ladder led up to a cluster of industrial-sized light bulbs in the very top covered with a red, white, and blue gel shade. A narrow opening half the width of a standard doorway led from the catwalk to the gallery outside. She went sideways through this doorway and stepped out onto the gallery. The door faced the lake. She looked down on the flagged patio and part of the house's roof.

She shook this wooden railing like she had the one inside. Good and solid. Heights weren't Giulia's nightmare, but it was reassuring to have a safety net of sorts. She circled the entire gallery, looking out over the beach, the lake, the town, and more beach before she reentered the lighthouse.

On her descent Giulia sought and found the wall scratches in the photo Mac had showed her. She didn't attempt to reach them.

One of the window recesses held a hurricane lantern and the other a ruby glass vase. Cobwebs covered both, perhaps to evoke the Halloween atmosphere even this early in the tourist season.

Giulia studied the suit of armor before leaving the vestibule. An effective prop as well. A man or woman could worm themselves into it and scare a year off a guest's life. In the twilight glow the metal visor appeared to be eying her with suspicion.

"I'm not Scooby-Doo," she whispered at it. "Go scare someone else."

At the doorway into the rest of the house, she stopped and listened. Everyone must have been out to dinner still, because the only sound was a brisk wind off the lake. The curtains in the living room puffed in the breeze. They whipped over the back of the sofa exactly like they had in the photo Mac had shown her in DI's office. Giulia snapped several photos with her phone. She'd have to look up this "Woman in White" legend to see if that kind of ghost preferred fluttery white dresses.

Next: Round two on the stairs. In the cooling air the second and fourth treads creaked.

Last: The foot of the attic stairs. Giulia wouldn't swear that floorboards settling in the attic didn't sound like a ghostly footstep. She cranked the volume on her phone and tried to capture the sound.

Two floors below, the screen door opened and voices returned to the house. Giulia dashed downstairs into her room.

Stone's Throw wasn't a business hotel and the room had no space for a desk and chair. Giulia piled the pillows against the headboard and propped her iPad on her knees.

True to her fears, the Wi-Fi took forever to connect. When the page of images finally loaded, it confirmed Giulia's white nightgown theory. Combining that with the Trip Advisor review about something rigged up in the attic, Giulia came up with Mac and the psychic working together to create a nightgown ghost.

She frowned. More ways to interpret that conclusion: Mac hired DI to boot the fake psychic and make a selling point out of it. Or the psychic wasn't fake and Mac hired DI to give cachet to her. Giulia's frown deepened.

She couldn't think of a casual way to meet the other guests until breakfast tomorrow. The rest of the night would be a waste of time.

An orange glow appeared in her windows. Fire! She jumped off the bed, iPad bouncing onto the quilt, and pressed her face against the glass.

Fifteen

Stupid of her to panic. She'd forgotten the bonfire. The tall woman with stooped shoulders at the fire pit had to be Mac. A shorter male in dark clothes stood on the patio coaxing the flames to grow.

Giulia's next thought: S'mores. Not a healthy supper, but sussing out possible ghost-making equipment had been more important than finding a place to eat.

Right after that thought: Here was her casual way to meet the guests. She closed her iPad, tied her sneakers, and headed downstairs.

The temperature had dropped at least twenty degrees with the breeze off the lake. Lights from the town prevented stargazing this close to the shore.

A single motorboat passed them headed east. Competing music from the beachfront bars reached as far as this section of beach, but not loud enough to be intrusive.

Giulia should've changed into jeans. She held out her hands to the bonfire.

Two men about her age sat on the patio sofa with their arms around each other.

Mac opened a cooler and passed out forks. As she walked around the group with an open bag of marshmallows, she said, "S'more's may be a way of reliving our childhood, but adulthood has its privileges. I have here regular chocolate and wine-infused chocolate. I recommend the dark with sherry."

Giulia toasted her marshmallow to an even golden-brown on all sides before choosing regular chocolate to accompany it. She smiled at the two men on the sofa and they waved her over.

"Did you just arrive?" the one with the close-trimmed beard said. "We didn't see you earlier today."

"Yes. I fought rush-hour traffic all the way. I'm Giulia."

"Joel. This is my husband, Gino."

Gino swallowed marshmallow and graham cracker bits once, then again before he opened his mouth. "Pleased to meet you. You're here all alone?"

"My husband got sucked into a work crisis right before we were supposed to leave. He's coming tomorrow."

A different couple arrived carrying half-empty martini glasses: The woman plump, with one of those haircuts designed especially for the customer, the man stocky and short, especially when he stood next to Mac. They declined s'mores and monopolized Mac's attention.

Joel and Gino wandered out to the beach. Giulia regretted the bit of chocolate and marshmallow because it emphasized her lack of real food. A third couple ran up from the beach and stopped next to the sofa, panting.

"Did we miss it?" the woman said.

Mac waved the bag of marshmallows as she listened to the perfect haircut and husband. The woman, tall with an afro, plucked the bag from Mac's hand. Her husband, the same height but with a buzz cut and built like a soccer player, found long-handled forks and the rest of the ingredients. When their snacks were ready, they sat down, *plump*, on either side of Giulia.

"Hi! I'm CeCe and this is Roy. I promise I'm safe to sit near. No birds are nesting in my hair despite its craziness."

"Your hair is beautiful," Giulia said, then gave them the same explanation she'd given to Joel and Gino.

"That's a bad start to a vacation," Roy said. "This your first time here? You'll love it. We've been coming here since the place opened."

"Mac's breakfasts are to die for," CeCe said. "You tell your husband that the rest of the week will make up for missing out on today. I can't wait for the séance on Sunday. Mac's always adding something new."

Roy leaned closer to Giulia. "We found a Ouija board in an antique shop back home. Haven't had the guts to try it yet. Are you game?"

Giulia said, "I've never tried one either."

"Let's do it," CeCe said, bouncing up and down on the hard cushion. "I've seen *Paranormal Activity* and *The Exorcist*, but movies aren't real life. We're on vacation. Let's live a little."

"Besides, what are you going to do all alone in that big bed without your husband?" Roy gave her an exaggerated wink.

CeCe aimed a slap at him. "He's a pig; just ignore him."

"You love it," Roy said. "Come on. It's dark out. I'll borrow some candles from Mac and we'll do this right."

Giulia followed CeCe up to the Starfish room on the third floor.

"We always have this room," CeCe said, opening their wardrobe. "I fell in love with the clawfoot bathtub our first year. Here's the board. Go ahead; look at how huge the tub is."

"Wow," Giulia said. "You could fit two people in that."

"You sure can." CeCe set the tattered-edged board on the starfish-shaped throw rug. "It's a good thing this rug isn't a pentagram or anything. Me and Roy and a demon would definitely not fit in that tub."

Giulia opened her mouth to lecture on the actual meaning of the pentagram, but shut it immediately. Undercover, undercover, undercover. Instead she said, "Don't these wardrobes make you think of Narnia?"

CeCe squeaked. "I say that every year! We ought to suggest that to Mac."

Roy opened the door carrying three shallow bowls and three tall candles. CeCe pounced. "Giulia says the wardrobes make her think of Narnia too. We should tell Mac to put fur coats in the wardrobes and open the first week of December for a Narnia winter getaway. They'd have to be faux fur, could you imagine the cost? What do you think, honey?"

Roy set one candle on the nightstand and two on the floor at the inner angles of two furry starfish arms. "You know I can't stand those books, doll."

"Yeah, but what do you think of the vacation idea?"

He struck a match and lit one candle. "I guess, if you could find enough adults willing to pay these prices to play kids' dress up for four or five days." As the wick burned, he said, "How are we going to make these stand up?"

Giulia came over next to him. "Like this." She picked up the candle and tilted it over the center of its bowl until several drops of wax had fallen. Then she pushed the base of the candle into the wax.

"Son of a gun." Roy nodded at Giulia. "Clever. You two set up the board?"

CeCe took a battered planchette out of a brown paper bag with "Blasts from the Past" stenciled on it. "We weren't sitting up here comparing nail polish. Too bad the glass in the center is cracked."

"Maybe we'll contact the spirit of a glassblower." Roy created wax bases for the other two candles. "Okay, lights out."

CeCe flipped the wall switch, made an annoyed noise, and walked around Giulia and Roy to turn off the bathroom light.

Giulia sat cross-legged facing CeCe. The candles combined with the canopied bed and antique furniture created a slumber party atmosphere.

Giulia kept her imagination on a tight leash. Too many Hammer films and Asian horror movies.

"Just a second." She took her cell phone from her pocket. "I don't want this ringing at the wrong time."

Roy and CeCe took out theirs. "Good point."

Giulia turned off her ringer and using small, quick movements turned on the voice memo function before she returned the phone to her pocket. At this point, everyone was a suspect. Especially complete strangers who just happened to invite her to their room for a Ouija board experiment on her first night in a haunted B&B.

CeCe giggled. "I've always wanted to try one of these, but my pastor would've beat my butt so bad. Mama would've beat it more when he sent me home."

"I've never seen one of these in person before," Giulia said.

"The class troublemaker snuck one into Bible camp when we were thirteen. It might've worked if we all hadn't giggled so loud the counselor came to check on us." CeCe sat on her heels. "Okay; everyone's fingers on the planchette."

Roy said, "Let's not imitate the movies. That never ends well. I'll try the straightforward approach. CeCe, stop shaking this thing."

She took several deep breaths, let out one last nervous giggle, and settled.

"Spirit of Stone's Throw, speak to us," Roy intoned.

They waited.

"Spirit of Stone's Throw," CeCe started, giggled, and started again. "Girl, come have a chat. Ignore that man over there."

They waited. Roy sneezed and the planchette skidded over to the letter "L."

"Sorry." He reset it to the middle of the board.

They waited some more.

"Giulia, you try," CeCe whispered.

Every Cradle Catholic molecule in Giulia's body rebelled. She couldn't. She really couldn't.

Yes, she could, because it was her job. Father Carlos would tease her to no end at next week's confession.

"Come speak to us," Giulia said in a coaxing voice. "It's a good night for some girl time."

Below them, on the patio, someone screamed.

Sixteen

Giulia jumped up. CeCe and Roy started. The planchette skittered over the board.

Giulia yanked apart the curtains and opened the window.

"Fire!" Several voices yelled.

"Oh my God, oh my God, the ghost started a fire." CeCe's voice quivered. "We're going to be arrested for arson."

"Cec, don't be ridiculous." Roy blew out the candles. "Come on, we've gotta help."

CeCe turned on the room light, glanced down at the Ouija board, and backpedaled until she hit the wardrobe. "Look at her message."

Roy and Giulia looked where CeCe's bright pink fingernail pointed. The planchette had stopped over the word "Yes," the letters cut in jagged halves by the cracked glass.

"Damn," Roy said.

Giulia shook her head. "We pushed it there when we all stood and ran to the window. It doesn't mean anything. Come on."

She opened the door and ran downstairs, a bodiless voice in her head repeating, "Too many horror movies. Too many horror movies." Which had to be the reason for all the little hairs on the back of her neck standing at attention. That was all. Period.

Through the sunroom windows, she saw a confusion of orange flames and black smoke whipping back and forth two feet above the ground. Mac shoved past her, carrying the kitchen fire extinguisher.

Giulia followed, right into a faceful of smoke. She bent in half, coughing and eyes stinging. The world stank of burning plastic. Mac's silhouette crossed in front of the largest flames and the hiss of spraying chemicals mixed with popping wood from the still-lit bonfire and ululating approach of sirens.

The smoke morphed from black to gray as it flowed over the house.

"Dammit, this thing is empty." Mac flung the small extinguisher aside. Someone hopped over it as it rolled onto the grass, possibly Joel or Gino.

The sides of the cooler melted in on each other. A small explosion whipped against the sparking cushions and reignited the stuffing. A new set of stenches joined the rest. Giulia pulled her shirt up over her nose and mouth and flattened against the sunroom windows as three firefighters appeared around the corner of the building, hose flopping behind them.

One turned on the pressure and another held the hose while the first one drowned the flames in a thick spray of foam. The third shouted orders and then all at once the fire was out and floodlights on the second floor overhang turned on to illuminate the wreckage.

That's when the police arrived.

The entire patio looked like the remains of a gigantic campfire doused with whipped cream. The firefighters clustered around the fire pit like Macbeth's witches as one detective conferred with the chief over the remains of the cushions. The noise level dropped by half. Giulia returned her shirt to its proper position. CeCe and Roy squeezed through the sunroom door together, looking exactly like all of Giulia's nieces and nephews caught pushing their parents' envelopes.

Giulia walked over to them. "Don't you dare tell Mac we goaded her family ghost into starting a fire, because we did no such thing."

With an "Excuse me, please," Mac brushed past them into the house.

"She looks angry," CeCe said. "I've never seen her angry."

Roy said to Giulia, "You seem to know a lot about ghosts, but how can you be sure—"

"Police!" Mac screamed from inside.

Giulia made a movement to run inside, but stopped herself. The uniformed officer walked inside. A minute later, he came to the door and called to the detective. When the opening was clear, Giulia caught CeCe's and Roy's attention and jerked her head toward the door. All of them went in. Giulia followed Mac's stressed voice to the kitchen area and the locked room, which turned out to be Mac's office.

Mac was cursing the beige walls blue. "My laptop and my purse. Miserable little drug addicts."

The uniformed officer called for assistance with fingerprints. The detective cautioned Mac not to touch anything.

"Do I look like I just crawled out of the underwater caves? Of course I didn't touch anything as soon as I saw that dust-free rectangle where my laptop used to sit." She cursed at the walls some more.

Giulia walked away and gestured Roy and CeCe to follow. When the three of them made it back to the sunroom, the firefighters were packing away their equipment. The remains of smoke clogged the air in the sunroom. Giulia went out to the edge of the patio and the others followed her. What she really wanted was Frank's perspective on this. What she wanted most after that was to drop this "guest" mask.

Too bad life didn't order itself to her wishes.

"Have you ever heard Mac swear like that?" she asked them.

"No way," CeCe said. "But she never got her purse stolen when we were here either."

Roy looked from the remains of the fire to the inside of the house and back again. "This is like a TV cop show. I bet someone set the fire to get everyone outside, and then the thief got in by the front door to steal her purse and laptop."

Giulia had never been so thrilled to sit back and let someone else voice the deduction.

"Excuse me. Did you say someone set this fire as a cover for a robbery?" A young woman channeling 1950s television Lois Lane *tick-tacked* across the flagstone patio in three-inch heels, pencil skirt, and matching jacket.

Giulia activated her best imitation of beige wallpaper. The young woman aimed a micro recorder at Roy.

"Well, yeah, it makes sense, doesn't it? Are you with the local paper?"

"Yes. My photographer is shooting the remains of the fire but we'd love to get an inset of some of the guests."

Perhaps to block out the noise from the people still around the patio wreckage, the reporter turned her back to the lake and by default to Giulia. Giulia slipped away, sidling among the croquet wickets in the grass. Once out of sight, she sprinted around the opposite side of the house and up the porch steps. Voices still came from the small office. Giulia entered the dark kitchen, avoided the spill of light from the office doorway, and used the antique stove as a shield for eavesdropping.

"Mac, we're going to need fingerprints from you and Lucy and Matthew for comparison."

"Fine. Whatever you want."

A series of clicks and snaps and footsteps.

"Lucy will be here tomorrow at eight. Matthew doesn't usually show up until after breakfast. If that's too late, you know where they both live. God, this ink is disgusting. I'll be right back."

Giulia leaped into the dining room. Mac stomped across the wood floor into the actual kitchen. The sounds of running water and splashing followed, then more stomping back to her office. Giulia returned to spy mode.

"We're all set here," a deep male voice said. "Lock the room, please. We'll call you as soon as we know anything."

"Thanks, Ronnie." Mac's voice sounded more tired than angry now. "I'll hide the key. The windows were locked already."

Three sets of footsteps neared the kitchen. Giulia dived into the dining room again.

"We'll get right on this," Ronnie said.

"I know you will. Tell Sheila I need more blackberry preserves, would you?"

"She'll bring a new supply over tomorrow."

The screen door closed a minute later. Giulia came out into the open.

"Oh. You." Mac sat on the end of the bench seat at the trestle table. "What did you hear?"

"Not enough."

Clomping footsteps came in from the direction of the sunroom. One of the firefighters stopped at the doorway, her braid coming loose from its elastic band.

"Mac, we need you out back."

Mac stood, her movements more like those of a seventy-year-old than Giulia had yet seen.

"I'll talk to you afterwards," Giulia said.

Mac palmed the office key into Giulia's hand.

Seventeen

Instead of taking Mac's hint, Giulia followed her out to the backyard. The floodlights illuminated a sad, dripping, filthy mess of couch cushion remnants and scorched iron. Off to one side, Ronnie the detective was typing into a small tablet.

"Call Jeanie for cleanup," the firefighter was saying to Mac. "Her team's not the fastest, but they're thorough. This won't take them more than a day. Can your Matthew repaint the furniture?"

Mac didn't answer right away. Her gaze kept moving from the fire pit to the furniture to the patio stones and back around again.

"Mac?"

"Yes, yes, sorry. Matthew can paint. He's done it before. I think I have some left over from last year."

"Okay. We triple-checked everything, of course. All that's left is the mess. Ed took all the pictures you'll need; he'll send them to your insurance rep for you since the firebug took your laptop."

Mac shook herself. "Thanks. I'm sure I'll see this tomorrow morning as a mess to clean, but right now all I want is a glass of wine and my bed."

The firefighter gave her a one-armed hug. "Understandable. Come on over and wrap things up with the police first."

Giulia couldn't get close enough to the detective to listen in without being obvious. She also knew better than to unlock the office and mess with a crime scene. Mac would be hearing about that from her before the end of this night.

A hand with pink fingernails shot out from the living room and grabbed her arm.

"Giulia," CeCe hissed. "What's going on? Where'd you go? That cute reporter would've put your picture in the paper too, I bet."

"I tried calling my husband, but he's still at work." Every so often Giulia Driscoll, former nun, was appalled at how smooth a liar Giulia Driscoll, private investigator, had become.

"He's not a caveman, is he? He won't swoop in and rescue you just because poor Mac got robbed?"

Giulia laughed. "I can take care of myself."

"Oh, good, because you have to be here for the real séance. Have to be! After what happened upstairs and down here, who knows what will happen when an actual psychic tries to contact the ghost?" CeCe yawned. "Sorry. I'm dead on my feet and it's barely eleven o'clock."

"I need a bed too." Giulia started upstairs and CeCe took the hint.

When Giulia was alone in the hall, she tiptoed downstairs and found Mac at the trestle table finishing a glass of chardonnay.

"Mac, here's the key to your office. It's a crime scene. You should know I can't go in there."

Mac ran her hands through her hair. "You're right. I wasn't thinking. I've got to call LifeLock and cancel every damned credit and bank card I own."

"I'll get out of your way, then. We'll talk tomorrow."

Giulia left Mac pounding the keypad on her phone and headed to her room for real. Not until she sat on the bed to call Frank did she remember she'd muted her ringer. Which turned out not to matter, because the phone was down to one percent battery. She'd never stopped the recording when the fire broke out.

"Professional of you, Driscoll. A good investigator shouldn't get distracted by a little arson."

She plugged it in, turned on the ringer, and four voicemails appeared. All from Frank. She hit redial.

"Hi, honey."

"*Cac naofa*, where the hell have you been? What happened? You were supposed to check in at eight."

"I, sir, have been participating in a séance, watching an amateur succeed at arson and theft, and eavesdropping on police and firefighters."

Silence.

Giulia chuckled. "I've never reduced you to silence before. Score one for me."

Something Irish Giulia figured was much worse than "holy shit" came from the phone. She kept her voice calm and even as she summarized the evening.

"Lock your door. Where's your gun?"

"I will, dear, and it's close at hand. I'm more interested in reading the police and fire reports."

"I am more interested in my wife taking precautions against nearby criminals."

"Frank, you're cute when you regress to Neanderthal. Don't worry. I'm alert and aware and will remain so even while sleeping. What time will you be here tomorrow?"

"After lunch unless we can turbocharge this wrap-up. I'll do my best."

Giulia woke from a Cinderella dream of scrubbing soot from endless floors. The room was so quiet without Frank snoring. She fluffed her pillow and turned on her side, sinking toward sleep again.

Someone in the hall started crying.

Giulia lay there, eyes closed, unsure if the noise was part of another dream. The sobs came again. She opened her eyes and gave herself a moment to adjust to the moonlight in the room. Then she slipped out of bed. Shirt. Underpants. Capris. It'd be enough. She checked the nightstand clock. If a real person was this miserable at two a.m., he or she wouldn't care if Giulia's boobs bounced with every step. And if it was a ghost...did ghosts care about boobs?

She picked up her phone and tiptoed to the door. Her hands remembered an old convent trick for Novices sneaking out of their rooms after all good nuns were asleep. Hold the door closed with the left hand and turn the handle with the right. If you kept the motion smooth and even, when the latch receded from the faceplate into the door it would make no noise.

Muscle memory triumphed. Without a sound she opened the door just enough to squeeze through, then closed it the same way.

Dark hall. The moon at the wrong angle to light the stained glass window. Library door open; other bedroom doors shut.

Giulia stood in place, her breathing shallow. The crying appeared to come from downstairs. She felt her way to the banister and counted the steps. The creaking ones were, she remembered, the fourth and second from the bottom. She used the banister to vault over both. She stopped on the wooden floor in front of the antique baby carriage. The moon shone through the floor-to-ceiling windows in the sunroom, making the doll's eyes glow.

That particular decoration could be put in storage any time and Giulia wouldn't miss it.

The first floor smelled ever so faintly of smoke. More weeping to her left distracted her from the blackened furniture outside, impervious to the moonlight. Was that a shadow of something (someone?) in the little souvenir room connecting the house to the lighthouse? The moonlight was bright enough for her to keep navigating without the flashlight app on her phone. The sobs receded as she entered the room. The small windows cut the available light by three-quarters. Giulia stood still and closed her eyes for a count of ten. The crying took a breath and restarted. When she opened her eyes she could see well enough to avoid running into that suit of armor and waking everyone in the house.

Another glimpse of something on the lighthouse stairs. Giulia followed into near-pitch darkness. The sobs floated above her. Giulia set one foot on the lowest step.

And stayed there. She'd seen this movie and read this book. She was not Daphne or Shaggy and this was not a *Scooby-Doo* cartoon. Her thumb flicked up the bottom of her iPhone screen and pressed the flashlight app. A second later she aimed the blinding light up the stairs. The sobs stopped. Nothing white moved above her as she angled the beam against the walls and the spiral railing. Now she heard no sounds.

Giulia climbed back upstairs, angry but remembering to skip the noisy steps. If this prankster liked games, Giulia would squash him or her like a hassled teacher corralling an unruly kid at the end of recess. She climbed into bed, wondering how many grade schools scheduled outside recess anymore. Wondering how the trick with the nightgown worked. If it had been a nightgown...

Eighteen

The aroma of coffee woke Giulia from a dream she didn't want to remember. This wasn't her bed. She reached out for Frank and her hand patted a quilt. A seagull squawked outside her window and she opened her eyes.

Right. Stone's Throw.

She showered and dressed and headed in the direction of coffee. Everyone she'd met last night stood at the sunroom windows staring at the patio.

"It doesn't look as awful as I expected," CeCe said.

Giulia's expectations must have been different, because it looked pretty much like her Cinderella dream had predicted. A ragged circle of smoke and soot discolored the flagstones. Charred wood floated in the miniature pool that used to be the fire pit. The remains of gutted patio cushions lay scattered on the grass. The couch and chairs, despite blistered and peeling paint, merely looked like they'd been antiqued by an amateur.

"Breakfast, everyone." Mac's voice was cheerful again.

"Oh, yes, the siren song of bacon," Gino said.

"And waffles," Joel said.

Mac and a young woman with short, straight blonde hair set a plate of waffles, bacon, and sausages next to a cup of melon balls at each place setting.

When all the guests were seated, Mac took the empty head chair and set a folded newspaper on the table.

"Good morning, and welcome to Stone's Throw. I apologize for last night."

Gino said, "Mac, you mean the police and fire truck and news reporters weren't part of this week's entertainment?"

Mac's smile seemed less than sincere. She opened the paper and displayed the front page. The huge sans serif headline read "ARSON AT STONE'S THROW." Below it, a three-column-wide photograph of the flames. Inset, as promised, a smiling CeCe and Roy. Below it, a formal picture of Mac.

"This isn't exactly the front page publicity I hoped for. My phone's been ringing nonstop since five a.m. The good news is, the idiot crackhead pawned my laptop already and the police promised to get it back to me today. It helps to know everyone's mother in a small town."

Roy chuckled and then found a sudden need to drink more coffee.

"There will be a lot of activity around the inn today. I'm sorry to have to ask everyone to stay out of the backyard."

A chorus of protests amounting to "Don't apologize. Of course we understand."

"Thank you. Now I'll leave everyone to enjoy breakfast. The syrup is the real thing, and all the other ingredients are locally sourced. Afterwards I'll conduct a tour of the lighthouse."

Giulia hated to rush a breakfast as perfect as the one in front of her, but business was business.

She played the old game of pretending to get a text that had to be answered, and left the table.

Mac was on her cell phone in the working kitchen and gestured Giulia inside.

"Thank you," Mac said into the phone. "You're worth your company's exorbitant monthly fee. I don't anticipate the same service when I go to the DMV today...All right. I'll expect your call before noon."

She hung up. "LifeLock," she said to Giulia. "Spent half the night on the phone with them. They're earning their money today."

"I'm sorry. Do the police have any leads they're willing to share with you?"

"They're not saying much, but they've rounded up the usual suspects. Conneaut Lake has a few. My money's on the meth addict or the crackhead, like I said in there. Quick cash for a fix and all that." She held up a black leather purse. "My perfect straw bag still hasn't shown up, and this is all wrong for summer. My mother is turning over in her grave."

Giulia didn't take the crooked path to distraction. "It would help if the police know why I'm here. That way I could ask for access to the reports."

Mac's short white hair flew around her ears, her headshake was so violent. "No. I want everyone here and in town to think you're just another guest. They won't let information slip otherwise."

Giulia made an acquiescent gesture. "Then I must ask for all information they give you as soon as you know it."

A nod replaced the headshake, the hair tickling Mac's chin. "That I can and will do. Anything it takes to get my property back under my control."

Giulia, mindful of good customer service, didn't point out the many contradictions in Mac's last few statements.

Mac stood. "They should be done eating. Come on the lighthouse tour. I give a sensational talk on our family history and the ghost. We can lock ourselves in the carriage house afterwards."

Giulia did not channel her years of teaching high school and point out that at least she knew better than to tell the client how to do her job. She returned to the dining room, made a despairing face over her cold breakfast, and dumped the melon balls on the top waffle. With a folded waffle in one hand and a slice of bacon in the other, she gave vague answers to CeCe's and Joel's questions about evil people who call during vacation breakfast.

Mac and Lucy cleared the dishes and Mac returned alone.

"I'm glad you all enjoyed breakfast. Now it's time for the history of Stone's Throw. All of you returning guests, please feel free to walk out on this anytime. After several visits, you probably know the stories almost as well as I do."

Polite laughter from all. Marion and Anthony, who turned out to be the plump woman and the silver-haired man from last night, excused themselves. "We rented a sailboat for the morning."

"CeCe, Roy?"

Roy said, "We're beach bums today and we take our jobs seriously." He looked at his watch. "We've already missed four minutes of prime morning swim time."

Mac gestured toward the bedrooms. "Far be it from me to hold you back."

They ran upstairs.

Mac turned to the last couple. "Joel and Gino, you too?"

Gino said, "We're in. We've only seen you perform with the spooky Halloween background. We want to see if it's got a different feel in the summer."

Mac smiled at him. "Okay, then. My great-grandfather built Stone's Throw as his family home. His business had prospered and he decided it was time to work on his bucket list. He'd always wanted to live in a lighthouse. The obvious fact that Conneaut Lake didn't justify one made no difference to him. He built the house and the lighthouse tower, moved his family in, and launched fireworks from the top of the lighthouse every Independence Day. The local authorities issued a summons for endangering the nearby residences each year, for which he dutifully paid the fine and the next year launched more fireworks." She winked at her guests. "My family has a history of seeing how much we can get away with."

She trailed her fingers over the back of Marion's empty dining room chair. "My great-grandmother was the queen of estate sales. The family who originally owned this furniture brought it over from their ancestral manor in England. Did anyone feel like you were being watched while you ate? The faces of the nineteenth-century family members are carved into the chair backs."

Giulia tipped her chair and found the face of a young girl with elaborate ringlets carved into it.

"Teak is sturdy," Mac continued. "Even after two hundred years of people sitting against the chairs, details are still sharp enough to recognize. Since everyone came here before caffeine, you may not have noticed the table legs. They're chess pieces: A king, queen, bishop, and knight."

On cue, Giulia crouched at the corner of the long table. She also gave the underside of the table a second examination, but found no added séance equipment. Joel and Gino took selfies with the calico cats that had wandered in during Mac's opening speech.

"We want to take Tweedledum and Tweedledee home with us, Mac." Joel radiated charm post-caffeine.

"You ask for them every year," Mac said, smiling. "Usually you try to lure them into your car with catnip. And the answer is still no."

They hung their heads in unison.

"You'll just have to come visit them next year. This way to the good part: The lighthouse." As she passed the doll and carriage, she said, "We found this little lady in a box in the attic. The box took the brunt of the weather and rodent damage. I think she looks happy to be down here with people again." Mac waited a beat. "I chose not to use the Stephen King-worthy clown doll we found up there instead. You're welcome."

Laughter.

Giulia and Joel both shivered as they passed the doll. Mac stood by the framed photograph nearest the doorway as everyone filed into the souvenir room.

Mac walked to the first occasional table. "My grandmother built these miniature lighthouses. She got the local stores to stock them and used the money to furnish her own trousseau."

Giulia said, "Entrepreneurship runs in the family."

Stone nodded. "Every generation of Stones has at least one self-starter. This spring my youngest nephew bought the boat rental and repair shop way down the street. The hat's been passed." She skipped the next photographs and crouched in front of the model. "Last stop before we climb into the lighthouse."

She turned a clasp on one side of the house and opened it to reveal a period-piece replica of the B&B. She picked up two of the many miniature dolls populating the open rooms. "My great-grandmother made a doll for every member of the family. One Christmas two of my cousins crafted tiny beer cans and cigarettes for all the dolls. The older generation was not pleased; that is, the women weren't, but the men thought it was a hoot."

Gino and Joel kept passing a small piece of paper back and forth between them. Joel wrote something on it as Gino said, "Mac, we give you points for family friendliness, but so far the Halloween version is tons better."

Mac laughed. "If I went through the whole Woman in White story with all its embellishments here in the middle of summer, I'd look like a loon. A ghost story needs the proper atmosphere."

"Nooo," Joel said.

"You have to give the new guest the full Stone's Throw treatment," Gino said. "What did you bring in Lady Solana for if not to make your family ghost work all year 'round?"

Mac smiled at them as though they were her favorite pupils. Giulia wondered in all seriousness if the men were plants, like in a stage magician's audience.

Mac walked over to a glassed-in bookcase filled with souvenir mugs, local preserves, and keychains with lighthouses that lit when you pressed a button.

From behind a plastic picture frame with a price list, she took an eight-by-ten photograph.

"This is one of the pictures I took during the remodel. We practically had to gut the first and second floors. It's a shot of the space where Giulia's room is now." She held it out.

Giulia took it. Joel and Gino stayed back, grinning.

"Something...white?" She walked over to the window. "Maybe. It could be glare on the lens."

"Oh, man, a skeptic," Joel said. "Don't you watch those ghost hunting shows?"

Giulia handed back the picture. "I'm more of a *CSI* type."

Mac said, "I didn't see anything when I took the pictures, and I was too busy for the next few months to think any more about them. When the carriage house, where I live now, was being remodeled in turn, I slept in each of the rooms here to get a feel for the place and to see what needed further improvements." A pause. "One night in the Sand Dollar room I saw something."

Giulia could hear Sidney's head explode all the way from Cottonwood.

"I'm a big old chicken. I didn't move from that bed 'til I heard the construction crew arrive. Then I set out to get my hands on every bit of family history I could scare up, no pun intended."

Joel and Gino said together, "What did you find?"

"We have a family tragedy. I always wonder if the poor thing appreciates the attention we give her or if she feels exploited. Come up to the lighthouse gallery with me and I'll give you the short version on the very spot it happened. The reconstructed spot, that is."

As they walked past the suit of armor, Joel and Gino handed Giulia their phones.

"Would you take our annual picture with Sir Rusts-a-Lot?"

Joel draped himself against the armor's right arm and Gino snuggled up to its spear. Giulia took several pictures as the men changed one silly expression for another.

Mac climbed two steps and delivered the rest of her pitch from on high. "We keep everything here in excellent repair, but the stairs are steep. Please watch your step."

Gino took the little paper and wrote on it.

The cylinder was stuffy and cramped with the sun on it, and their steps bounced around the tapering space as they climbed higher. Mac reached the catwalk and walked around it to the narrow opening in the glass.

A breeze touched Giulia's face. She hadn't realized how hot she'd become.

One by one, they climbed up to the catwalk and stood in a circle around the light.

"Now we pretend I'm telling spooky stories around a bonfire up here, where no thieving crackhead can ruin the fun. One autumn night a young bride of one of the many Stone brothers waited for her husband to return from a trip to the far end of the lake. She paced the Widow's Walk. That's what lighthouse galleries used to be known as. Isn't Widow's Walk much more picturesque? As the moon rose, she saw her new husband sailing toward her in his dinghy. When he was only a quarter-mile away from the lighthouse's shore, the wind changed directions and ripped the boom out of his hands. While she watched, horrified, it whipped around and cracked open his head. He fell into the water, leaving a trail of blood gleaming black in the moonlight. His wife instinctively reached out as she cried his name. The wind caught her skirts, unbalanced her, and she plunged over the wooden railing to her death on the paving stones below."

She paused and took in her audience.

"Joel and Gino, are you passing notes in class?"

They started and looked guilty for a second. "Mac," Gino said, "you're one square short of Stone's Throw bingo."

"I'm what?"

He held up a paper divided into nine squares. "So far you've hit the dining room table, the doll and carriage, the clown doll no one has ever seen, the doll house, the miniature beer cans, the suspicious photograph, the night you were too scared to get out of bed, and how the stairs here are in excellent repair, but be careful so you don't ruin everyone else's holiday by falling and breaking your neck. Just one more and we fill the bingo card."

Giulia bit her lips to keep her composure. Mac looked startled, but a moment later she laughed. "You two could be my wayward nephews. If I catch you distributing that bingo card to anyone else, I'm adding fifteen percent onto your bill."

At that, Giulia managed to turn a laugh into an unladylike snort.

"As I was saying," Mac scowled at the bingo players, "the family legend concludes with the hint that on windy nights or nights with a bright moon, the widow's ghost wanders up and down the lighthouse stairs and Widow's Walk, waiting for her husband to rise from the lake and join her."

"Bingo," Joel and Gino whispered together.

Mac didn't acknowledge them. "That's all I can tell you about any ghost who might or might not haunt Stone's Throw. But no one really believes in ghosts, right?" She cut off any possible discussion by stepping through the glass door. "If you follow me to the gallery, I'll show you the best view of Conneaut Lake you'll ever see."

When Giulia stepped outside, the breeze hit her like a breath of winter. Ahh. She moved to the side, squinting against the glare of the sun on the water. The brown shingles of the B&B's roof directly below her brought out the greens of the grass, and far ahead of her, the darker green of the pine trees lining the lake. The sky above her rose up forever and the breeze smelled of cool water and fresh hot dogs and cotton candy.

Off to her right, Mac pointed out the spot in the lake where the long-ago Stone husband met his untimely demise. "Where Giulia is standing would be the approximate spot the young Mrs. Stone fell to her death."

Giulia looked down at the wide patio stones. She gripped the railing and shook it because that's what anyone would do, even though she'd already performed this railing test last night.

Mac said, "Every guest who stands in that spot shakes the railing."

Giulia conjured a faint blush. "It's your storytelling skills, Mac. Plus my strong self-preservation instinct."

"This railing was one of the few things I changed in the restoration," Mac said. "I hired a local woodworker to carve all the pieces in this swirl pattern. It reminds me of waves."

"What else did you change?" Giulia asked. "Authenticity is one of the charms here."

"Modern plumbing," Mac said.

Giulia pictured a quaint and malodorous chamber pot in her bedroom and shuddered. "I can't argue with that."

Nineteen

"Mac?" A hassled voice came from the foot of the spiral stairs. "The cleaners are here."

Mac poked her head through the opening in the glass. "Be right down, Lucy." She reentered the catwalk and gestured Giulia, Joel, and Gino in after her. "That's the Great Stone's Throw Ghost Story. What do you think?"

Gino started down the stairs and Joel said, "It's all wrong for a beautiful summer morning. I think you should tell the story over the bonfire, adding that the ghost sometimes crawls out of her grave when she hears her story being told. Then Lucy could creep up behind the newbies wearing a beat-up wedding gown all covered with dirt. Have her wear fake fingernails that are really long when she puts her ghostly hand on someone's shoulder."

Mac paused by the suit of armor. "I may steal that idea."

"Anything for the baker of Sunday's Bananas Foster pancakes."

They headed upstairs with Giulia behind them to retrieve her iPad. When she came down to the sunroom, two men and a woman had taken over the backyard. The woman, in a muted mauve plaid business suit, had to be the insurance adjustor. She and Mac conferred over several papers on a clipboard while the men walked around and over the patio. A third older man in jeans and work boots joined them. Giulia took several pictures with the iPad. Mac signed papers and the men attacked the cleanup. The insurance adjustor disappeared around the parking lot side of the building. Mac came into the sunroom and picked up two stray coffee cups from a shelf of board games.

"They promise me I'll have my patio back tomorrow. It would be tonight, but the paint on the furniture has to set," Mac said. "Now my house insurance rates will go up. Come on. I'm all yours."

Mac deposited the coffee cups in the kitchen and Giulia went out to the porch to scratch the white-muzzled beagle behind the ears.

"All the guests spoil Jabberwocky." Mac continued down the steps.

Giulia followed her into the carriage house. Unlike the studied antique restoration décor of the B&B, Mac's private house was spare, clean, and modern. Giulia slipped off her sneakers to walk on the cream-colored rugs.

Mac sat on the center cushion of a pale green couch. Giulia chose a complementary armchair in coral and opened her iPad. "No ghost has visited me in the Sand Dollar room."

Mac fidgeted with something in her pocket. Giulia refrained from quoting Tolkien, even though Gollum's voice in her head said, "What has she got in her pocketses?" She also kept last night's spectral sobs and white nightgown sighting to herself for now.

"Is today's newspaper correct? Was it arson last night?"

Mac leaned forward as though she were leaping at a safe conversation opening. "Another advantage of small town life: No official backlogs. They found a small container of lighter fluid in the fire pit. It wasn't the brand we use here."

"And the office?" Giulia typed it all in.

Mac made a face. "No fingerprints except mine and Lucy's, of course, and a solid smudge of prints on the screen door. Useless."

"That's unfortunate."

Mac snorted. "You could say so." Her phone rang. "Excuse me. Yes?...Damn that thieving bastard...Thank you...Good...Thank you." She stopped her hand's downward motion only a few inches short of slamming the phone on the coffee table. "Our firebug used my credit card at the Walmart over in Meadville. Kept it to twenty-four dollars' worth of stuff so he didn't have to sign for it. The police are checking the video feed."

Giulia hit save. "Ghosts don't need to shop at Walmart."

Mac didn't smile. "Maybe not, but this ghost could be causing this run of bad luck."

Excellent. When the client gives the proper opening they don't feel coerced.

"What bad luck? Specifics, please."

"Right. We've had two other accidents in the last three weeks. A water pipe burst last week. Pipes don't burst in summer weather. Before you ask, yes, I had all new pipes installed as part of the renovations. The break flooded part of the cellar. I lost some supplies and my guests had to take cold showers for two days. I took a percentage off everyone's bills for that."

"What did the plumbers say?"

"A fat lot of nothing. They tossed a bunch of jargon at me that netted out to they had no clue what caused the accident."

Giulia flexed her hands. The miniature keyboard on her tablet took some getting used to.

"Are you ready? Three days ago I came over to the B&B earlier than usual and the whole working kitchen reeked of gas. I ran downstairs and shut off the feed. Everything down there was normal. I called Lucy and she came over early. Together we took apart the stove. One of the hoses at the back was unscrewed."

Giulia opened her mouth.

"Don't you tell me that ghosts can't tamper with gas lines."

Giulia's "no snapping at the client" count got as far as seven when Mac said, "Now get ready. This is what I expect from you."

"No." Giulia didn't snap, exactly. "First I need several things from you. A list of your recurring guests and the weeks they usually stay, with addresses and phone numbers. The addresses and phone numbers for you and your employees, including the new psychic. Any threatening emails or letters you may have received since the date your problems began."

A mottled red flush crept from Mac's collar up her long neck. Her lips thinned to invisibility. If the waves of anger and offense surging from her were supposed to intimidate Giulia, Mac was about to be disappointed. Her upper-management ire was cake compared to one of the convent's spiritual reviews. Giulia had survived five nuns with the most authority grilling her on how deeply she embodied Franciscan ideals, how the world viewed her as what a true, proper, devout Sister should be, and their dissection of the holiness of her spiritual life. Annually.

A client going all self-righteous and "I'm in charge" at her? A Care Bear.

The next moment, the tension snapped. Mac's lips reappeared as she said, "I'm much too used to ordering people around." The flush receded. "A hazard of being queen of all I survey, I suppose. Why hire an expert if I'm not going to listen to you? I can't get those lists until I have my laptop again, but I can get you the possible start date of my troubles. I'll be right back."

Giulia stood and walked back into the entrance hall to inspect the watercolors hanging there. The sunsets and fishing boats and lighthouses in all four seasons shrieked "amateur." Sure enough, "Mac" and a date hugged the lower right-hand corner of each painting. Eh. Giulia's hobby was growing her own food. No finger-pointing here.

"Where are you? I found it. Oh. When I have any free time, which isn't often, I drag out the easel and floppy hat and go all artiste on the lawn. Here."

Giulia took the newspaper dated this past May fourteenth. Mac pointed to the callout above the masthead. "This Week's Local Spotlight: The Stone's Throw B&B: Page 8."

"The paper ran one article a week in the month before Memorial Day," she said. "My article didn't go viral or anything, but I got reservations from a handful of first-timers."

Giulia scanned the article as Mac kept talking. "I pulled out all the stops: Great-Grandpa's lighthouse where none was needed. The legend of the family gold. The family ghost's death and haunting.

The eager young intern was astounded that an old lady ran this place all by herself."

"That astonishment comes across in his writing."

"I know. He made me into a combination of Wonder Woman and Julia Child."

Giulia kept reading.

> Mac Stone's great-great-great-grandfather, Joshua Aloysius Stone, spent his life despoiling rich travelers. That's right, readers. Our peaceful tourist haven boasts a descendant of a real Wild West highwayman. He was a fastidious highwayman, according to his great-great-great-granddaughter: He only took the travelers' gold. Alas, the law caught up with him and hanged him for his deeds. But our Mac says the family has an enduring legend of Joshua Aloysius' secret hoard.
>
> "No one's ever found it," she told this reporter as we stood high up on the Widow's Walk of Stone's Throw lighthouse. "As kids we were told our family black sheep revealed the location of the gold to his wife before he died, but no other Stone has ever found it."
>
> As Mac finished my tour of her luxurious yet affordable inn, I asked her about the Herculean labor she undertook when she chose to turn the abandoned Stone house into a working Bed and Breakfast.
>
> "It didn't come cheap," Mac said as we watched the sun set over Conneaut Lake from Stone's Throw's flagged patio. "People have asked me if I had to discover that stash of highwayman's gold to pay for all of this, but the truth is I emptied fifty years' worth of savings to make Stone's Throw happen."

Giulia looked up from the newspaper. From that suspicious pocket, Mac brought out a single gold coin. "Behold the Stone family treasure. One Liberty five-dollar gold coin. Depending on which collector I show it to, it's worth between two hundred fifty and four hundred dollars."

"So you've embellished a colorful legend?" Giulia handed the paper back to her.

Mac chuckled. "That's a polite way of saying I'm a big fat liar."

Giulia's "displeased teacher" face appeared. "That's not at all what I meant."

Mac's spine stiffened. "Did you used to be a teacher? My college science teacher used to get that look and it never meant anything good."

Giulia let her teacher face return to the past. Oh, yeah. She still had it.

Mac returned the coin to her pocket. The doorbell rang. The detective from last night stood on the asphalt.

"Ronnie, tell me you have good news."

"Yes and no. Here's your laptop. Sign, please." He held out a carbonless receipt form on a clipboard.

Mac signed and took the bottom copy. "My tax dollars are well spent. What's the bad news?"

"No sign of your purse or anything in it besides the MasterCard used at Walmart."

"Out of respect for your official status, I won't give voice to what I'm thinking."

The detective's face gave nothing away. "I have more good news to make up for the lack of purse contents. We also caught the guy who pawned your laptop."

"Yes." Mac punched the doorframe. "Was it our friendly neighborhood crackhead?"

"Sorry to disappoint you, but this time it was one of the meth addicts. He and his friends have been particularly active since we busted up their lab in the woods behind Anderson's farm."

"Tell me you can pin the arson on him and I'll give you and Sheila a free overnight stay here."

"Mac, please don't bribe your local law enforcement." He shook his head. "We will use everything in our power to find the firebug. Arson is bad for tourism." This time he allowed himself a small smile. "Since this charmer scored heroin with the pawnshop money and is coming off the high as I stand here, we expect him to vomit every thought in his useless head before my shift ends."

"Good." Mac's voice was hard. "Did he screw with my laptop?"

"Our guy says not as far as he can tell. According to the timeline of events, he pawned it right after he left here and used all the cash on horse. You should change all your passwords anyway."

"Miserable waste of skin." Mac shook the detective's hand. "Thanks. Maybe I'll have my psychic curse him with genital rot."

The detective's smile became derisive but he left without comment.

Giulia left her spot in the hallway and returned to the living room before Mac.

Mac gestured with her head to a nook opposite the television. "It's a good thing I moved my old printer over here since my office is still off-limits. This one is slower but I'll be able to give you all the documentation you asked for."

Twenty

Giulia returned to the inn with a large envelope full of printouts. Neither the cats nor the dog were on the porch, despite multiple pools of inviting sunlight on the wicker chairs.

The screen door opened before Giulia could grasp the handle.

"A pall surrounds your head," a resonant alto voice said. "It is black as the deepest night, yet glimmering with the brightness of many stars."

A tall woman in linen trousers with a knife crease so severe they ought to have a warning label blocked the entrance. Her asymmetrical black hair hung to her right shoulder and brushed the bottom of her left earlobe. Every strand kept to its assigned place even when she moved. Giulia envied hair with such ingrained obedience.

"What are you, with this veil about you?" The woman's hands sketched a swoop around Giulia's head and past her shoulders.

CeCe stood in the hall doorway, her phone up.

A male voice behind Giulia said, "I told you these new swim trunks would get me..."

Joel. That meant the next voice would be Gino's.

"Get you what? More ego-stroking? Out of my way, Mr. Pinup. I need a shower. What the heck?"

"Yes. It is a veil of some kind." The woman's hands kept fondling the air around Giulia's head. Her eyes rolled partway up, revealing their white undersides.

Gross. Giulia considered her options. If she broke up this tableau by walking around Ms. Obedient Hair, would it simply create another ring to this circus?

Where was a Woman in White when Giulia could've used a ghost to steal the spotlight?

Movement from the dining room caught Giulia's eye. Mac's assistant Lucy peered around the doorframe, texting. Either Gino or Joel snickered.

In an instant, the theatrics evaporated. The woman's arms dropped, her blue irises reappeared, and she smoothed her hair as though one strand on the longer side had entertained a thought of rebellion.

"I am Solana," she said. "You are a new guest here. I will return tomorrow and we must meet then."

Giulia clutched the oversized envelope to prevent her hands from adjusting a phantom veil. It had been four years. She'd thought she was long past that reflex.

"Giulia Driscoll. Is there a particular reason you'd like to meet with me?"

Solana's laugh was an octave higher than her psychic revelation voice. "You have so many walls erected around your spirit. I see the unusual in you despite them. This is why I am here. If you will allow me an entrance into those walls, I will show you the deeper meanings in your ethereal veil."

Neon message boards lit up on all Giulia's supposed walls: Not if we were stranded in the middle of Conneaut Lake in the dead of winter with a hungry Lake Monster circling us.

Giulia's self-control held. She said, "How interesting. I'll see if I can manage some time for a meeting. Thank you."

Now she walked around Solana, who never stopped staring at the air surrounding Giulia's head. CeCe slipped her phone into a pocket when Giulia passed her.

Joel and Gino caught Giulia in the second floor hall.

"Hey, Giulia. If CeCe uploads that video to YouTube, you're gonna go viral." Joel still looked hugely entertained.

Giulia didn't bother to hide her grimace from them. "This was supposed to be a peaceful getaway. My husband and I haven't taken any time off since our honeymoon last year."

"Ouch," Gino said. "Well, it sure won't be boring. Best I can offer."

"I gather Solana is Mac's tame psychic?"

Joel snorted. "Tame psychic. That's perfect. All she needs is a Goth collar with a tag."

Gino gave him a "duh" look. "Did you see her clothes and hair? She'd only wear a collar if Paris Hilton gave her a hand-me-down from one of her yappy little purse beasts."

"Yeah, I don't see Solana shopping at Costco."

Giulia cataloged their naked delight at the free entertainment. Toyed with and discarded the idea of asking CeCe to delete the recording. Added Mac's friend Lady Rowan sending Mac to DI for the "veiled woman" to Solana's "sparkling black veil" performance. The result: DI was being played by an expert trio. Or by Mac, and the other two were on her payroll. Or by the psychics and Mac was their dupe.

Giulia knew a few Irish curses by now. She didn't let loose with any of them as she forced a rueful smile. "If this turns out to be my fifteen minutes of fame, I'll be signing autographs tomorrow after breakfast."

"That's the spirit," Gino said. "We'll be first in line."

"Right now I want to be first in line at the lunch truck," Joel said.

"Yes, dear."

They opened their room door and Giulia locked herself into the supposedly haunted Sand Dollar room. First she set the envelope on the dresser. Second, she closed the windows. Third, she climbed onto the bed. Fourth, she shoved her face into her pillow and screamed.

The quasi-military *Godzilla* theme played from her phone. She raised her head, shoved her always disobedient hair out of her face, and punched the button beneath her husband's picture.

"Please tell me you're on your way."

"Better than that. I'm in the parking lot next to a certain copper Ion."

"I'm already there."

Giulia slid sideways down the banister. Hey, she was on vacation. The beagle had returned to the porch, but not the cats. Maybe they enjoyed Solana's presence as little as she did. She jumped from the bottom porch step into Frank's arms.

"You are the best thing to happen to me in days."

After a prolonged public display of affection, Frank said, "Not another fire?"

"A psychic encounter which may have been uploaded to YouTube already."

Frank guffawed. "I have to see this. What did you do?"

"Me? Absolutely nothing. Come on. You need to be briefed."

He took a small rolling suitcase out of the Camry's trunk. "I remember. I'm an IT consultant because I know enough about setting up networks to convince anyone at this place who wants to score some free advice."

"And you're here a day later than me because you had an emergency network failure to fix. I manage a local coffee shop. Have I mentioned how much I despise lying?"

"Too many times to count."

"I pre-confessed to Father Carlos for this entire week last Saturday. He absolved me for the fake job interviews to catch Flynt the scumbag and for this cover assignment."

"I won't begin to pretend to understand the system you and Carlos have worked out so you can attend Mass with a clean slate." Frank surveyed the front of the inn. "Give me the layout of this place, please."

Giulia pointed over her shoulder. "Behind you is the carriage house, which Mac—everyone calls her Mac—converted into her own living area. The first floor of the inn has the kitchen, dining room, living room, music room, and sunroom. Also a pass-through to the lighthouse. The second floor has two bedrooms and a reading room which she calls a library. The third floor has three bedrooms and that's it, except for the attic and cellar."

Frank stooped to scratch the beagle's ears. "Sounds like a plain old renovated house."

"Bingo." Giulia looked in vain for the cats. "There are no TVs." She cut off Frank's groan. "But there is Wi-Fi."

"There's hope for my fantasy baseball league yet." He stopped just inside the kitchen and checked the placement of all visible doors.

"Stop being a cop," Giulia whispered.

"Never off-duty," he said, "especially when my wife is here to evict a territorial ghost with an affinity for setting fires."

"That's not what happened."

Frank stopped at their doorway. "Sand Dollar room?"

"It has atmosphere." Giulia opened the top dresser drawer.

"What it doesn't have is a TV." He tossed underwear, shorts, and shirts in more or less the same order as hers. "What's the Wi-Fi password? Never mind. I see it here." He typed into his phone, scowled, and waited.

"Ah, ESPN, how I love you." With the phone in his left hand, he spread out the other papers. "We can get pizza and beer delivered. Shrimp baskets too. I like the beach."

Giulia opened the top drawer and fluttered her slinky nightgown until Frank looked away from his phone.

His eyebrows arched, but he didn't comment. Instead, he set down his phone, walked to the bed, and pushed on the mattress several times until it bounced. "No creaks," he said. "Good."

"Come outside and I'll give you the whole fire story."

"Not yet. I have to find this YouTube video."

Giulia groaned. "You're supposed to be on my side."

He typed into his browser, typed again; a third time. A fourth. His finger touched the screen and after a good twenty seconds Giulia heard Solana's voice describing Giulia's "pall."

Frank's face got redder than his hair until he laughed so hard he drowned out the sound from the phone.

"*Muirnín*, that's priceless. Who do I thank for this?"

Giulia left the room without answering. Frank caught up to her on the stairs. The cleaners were still working on the patio so they walked out to the porch.

The driver's door of a slate blue Prius closed on Solana's dark hair. Giulia put a hand out to stop Frank. They didn't move until the car drove away down the street.

"That was the psychic."

"But I wanted to ask her about the Veeeiled Woooman."

Giulia stomped down the porch steps. Frank followed, laughing again.

Twenty-One

Giulia bought a tangerine snow cone and Frank a hot dog as they walked along the boardwalk parallel to the beach.

She started with last night's three-way Ouija board session, segued to the fire, recited a précis of everything she knew about the guests, and ended with the sheaf of printouts waiting for her in their room.

The beachfront was packed. Jimmy Buffett songs played from the speakers at one bar. A block farther on, a second bar played sixties retro. Down the streets between the bars, different shops sold t-shirts, salt water taffy, sunscreen, magazines, and disposable cameras. "I didn't know those still existed," Giulia said.

They hung a right down the street with the least crowded sidewalks and tossed their food papers into a trashcan shaped like a sandcastle.

"It sucks that the fingerprints were a bust," Frank said.

"I know, but the suspect pool is small enough for that not to matter."

One storefront appeared to have the swimsuit market to itself. A coffee shop advertised banana daiquiri smoothies. Frank pointed out three restaurants for them to try. When they returned to the beach, speedboats and Sea-Doos crowded the water farther out on the lake.

"Ever been on a Sea-Doo?" Frank said.

"Never."

"We need to shoehorn in an hour for that. All in the name of our cover story, of course."

"The rental place should be right around here. Mac's nephew runs it."

Frank pointed. "Second pier to the right."

A tall, white-haired man was choosing between small motorboats when Giulia and Frank walked onto the dock. Two grade school kids sprawled on the dock flat on their stomachs, staring into the water. Three sets of fishing gear, two small and one large, lay at the adult's feet.

A man about Giulia's age was describing the different features of each boat. His retro-preppie look wasn't completely out of place. Where else to wear deck shoes minus socks if not on the waterfront? Although no preppie worth the name should have the beginnings of that beer gut. He wore his brown hair in the 1980s blow-dried style too. To complete the look it really ought to have been blond.

The old man chose a boat and paid. The kids grabbed their paraphernalia and bounced into the boat, rocking it something wicked. The old man got them settled and the preppie cast the boat off. Then he turned to Frank with a business smile.

"Morning. Looking to rent a boat?"

"Yep," Frank said. "We're staying at that lighthouse place and it's girly. I need some real recreation."

"Liar," Giulia said. "You said it reminded you of your grandmother's." She wasn't quite sure if Frank was trying to create a male bonding moment to get the nephew to open up easier, so she waited for a cue.

"What do you have in mind?" the preppie said. "Fishing? Water skiing? Sea-Doo?"

Frank turned to Giulia. "Yeah, babe—Sea-Doo. Don't you want to scream across the lake, sending up fountains of spray with the wind whipping your hair?"

Giulia made the face she got when a skunk walked by their house. "My new bathing suit is meant to be seen, not to get wet."

Frank rolled his eyes as he turned his head toward the preppie. "Guess it's fishing."

Giulia walked away to the souvenir shop where the street met the dock and made a small show of evaluating the handcrafted jewelry in the window. The window also gave her a faint reflection of Frank and his new bud. They laughed. Frank mimed the length of a caught fish; the preppie acted impressed.

They walked several steps over to a narrow two-story house farther back from the water's edge. The first floor was taken up by the rental and repair shop.

The preppie took a brochure from a rack outside the door and pointed out several things in it to Frank. After a few more words, Frank came over to Giulia.

"I have a new soulmate," Frank said as they walked back onto the crowded beach. "Walt and I can't understand why women buy bathing suits that aren't supposed to go in the water. Also, I may have embellished the length of that pike I caught on my last fishing trip."

"Father Carlos is always ready to hear your confession," Giulia said.

"That's still better than confessing to my own brother," Frank said.

"It's the hazard of all families with a priest as a sibling. If you ever have to confess to Pat, I will wheedle a recording out of him despite the seal of the confessional."

"Hell will freeze over first."

Three preteens ran into them, apologized, and kept running. Two smaller children chased after the older ones, trying and failing to aim gigantic squirt guns.

Frank said, "My pal Walt could be a Casablanca-like fount of information. Everybody comes to the boat dock on a lake."

"Then by all means spend more time with him."

"I hear and obey." Frank stuck the brochure in his pocket. "A two-hour small boat rental is only fifty bucks. I can get in some fishing and take him for a beer afterward."

Giulia said, "This afternoon is dedicated to research on guests and staff. If the Wi-Fi is always as slow as it has been today, I'll have to go back to Cottonwood Monday to get in any useful searching."

"Leaving me on my own with Sea-Doos at hand. Awesome."

They reached the Stone's Throw area of the beach and climbed the short hill. The patio was empty but large "WET PAINT" tent signs blocked the cushionless furniture. The older man who'd tended the bonfire last night was hammering croquet wickets into the abused grass. A bocce ball court on the opposite side of the patio still needed raking, but the sides had been replaced.

"Game later?" Frank said.

"Always. First, though, studying."

"For you. For me, ESPN."

They entered the sunroom, where Roy and CeCe were playing Monopoly with Marion and Anthony. Giulia introduced Frank. Roy and Gino gave Frank elaborate, in-the-know winks when he left to take Giulia to their room.

"Afternoon sex. Ah, vacation," Frank said. But when they closed themselves into their room, he left the bed to Giulia and her research and took his phone into the bathroom.

"What the hell kind of a shower is this?"

Twenty-Two

At least three hours had passed and Frank was asleep next to Giulia's piles of paper on the bed when shrieks filled the hall on the other side of their closed door. Giulia reached it first and yanked it open. The shrieks quadrupled in volume.

Marion stood on the polished hall floor covered only with a bath towel.

Brown goo oozed down her hair and glopped onto her shoulders. Tendrils of gunk stretched thinner and thinner as they dripped onto her chest and rolled off toward her feet.

"Mac! Oh my God! Mac, where are you?"

The gunk oozed onto her cheek. Marion opened her mouth again and a tendril ran into it. Her resulting shrieks threatened to shatter the stained glass window.

Anthony came out of the room behind her, towel in hand. Marion swatted it away.

CeCe and Roy, in matching bathing suits, stood on the stairs to the third floor, open-mouthed. Mac and Matthew the handyman, whose face mimicked Grumpy Cat in human form, pounded up the stairs from the first floor. Both of them stopped and stared for a few seconds.

Marion's latest screech cut off in the middle and the eerier noise of groaning pipes replaced it. She flung out her arms at Mac and the bath towel slipped. Anthony grabbed it in time to prevent a wardrobe malfunction.

"It's coming out of the shower." Marion's voice acquired the tones of a supervisor chastising an underling.

Mac deflected her guest's wrath with action. "Matthew, the shower."

Grumpy Cat clomped into the room and the pipes stopped moaning a moment later.

Giulia came forward and touched Marion's shoulder. "Would you like to use our shower while yours is being fixed?"

More brown gunk hit Marion's shoulders. She shuddered. "Thank you. Yes, I would very much like to use a shower that works."

Mac's expression said she was calculating the odds the couple would cancel their stay and demand a refund. Giulia led Marion past Frank into their room.

"Honey, could you maybe go check out boat rentals for tomorrow?"

"Sure." He headed downstairs.

"Mac," Giulia said, "may we have a few extra towels?"

"Of course." Mac turned to Anthony. "Can I offer you some lemonade or iced coffee while your room is being attended to?"

He called after his wife, "Honey, I'll take your purse with me," returned to the room and came out with a tasteful white leather bag. "Iced coffee, thanks, Mac."

Giulia repacked all the papers and sat in the room's single chair, reading the latest issue of *Cosmo*. More clomping and pipes banging came through from the hall. When the shower stopped, she turned on her phone's voice memo function and slipped the phone into the front pocket of her capris.

Marion came out of the bathroom, hair plastered to her head and wrapped in clean towels.

"I used both of your bath towels. I'm sorry."

Giulia put down the magazine and stood. "That's quite all right. Mac is bringing up some more."

"Thank you for the use of your shower. I've never been so disgusted in my life." Her voice had reverted to its usual sophistication now that she wasn't imitating an angry crow. "Now that your husband's arrived, do you have plans for dinner?"

"Not yet. We've been celebrating our first day by taking a nap."

"Why don't you come to dinner with us? The Oyster Shuck caters to the boating crowd. The owner knows us well."

"We'd be happy to. I'll track down Frank and meet you...downstairs?"

"Excellent. I'll be only fifteen minutes. I need more than one martini tonight."

Giulia erased the unprofitable voice memo and went in search of Frank. She found him practicing bocce on the restored court.

"You're letting your wrist snap too much on release," she said.

"Yeah? Show me."

Giulia stepped into the long, rectangular bocce pit and picked up a ball. "Like this." She raised the ball in both hands and sighted along them for the *pallino*, cocked her right arm.back, and half-threw, half-rolled the ball off her hand, following through with her entire arm aligned. The larger ball stopped three inches to the right of the tiny target ball.

"Bah. I'm out of practice."

"Jesus, Mary, and Joseph, you call that out of practice? Let's find someplace to eat so I can drown my athlete's sorrows."

"We already have dinner plans. Marion invited us to dine with them at the restaurant all the boating people patronize. They know the owner."

Frank stepped onto the grass. "Dine, huh? Guess they don't serve regular old fried fish and beer at this joint?"

"Oh, but of course. Overpriced imported beer and panko-crusted trout with truffle sauce."

The waiter seated Frank, Giulia, Marion, and Anthony, and handed them menus. Giulia opened hers to the clipped-in paper with today's specials and almost lost it when she read the top one: Panko-encrusted smallmouth bass with a Guinness reduction.

"Giulia, I forgot what business you said you were in," Marion said after she'd partaken of the life-giving elixir called martini.

"I manage a coffee shop." Giulia sipped a Guinness.

"Oh, how nice. Do you have much employee turnover? Anthony has such a difficult time finding a manager whom he can trust to keep the workers in line."

Giulia put on Polite Smile Number Three. Marion had slotted her into a lower social sphere, which was fine with Giulia. Whenever people considered Giulia beneath themselves, she took it as a gift. People didn't bother to censor their discussions around the lower classes.

"Our turnover isn't too bad. It's worst when college starts up every August."

Anthony and Frank were talking network configurations over Coronas. Like at the boat dock earlier, Frank once again proved himself the perfect partner. He ranked Corona a notch above "lite" beers; in other words, only to be consumed under extreme duress. Yet here he was, using it to bond with a possible suspect to pump information.

Marion patronized Giulia as they ate panko-encrusted bass. Giulia asked her advice on hiring high school seniors versus college students. Marion instructed. Giulia splashed hot sauce on her hand-cut fries. Marion's expression patted Giulia on the head for her plebian tastes.

Giulia struck. "Thank you for recommending this restaurant. The food is excellent."

"We eat here at least twice every time we stay at the Stone's Throw. This is your first time, you said?"

"Yes. We're both so busy we had to find a place on short notice. We seem to have chosen well."

Marion finished her second martini and signaled for another. "This is our fourth year. Stone's Throw is our exception. We stay at Westin resorts as a rule."

The martini arrived along with the dessert menu. Giulia nudged Frank. "Split a brownie sundae with me?"

"I'm ready to do my duty as a husband." He ordered coffee for both of them.

Marion ordered strawberry shortcake and a small kirsch. Anthony chose coffee and brandy. Giulia hadn't felt this bourgeois in years. No, in ever.

"Stone's Throw is roughing it," Anthony said, "but it's also research. There's money in a bed and breakfast if the location is right. The historic value and the personal touches are what we're looking for."

Dessert arrived. Marion poured the kirsch over her shortcake. "A chef who wants to be away from the pressure of a four- or five-star restaurant or a recent graduate of a good school is necessary."

Giulia swallowed a mouthful of brownie, ice cream, and real whipped cream. "So you're not looking to run a B&B yourself?"

"Oh, no. I don't cook."

She sure drank, though. Three martinis and one liqueur and not a slur in her voice. Giulia's limit was two beers.

Anthony sipped his brandy. "We've recommended Stone's Throw to several friends. No one's been disappointed. Frank, tell me more about using terminals instead of separate towers."

The couples split after dinner. Marion and Anthony had an appointment with a local artist whose lake views Anthony was considering for one of his offices. Frank took Giulia by the arm in a proper protective manner and turned toward the beach.

"My cheeks ache from keeping up that empty smile," Giulia said after a few minutes when they'd walked far in the opposite direction.

"That coffee didn't wash out the taste of Corona." Frank squeezed Giulia. "I haven't seen you work for quite a while. I rather enjoy you as a Stepford Wife."

She shuddered. "That's the scariest movie ever made."

"Still, good call on letting her patronize you."

"If there's one thing I do well, it's stealth mode. Wait a sec." She took off her sandals. "Come walk along the water's edge with me."

He kissed the top of her curls. "You are such a romantic. All right, I'll play." He removed sneakers and socks, stuffed the socks in the toes, tied the laces together, and hung them over his left shoulder. "I'm reliving my childhood."

"It's a beach. It's calling to us. Ooh, chilly water." She opened a voice memo on her phone. "Back to business. What did Anthony have to say?"

"He was less patronizing than his wife. We talked of manly things: Basketball and scotch. Then he switched the discussion to network builds. Probably wanted free advice; doubt he was trying to see if I'm for real. There's no reason for anyone to think we have ulterior motives."

"I'll make a note in your employee file. Marion holds her liquor well, but it makes her talkative. I first learned all about how difficult it is to hire competent managers."

"Ouch."

"I switched to full-on Barbie doll female after that. I conveyed all eagerness to receive her wisdom and experience. She gave me advice on how to choose employees and then told me how they've been coming here for years and recommending it to their friends, because it's quaint."

Frank said, "Yeah. Quaint."

"Oh, stop. This is not a hardship. Anyway, after she impressed me with her patronage she confided they have a plan to buy their own bed and breakfast."

"Do they now?"

"Indeed. Behind my empty smile I was measuring her for a saboteur hat. What if she or her husband put that gunk in the shower themselves?" She danced away from an aggressive wave.

Frank followed her. "You can't capture my wisdom if you take away the recording device. Do you think she's capable of making herself into a mess on purpose?"

Giulia tried the waves one last time and quit. "I've got goosebumps in places that shouldn't have goosebumps. I'm not sure how driven she is. That's what's holding me back. If image is more important than acquiring what she wants, then no. But we have a few more days to get under their skins. At least one of our first possible suspects walked right into our shower."

Frank angled them toward the lighthouse's beach fence. "If you give that to Zane to transcribe, he'll freak out."

Giulia laughed. "I'll warn him first." She stopped recording. "I have to scrape the sand off my feet before I go inside."

Frank sat her down on the grass. "Let me see." He faced her feet to the setting sun. "Allow me, ma'am." He brushed her feet clean with his hands, then started tickling.

Giulia gasped and shrieked and squirmed. "Stop—stop—stop."

"Kiss me in public first."

"Stop first." She butt-walked farther up the grass. Frank sat next to her and kissed her. Giulia didn't keep her eyes open to make sure no one was watching, either.

When Frank broke the long kiss, he said, "Honest answer: Did you check to see if we were alone?"

"I did not."

Frank stared into her eyes.

"I only lie to catch a suspect. You know that." She pecked his nose. "Maybe I'm mellowing."

"Excellent." He pulled her to her feet. "Next we'll find a secluded corner of beach and have sex outside."

Giulia squeaked.

Twenty-Three

Giulia ran into the sunroom, laughing, with Frank a step behind her.

The glowing twilight outside didn't extend to inside. Frank groped along the wall and switched on the sconces.

"So what do we do here in the evening? Get the game on the radio and sit around playing bridge?"

Giulia shook her head. "You never had to make your own entertainment, did you? Not with your huge family." She walked through to the music room and turned on the fringed lamps.

"*A Dhia dhílis.*"

"Frank, please don't blaspheme."

He brought his face closer to a floor lamp with six different crochet panels in shades of rose terminating in gold fringe. "'My God' is a simple reaction to unexpected events. Trust me, when I blaspheme, you'll know it. This lamp is like something out of a time travel nightmare."

Giulia lifted the piano's fallboard and played an arpeggio. "If my relatives still spoke to me I could take you to visit Aunt Cherubina. The last time I saw her, six years ago, her entire house was packed with furniture like this. Gloomy old paintings of Christ Crucified and Our Lady of Sorrows covered the walls."

"I've never been so glad my relatives chose to become as American as possible. The worst I remember was Uncle Fionn. He mashed Auld Country styles with kitsch from the nineteen fifties."

A shudder. "It was like a flea market dumpster unloaded in his house."

Giulia played the opening bars to "When Irish Eyes Are Smiling."

Frank stalked over to the piano and banged out the beginning of the Tarantella.

Giulia countered with "How Are Things in Glocca Morra" from *Finian's Rainbow.*

Frank blew her a kiss and began "That's Amore." Giulia started singing by the second verse and they finished the duet together. Without a beat in between, Giulia segued to "The Wells Fargo Wagon." Since they'd spent several weeks rehearsing and performing this musical in the Cottonwood Community Theater orchestra pit, both of them could sing it like loud karaoke.

Applause after the last chord made them both jump. Everyone except Marion and Anthony had squeezed into the music room.

"More, please," Roy said. "Do you know anything from *Hello Dolly?*"

Frank tried "Before the Parade Passes By." CeCe and Roy sang along. The instant that song ended, Mac asked for "Ten Minutes Ago" from *Cinderella.* Giulia played that one as well as she could with Frank holding her by the waist and waltzing in place. She glanced sideways once to see two of the couples waltzing. Not Marion and Anthony, who'd arrived when she'd been concentrating on the keyboard.

Lucy said with a slight duck of her head, "By any chance do you know the marionette song?"

Frank said, "You mean, 'The Internet is for—'"

Giulia elbowed Frank. "I am not playing anything from *Avenue Q.*" To Lucy: "Do you mean 'The Lonely Goatherd' from *The Sound of Music?*"

"Well, yeah, of course."

Giulia gave her the smile she used to reserve for the students whose mouths she wanted to wash out with soap. "I don't know that one by heart. What about 'My Favorite Things' or 'Edelweiss?'"

"My Favorite Things" won the vote. Frank took the left-hand part and Giulia the right-hand. She could play this song in her sleep, so under the cover of adjusting her position on the piano seat, she sneaked glances at everyone.

Joel and Gino sang along with their arms around each other. Next to them, Marion and Anthony tried not to enjoy themselves. Giulia could tell by their facial expressions. Every year she'd taught English literature a few students fell in love with the Gilgamesh and Beowulf unit but pretended not to because it wasn't cool.

When the song ended, Frank changed keys and vamped the opening to "Singin' in the Rain." Mac said something to Lucy and they both left. Before the song finished, Lucy returned with a pitcher of lemonade and a stack of glasses and Mac carried a plate of chocolate chip cookies.

More applause at the end of the song. Giulia glanced at Frank, who nodded.

"Just one more, okay?" Giulia said to the room.

"'Cabaret?'"

"'Everything's Coming Up Roses?'"

"'Brush Up Your Shakespeare?'"

"Yes!"

"Yes, please."

Frank started the intro and Giulia scanned her memory for the order of verses. The guests divided themselves into two groups on their own and tried a proper call-and-response but they kept messing up the order of Shakespeare plays.

Halfway through the second verse Gino pulled up the lyrics on his phone. Everyone crowded around the tiny screen to sing. By the last verse they all had their arms around each other's shoulders and were swaying in time to the music. Even Marion and Anthony joined in.

Laughter and applause followed the final chorus.

"That's thirsty work, everyone," Mac said. "I've got lemonade and fresh-baked cookies set out on the coffee table in the living room."

The party shooed themselves into the other room. Mac stayed in the music room. Frank went to get Giulia something to drink.

"Matthew found a long mesh bag filled with sludge in the Haswells' shower pipe," Mac whispered to Giulia. "It looked like one of those lint traps you see on washing machine hoses."

In a low voice, Giulia said, "No ghost did that."

Mac looked doubtful, but Anthony and Marion returned to the music room before she could answer.

"Thank you both for that impromptu concert," Anthony said. "You must be in theater as well as coffee and IT."

"Yes, we both work in the orchestra pit on occasion. We know a lot of standard musicals."

Frank slipped a warm chocolate chip cookie into her hand.

"Thank you, honey."

Anthony jogged Marion's elbow. "Come on; let's top off our coffee in our room." He winked at Giulia and Frank. "We have a stash of liqueurs. It's our not-so-secret vice."

"I missed a possible drawback to this place," Frank said when they were in their own room.

"Which is?" Giulia said from the tiny round nightstand. Her iPad took up half its surface.

"The cute element." Without raising his eyes from his phone, he said, "That video of you only has a hundred and thirty-four views. You'll never go viral that way."

"I would love to wring CeCe's neck." She typed a set of bullet points while Frank texted one of his fantasy league rivals, from the gloating sound of his chuckle. "I can think of at least four different ways that sludge got into the shower pipe, and none of them involve otherworldly intervention. Also, I want to wangle lunch or dinner with the psychic tomorrow."

"Sure. I'll run out and buy you one of those big rectangular swimsuit cover-ups and you can wrap yourself in it. See if that brings out any more about the Veeeiled Woooman."

Giulia facepalmed. "Seriously, why couldn't she see me as my Italian great-grandmother far in the past? Lady Rowan back in Cottonwood did it too. If I'm going to give off psychic vibes to total strangers, how much longer will it take for the signals from my old life to fade?"

Frank set his phone on the nightstand next to the iPad. "Come to bed and we'll work on it."

Twenty-Four

"Hey, it's eight thirty. Wake up. I'm starving."

Giulia opened her eyes and squeezed them shut a second later against the morning sun. "It's what?"

Frank's voice smiled. "It's eight thirty, breakfast is at nine, and we're supposed to show up together, right?"

Giulia sat up like a Jack-in-the-box. "It's eight thirty? I've got to shower." She stripped everything off and ran into the bathroom.

They took the last two available chairs at the dining room table at one minute to nine. Frank got back up half a second later to pour coffee for them both. Giulia sipped and controlled her instinctive grimace; the coffee was still thin and bitter.

Breakfast made up for it, though. Fresh strawberries to start, followed by pancakes covered with sliced bananas and nuts in a spiced rum and brown sugar syrup.

Mac and Lucy served and removed plates, refilled the coffee carafe, and graciously accepted compliments on the food.

Marion set down her fork. "So, Giulia, what did you and Frank think of your first night together at Stone's Throw?"

"We slept the sleep of the truly relaxed."

Joel and Roy winked at each other. CeCe and Giulia rolled their eyes in the classic "men" expression.

Giulia bailed on the lighthouse tour, but Frank took his cue and played new guest. He came up to their room after and dragged her away from research with the creaking Wi-Fi.

"Outdoors with you. You want to compare lighthouse notes with me."

"I do, actually." She stretched her back as Frank jogged the printouts back into their envelope.

Sunshine enveloped Giulia when she stepped onto the porch. "Another gorgeous day. Let's go around the lighthouse side of the building. Maybe the beach will be less crowded."

"Mac gave me the full treatment," Frank said. "Emphasis on the miniature beer cans and cigarettes in the dollhouse."

"I got the emphasis on the dramatic and tearful story of the long-ago Stone bride. Look, the cushions are back on the patio furniture. What do you say to—"

A brick shattered at Giulia's feet. Missile-shaped shards of red clay exploded like a starburst. Giulia blocked her face with her arms. She felt three slice into her forearms before Frank tackled her onto the grass.

"Are you okay?" His voice was breathless.

"Yes." So was hers.

He climbed off her. "You have hair accessories." He tugged at her curls and showed her two slivers of brick.

She felt her arms and her hands came away painted with narrow lines of blood. "Look at me." She inspected his face and neck. "You're clean."

"You were half a step ahead of me. Come on. We need to wash that blood off you."

She stood. "Is there a rectangular hole in the lighthouse?"

They shaded their eyes and looked at the rows of bricks.

"Second row from the top," they said together.

"The ghost doesn't want us here," Giulia said.

"What?"

Giulia smiled. "Watch. Mac will blame it on the family ghost."

"Not in front of me, I hope."

They entered from the front porch. The uniformed police officer was at the office door telling Mac she could use it again. They both turned when Giulia said, "Mac, where's the first-aid kit?"

Lawsuit terror filled Mac's eyes before she ran for the kitchen. Frank explained about the brick to the police officer. Mac returned with a fishing tackle box stuffed with everything from alcohol wipes to three different kinds of antibiotic ointments.

"Mac," the officer said, "I'd get your contractor back here to check his work. Looks like the last couple of freeze-and-thaw winters did a number on his mortar."

"I'll take care of things in my room," Giulia said.

"You probably want pictures for insurance before you clean the mess," Frank said.

"Yes. Yes, of course. I'll come up and check on you in a minute." Mac scurried darn well for a seventy-four-year-old woman.

In her room, Giulia set the tackle box on the toilet lid and inspected her forearms. The cuts must have been shallow because the blood was already dry. Nothing else in her hair; nothing on her clothes; nothing on her face, thank God for small favors.

She ripped open an alcohol wipe and applied it to the crusted blood near her left elbow.

"Ow ow ow." She checked the result. A little seeping blood, but not bad at all. She applied ointment and a long bandage created from two regular ones because of the cut's dimensions. The other two slices, one long and one short, reacted much the same.

"It's me." Frank's voice.

"In the bathroom."

He surveyed the debris. "Should I be concerned?"

"About these? No. The worst damage they'll cause is messing up my tan."

"I'll still love you." He kissed the back of her neck.

She closed the tackle box. "About that brick."

A knock at their door. "May I come in?"

"Yes, please, Mac." Giulia stepped into the bedroom and set the tackle box on the dresser. Frank leaned against the bathroom doorway. Mac looked from one to the other, then at Giulia's bandaged arms.

"I'm sorry, I'm so sorry. I have no idea what happened."
Twittery Mac was someone new to Giulia. "Nothing like this has
ever happened to the lighthouse since the restoration."

"Some basic first aid took care of me," Giulia said. "But if your
repair work is sound, then the important question is who wants one
of your guests dead?"

"The ghost. It has to be the ghost." Mac stared at the corner of
the room near the windows. "Are you watching us?" she whispered.
"What do you want from me?"

"Mac? Are you here?" The call came from downstairs.

Mac's head swiveled toward the door. "Solana's here? She isn't
scheduled until seven." She called at the doorway, "I'll be right
down."

"Please come back up here when you're free," Giulia said.

Mac gave her a still-twittery nod and left.

Giulia waited five seconds and ran on tiptoes to the railing.
Her hunch was correct: Solana's voice carried as well as that of a
trained stage actor.

When listening to the YouTube video, Giulia had recognized
the diaphragm support.

"Mac, dear, you didn't tell me a friend of Rowan's was staying
this week."

"How did you know?"

A touch of condescension instilled itself into the professional
voice. "Those few of us with the true gift form a tight cluster. We
communicate often."

Successful Manager Mac replaced lawsuit-fear Mac. "I don't
see the need to discuss my guests."

Solana's laugh was the equivalent of head-patting a stubborn
child. "You will never need to. We'll be back at seven to meet
everyone in the usual way."

"Why are you here now?"

"The weather is so beautiful today, it would have been a crime
against nature not to spend it on the beach." The screen door
clapped shut.

Giulia made it back to her room and repeated the conversation to Frank before Mac returned. First things first. "Mac, we have no intention of suing you for this, so please stop worrying about that. I want to remind you I haven't encountered any ghosts in this room."

Another vigorous headshake. "Rowan has always said that disbelief may cloud your vision, but it doesn't affect the spirit's existence."

So many replies. Giulia chose, "Is the hole from the missing brick visible from the Widow's Walk?"

"What? Yes, if you get flat on the gallery and stick your head over the edge, but it's not safe to do that."

"We're going up to check. We'll make sure no one sees us."

She walked out before Mac could protest.

The beautiful day worked in her favor: All the guests appeared to be away from the inn.

Frank whispered in her ear as they reached the first floor, "Confident women are sexy."

Giulia just managed to control a spurt of laughter. "Mac respects a take-charge attitude. Earlier today she tried to tell me how to do my job."

"Like I said."

"Shush, you, and let's get up to the Widow's Walk before someone comes in from the beach."

Giulia hung over the side with Frank holding her by the legs.

"I can reach the top edge of the hole with the tips of my fingers, but Solana is at least six inches taller than me. She could get to it without a problem." She explored the ragged mortar. "The outline is chipped away in a pattern, not random like it might be if ice had crept in and expanded it over a few years." More exploring. "The pattern isn't completely regular. Someone is clever and ruthless. Okay, help me up, please."

She sat against the glass and dusted off her hands. "It's a good thing I'm not afraid of heights."

"Which is why you're pushing into the window behind you."

"You lean out there."

"My employee agreement doesn't include hazard pay." He sat next to her. "I admit to not liking extreme heights. A chisel, you think?"

"Easily. Even a sturdy nail file could have done it over time. Not an emery board, a real metal file." Giulia tapped her foot on the walkway. "Mac could be responsible for this, you know."

"Why?"

"Mac knows Rowan, who knows Solana. Mac played up the ghost angle in this puff piece the local paper ran a month ago. I forgot, you haven't seen that. It should be online. So Mac could be staging the hauntings to boost business. Or Solana could be staging them to boost her own business. Or Rowan and Solana could be in it together against Mac." She blew out a breath. "I could use the help of a legitimate mind reader. Or a priest who'd be willing to break the seal of the confessional. I wonder if any of these psychics are Catholic."

Twenty-Five

Giulia paused by the suit of armor. "I forgot to check him for hidden haunting devices. Tonight for that." She looked toward the house. "I don't want to meet Mac again just yet."

Frank took them out through the vestibule door. "It's time for a romantic walk on the edge of the water."

Which might have worked if the water's edge hadn't been inundated by a few hundred other vacationers with the same idea. Giulia dodged two beach balls and five shrieking children in the first four hundred feet of beach.

"Bad idea on a Sunday," Frank said. He inhaled. "Hot dogs. No, not today. Where's that shrimp place that delivers to the B&B?"

They plodded through sand up to the boardwalk.

Giulia looked up and down the street. "Not here. Maybe the next one." When they walked another block she pointed. "There. Next to the bookstore."

They landed in the middle of the lunch rush, but technically this was vacation, so Giulia didn't stress over the minutes in line. So many people sitting at the square tables with shrimp baskets convinced her that Frank's lunch choice was the correct one. They walked back to Stone's Throw with shrimp, fries, packets of cocktail sauce and ketchup, and extra-large Cokes.

Joel and Gino were already on the patio eating burgers, chips, and giant pickles.

"Room for two more?" Frank said.

"Sure, drag over a chair." Joel moved his chair closer to one end of the rectangular glass table, giving Frank and Giulia the opposite end.

"Shrimp," Gino said. "That's what's for lunch tomorrow."

"Where did you get those pickles?" Giulia said.

"You know that bar with the Jimmy Buffet obsession?"

Giulia squeezed a mound of cocktail sauce next to her shrimp. "Of course. What else would a Jimmy Buffet place serve except burgers, fries, and pickles?" She bit into her first shrimp. "You were right," she said to Frank around the mouthful.

"The patio looks as good as new," Joel said. "I heard they caught the guy who did it."

Giulia nodded.

"Poor Mac," Gino said. "If the place keeps having accidents it'll get a rep of being cursed."

Joel plunged three fries into barbecue sauce and swallowed them. "You really have to come back for Halloween. Mac goes all out."

"What makes Halloween here so much better than this?" Giulia swept the beach, lake, and hot, sunny sky with one arm. Even with the cacophony of a crowded beach and motorized craft on the water, the patio was far enough up and back to create a natural sound barrier. The noise was muted enough not to assault the ears.

Gino set down his beer. "The lake in summer is great, but you can get that anywhere. The chain hotels around here all have beach areas and breakfast service. Mac's place is all about the personal touch, which is what makes it better in the summer, but nobody does one-tenth of what Mac does for Halloween."

Joel gulped the last of his fries. "Every single room is decorated. The tablecloth and napkins change every day. It's more than her usual prices because she brings in a dessert chef for the evenings."

"Oh, God, the tiramisu," Gino said.

"The pot de crème," Joel said.

"The homemade ice cream."

"Last year she worked out a deal with a palm reader to come in on Halloween," Joel said. "Made for an epic party. The younger kids in town come here to trick-or-treat and Mac finds a way to scare them shitless."

Frank said, "Does she use her family legend on the trick-or-treaters?"

Gino said, "Nah, that's just for the guests. She won't let kids climb the lighthouse, either. Think of the liability premiums."

Joel groaned. "Spoken like an insurance salesman."

Gino hung his head. "I'm on vacation. I'll remember."

"Does Mac ever give a hint whether the ghost legend is real or not?" Giulia said.

"Never," Gino and Joel said together.

"She has the story letter-perfect and she never cracks her game face," Joel continued. "I can't wait until this psychic does her stuff tonight. We're divided on whether she's an actor on Mac's payroll or if she's the real thing. Her surprise attack on you sure looked genuine."

"We watched it on YouTube last night," Gino said. "Have you checked your viewing stats, Giulia?"

Giulia hung her head. "Yes."

They both laughed. Joel took out his phone. "You don't have a Twitter hashtag yet. Gotta work on that."

"I could email my in-laws."

Frank choked on a shrimp. "Why didn't I think of that? Pat could use it in a sermon. My brother is a priest," he said to the other two as the ESPN *da-da-da, da-da-da* signal went off from his phone. He poked it. "Pirates got a grand slam. Eat my dust, Jimmy." He finished with a mad scientist laugh.

Gino said, "Fantasy baseball?"

"Yep, I just kicked my boss's butt."

Giulia happily let the conversation turn into a three-way discussion of fantasy sports statistics. The breeze ruffled her curls. Kids splashed in the lake, squealing and laughing. The sun soaked into her bare arms. She stretched out her legs and leaned her head back to catch more of it.

Her inner work alarm stopped her from falling asleep. What was she thinking, sunbathing on the job? She sat up and all three men jumped.

"Thought you were asleep," Frank said.

"Just keeping you off-guard." Giulia gathered their takeout paraphernalia. "See you later."

She swore she could feel a wave of confusion from all three of them pushing at her back. *Cosmo* would be proud.

Twenty-Six

Giulia went back to the room to change into running gear. Frank arrived a few minutes later and switched into beat-up cargo shorts. Odd-sized miniature boxes of lures went into several pockets.

Giulia adjusted a Spandex racerback shirt. "I'll buy cheap sparkly sunglasses and run past the boat dock doing my best to look annoyed and vain."

"I'll tell a reasonable lie about how I refused to take you shopping last night."

She tied her sneakers. "Was he wearing a wedding ring?"

"Don't think so, but it doesn't mean much. Not all men do."

"Good point." She strapped on her armband and Velcroed in her phone. "I'll expect your report when you get back."

At the end of what became a ten-mile run that looped through most of town, the only thing stopping Giulia from a dive into the lake was the thought of a soaked wedgie.

The glorious weather brought crowds to the stores, the bars, and the beach. She was the only one running at three in the afternoon. Stupid time of day for it, but when you have to squeeze things in...Her glitter-encrusted sunglasses pinched her nose and she was certain they were creating a gold-flecked raccoon mask on her sweaty face. She bought bottled water at the souvenir store before finishing the tenth mile at the Stone's Throw driveway and plopped onto one of the patio chairs. The sunglasses came off before she drank half her bottled water without stopping for breath.

Then she poured another third of it over her head and down her neck.

Mac joined her. "Is it too soon to ask if you've had any breakthroughs?"

Giulia gave her Polite Smile Number Two. "You know it is. I'm heading back to Cottonwood tomorrow morning to research. My computer at work is fast and powerful. It'll keep me away from the scene here only a few hours."

"The contractor who repaired the lighthouse retired, but his son is running the business now. He wasn't happy when I suggested his father may have cut corners and endangered lives."

Giulia stopped in the middle of another long drink. "Not when you phrase it that way."

"People need to know when they screw up. I may look like a quaint old innkeeper now, but they forget that under these flowered shirts I'm still the woman who oversaw my hotel chain's entire east coast management."

With a wide-eyed expression, Giulia said, "So you agree with me that this incident wasn't ghost-powered."

Mac didn't rise to the bait. "Not at all. I'm merely covering my bases."

Frank met Giulia on the bocce ball court an hour later. She and Gino stopped their game for a moment.

"We're tied at one end apiece if you want to shower, honey," Giulia said.

"What, you don't like my new Eau de Fish cologne?" He kissed her and she waved a hand in front of her face. "Fine. I'll scrub up. Joel, are you playing the winner?"

Joel nodded. "Want to play the winner of my match?"

"Sure. Be back down in ten."

Giulia aimed her ball and released. It knocked one of Gino's out of play. She gave him her sweetest smile.

"You're killing me. Joel, check for weighted balls, will you?"

Giulia fluffed her hair. "It's called skill, gentlemen."

Gino pointed up toward Heaven. "My grandfather, God rest his soul, is going to haunt me worse than the Stone's Throw ghost if I lose this. Nobody beats me at bocce."

"You do recall that I wouldn't take a wager on our game," Giulia said.

Gino threw his ball, which knocked one of Giulia's closer to the *pallino*. He cursed. "I thought you wouldn't bet because you figured you'd lose."

She stared at him. "I told you I had experience."

"People brag. Like Joel here when we first met. He doesn't like to admit defeat in any sport."

"Rugby," Joel said. "I admit defeat in rugby, lacrosse, and the high jump."

"And bocce." Gino heaved his set of balls down to Giulia's end and followed them with his hand out. "Good game. I underestimated you."

Giulia shook hands. "I'm my own secret weapon. Joel, are you ready?"

He stood. "I will redeem the honor of my household."

"Challenge accepted," Giulia said.

They played to a tie and needed two additional ends to break it. Giulia won by putting a touch of English on her last ball, snaking it between two of Joel's to within three inches of the *pallino*. As one, Joel and Gino got on their knees and bowed, hands and faces on the grass. A *click* made all three turn their heads. Frank lowered his phone. "For my own gallery, guys. I won't post it on Facebook."

Gino stood, dusting grass off his knees. "If she beats you, we want to see you kowtow to her like us."

Giulia grinned. "Oh, yes, please, honey."

Frank scowled. "Only if you do the same for me if I win."

"Deal. Give me your phone." She handed both their phones to Gino. "You're in charge of the incriminating photograph."

If bocce had a mercy rule, a referee would've called the game after the third end. Frank, muttering Irish maledictions against the balls, the wind, the court, and life in general, played the last end as though he had a chance. Giulia was gracious in victory, even when she stepped up on the railroad tie that marked the end of the court and waited for the promised homage.

Gino put the sun to his back and readied both phones. The smile on Frank's face appeared a little forced, but he got down on the grass and made obeisance to the bocce champion.

"Thanks, guys." Giulia hopped to the grass and retrieved the phones. "Lovely picture. I might make it into our Christmas card this year."

She reset the balls at one end of the court. Joel and Gino took off toward the beach. Giulia waited until they were gone to drag her husband into her arms and kiss him.

"Thank you for being such a good sport. I think everyone here considers us to be nothing more than a couple on vacation."

Frank growled. "My manhood is affronted by that beat-down you administered. I may have to endure another beer session with Walter the Whiner to regain it."

"If you need to regain your manhood by winning a sporting contest with me, may I remind you of the last three times we played Horse, in our driveway, in full view of the neighbors?"

"Hey, a basketball hoop on the garage is meant to be used." He scanned the yard and beach. "Everybody seems to have gone out for supper. Do you want to hear my fishing rental story?"

"Yes, yes, yes. Come over here and we'll pull two chairs together." When they were seated next to each other, she unlocked her phone. "Let me turn on the voice memo. Okay, go."

"So the boat dock owner does not possess the family name and is Mac's nephew from a Stone daughter's marriage. He's got a bachelor's degree in business but quit working for The Man in January. He came here last Thanksgiving for a family reunion."

"All those Stones?" Giulia said. "There aren't enough beds."

"It was a one-day party, picnic, boating, swimming binge. The boat dock business was up for sale, so Walter seized his opportunity."

"That seems to be a Stone trait."

A seagull flew over to the bocce court and landed on one of the railroad ties. Another settled on the sunroom roof and began a squawk-off with the one on the bocce court.

Frank lunged at the bocce seagull, yelling and throwing his arms forward. The seagull flapped to the grass and waddled away, head in the air.

Giulia chuckled. "I think you offended its dignity."

"Too bad. Its droppings offended my car. I had to borrow paper towels and glass cleaner from Mac."

"Yuck. So Walter bought the boat rental business. When?"

"February. I couldn't get a handle on his finances, but if I had to guess, I'd say he's stretched pretty thin. He let me buy the beer. He and his girlfriend live over the rental shop. I gather the spectacular view doesn't offset the tiny rooms and free fish odors day and night."

Three young women in itsy-bitsy bikinis spread out blankets below the B&B's grass and turned on U2 at top volume. Giulia brought the phone closer to her mouth.

"What kind of person is he?" She held the phone to Frank's mouth.

"Lazy. He's slow to get equipment, slow to make change. He slouches like it's too much effort to stand up. I wonder if he quit his last job before they fired him."

"Are you sure he wasn't playing a part? You know, life is slow and easy here at the lake?"

"Pretty sure. He really hates waiting on customers and his cheerful smile vanishes the second they walk away. Oh, and get this: He skeeves blood. He griped every time a kid interrupted us to ask him to take out a hook from a fish they'd caught off the dock."

"He must have really hated his last job."

"Or his need to suck up to Auntie Mac overrode all other considerations."

Creed replaced U2. Frank looked pained. "Somebody made a mix CD."

Giulia saved the voice memo. "You still have the touch. That was everything I needed and hardly anything I didn't."

"You think the nephew's pulling all this haunting stuff because he wants the B&B?"

"Actually, no, because it's way too much effort for someone who's allergic to hard work. I'll check up on him tomorrow with the rest, though."

"Tomorrow? Oh, right. Research on DI's internet."

"My tablet has limits too. I need my tower."

Nickelback took Creed's place.

Frank stood. "I'm on vacation. That means I don't have to eat Brussels sprouts, do homework, or listen to overhyped musicians."

They headed inside.

"What's next for me?" Frank said.

"All the poking around possible. I'm going to search the library and the upstairs halls again for hidden switches. Could you take downstairs, the souvenir room, and the suit of armor?"

"Break's over." Frank walked through the sunroom and down the hall to the lighthouse entrance. "Empty. I shall seize the moment."

Giulia went up to the third floor and started with the red-fringed light. She ran her hands over the lace panels, but felt no unusual bumps. Crouching, she slipped under the lampshade to look for extra switches or a computerized gizmo. She was disappointed that the lamp appeared exactly as it should: An ornate, old-fashioned lamp.

Next the strip of carpet. No lumps or hidden wires. Nothing had been attached to the skinny hall table either. Maybe the attic, if Mac ran her Halloween week from a different, hidden computer. At the moment, Giulia couldn't think of anything else powerful enough to coordinate a whole-house haunting.

On her way down to the second floor, she felt under the banister and checked the newel post for a secret hinge. Clean. She headed into the library and went straight for the five bookshelves. A thin layer of dust coated the highest shelves and the books on them.

All the lower shelves were slightly above or at Giulia's eye level. No dust on them. She started at the bookshelf farthest from the door and tilted out each book one by one.

Dialogue from *Young Frankenstein* popped into her head: "Put. Ze candle. Back." She stifled a giggle. What would she do if one of these books triggered a secret passage? Besides follow it, that is. Call Frank? No. Explore the passage and hope it came out in front of a shocked Frank's face. Maybe the exit would be in the suit of armor. Frank's buzzed hair would find new ways to stand up higher if that happened.

"Looking for a book, Giulia? How was your day?"

Giulia did not jump. She turned to Marion with a smile. "A lot of fun. I beat Joel, Gino, and my husband in bocce ball."

"In all the years we've been staying here we've never tried that. Anthony?"

Her husband joined her in the doorway. "Tried what?"

"Bocce ball. You know, that narrow court on the opposite side of the patio from the croquet wickets. Giulia is quite skilled at it."

"Really? Could you give us a lesson? If we're going ahead with our plan to buy a bed and breakfast or two, we need to learn the best entertainment to provide the guests. Perhaps tomorrow or Tuesday."

Giulia's smile didn't waver. She'd dealt with worse condescension. "I'd be happy to. Let me know at breakfast the day you want to learn the game."

They went into their room, forcing Giulia to be stealthy.

She moved and replaced one shelf of books after another, but not a single creak or snap of a secret lock opening rewarded her search.

She gave up at eight o'clock and went to find Frank.

He was studying the suit of armor and beckoned her over. "What this needs is a mace. Raise the arm and set it at an angle to threaten visitors."

"You're so romantic. Find anything suspicious?"

"Not a hidden lever or a secret nook anywhere."

"I refuse to believe that a Woman in White is actually haunting this place."

"A sound basis on which to work." Frank stretched his back. "It's got to be beer o'clock by now."

"Long past it. Want to walk to that little Mexican place by the boat dock?"

A crash of thunder cut her off. Wind and rain attacked the lakefront door.

"Check that," she said. "Pizza, delivered?"

As they walked past the sunroom, the living room lights came on. Mac and Solana entered, accompanied by a short, middle-aged man in flowing trousers and tunic.

"Anyone down here?" Mac called.

Giulia and Frank walked into the room. Marion called down the stairs, "We'll be right there."

Mac continued, "Does anyone know where those truant young men are? What about Roy and CeCe?"

"We've only seen Marion and Anthony this evening," Giulia said.

Joel ran in from the kitchen hallway. "Are we late? Did we miss anything? Tonight of all nights my husband wants to eat at a fancy restaurant."

"There's still time," Mac said. "We're getting everyone together."

"There is a God. Gino! Hurry up!"

"Coming." Gino passed Joel and ran upstairs. "Back in forty seconds."

"Serves him right for eating all that prime rib on a hot night." Joel used his jacket to rub most of the rain out of his hair.

Giulia watched Solana and Flowing Clothes. Solana walked the perimeter of the living room. He set five dining room chairs around the coffee table.

CeCe and Roy entered through the sunroom, laughing and kissing and only a little soaked.

"You're my babycakes," she said.

"You're my honey muffin," he said.

Gino came downstairs in time to hear the endearments and shared an eye roll with Joel.

"I hear tequila talking," Frank said.

CeCe hiccupped. "Only a few margaritas."

Roy kissed her again. "Four and a half, baby. We split that last one." He looked around at the gathering. "What's up?"

CeCe spotted Solana and jumped up and down. "It's séance night, it's séance night."

Solana finished her tour of the room and said to the guests, "Is anyone easily frightened?"

"No," Giulia said.

"Not unless you brought a box of pet tarantulas," Joel said.

Anthony and Marion joined the group. "I'm a business professional," she said. "The only thing that frightens me is a tax audit."

"Good." Solana nodded at Mac, who left the room. "I have the ability to contact the spirits of those who have passed over. The lighthouse's Woman in White is why Mac has asked us to come here each week. She wishes me to contact her, but we have yet to succeed. Is anyone here familiar with how a séance works?"

Several headshakes. Marion said, "I have a little knowledge from movies our children begged us to take them to see."

Solana waved that away. "Hollywood. Please. Cedar, would you draw the drapes?" To the guests again: "This is my husband, Cedar. He is also my business manager and webmaster."

Mac returned, carrying a tray of pillar candles in several colors.

Cedar directed their placement: Two near the center of the coffee table, two on the mantelpiece, and two more on a spare card table from the sunroom.

Cedar positioned an antique Ouija board and planchette in the exact center of the coffee table and set the candles on either side of it. "Solana inherited this from her mother, who inherited it from her mother. It's the William Fuld 1917 design. Solana's grandmother could see complete words from the spirits in the wood grain surface."

The thunder came nearer. Giulia glanced at Solana for a reaction to this aggrandizement.

The businesswoman was already seated on the middle couch cushion, feet on floor, hands in lap. At least she wasn't focused on Giulia as the Veiled Woman.

"Cedar and I are accountants during our day jobs, but I have some small notoriety and some equally small fame in the spirit realm." A brief smile. "I don't have a set rate for my services but I do take payment. That fact sets the hounds on me. If anyone has ever heard of CSICOP?"

Several headshakes.

"They investigate the paranormal, living and transitioned. That includes people like me. I spoke at length with a kind man who did his best to prove me as much a fraud as those television preachers who pretend to heal people they've planted in the audience."

"He had these prominent veins on either side of his neck." Cedar drew imaginary lines on his own neck. "Every time Solana passed one of his tests, the veins bulged. His cameraman was supremely bored for most of the session."

"He was, until I brought out the board and the debunker's grandmother contacted me. She used the planchette to spell out three words in the Basque dialect." She looked over at her husband.

"Solana was concentrating with her eyes closed, so she didn't see his reaction. I was honestly worried that the man would have a stroke in our living room. He made a strangled kind of noise and Solana opened her eyes."

"The poor man was staring at the planchette like it was a scorpion," Solana said. "He repeated the words to me and asked me how I knew them. I don't know that dialect and told him so." She sighed. "He got the witch hunter's look in his eyes then and I started to end the session. He put his hands on the planchette and demanded more. Before Cedar could toss both of them out into the street, the man's grandmother took over the planchette through my hands and spelled out several more words."

Cedar chuckled. "He shrank in his chair like a little boy who'd just been spanked. When the grandmother's spirit left us, I asked him to translate. He got belligerent again and insisted we were frauds preying on the vulnerable. That's when I tossed his ass out."

After a pause, Giulia said, "Did you ever get a translation of the words?"

Solana nodded. "A few months later he emailed us with a backhanded apology. He'd researched us all that time and couldn't find irrefutable proof we were frauds. How nice of him. He also said that on the slim chance I hadn't tried to dupe him, his grandmother had spelled out her pet nickname for him and the location of the two-hundred-dollar Christmas bonus he'd misplaced. It was in the torn pants he'd stuffed in a Goodwill bag. The bag was in his car trunk to donate that weekend."

Marion took out a Moleskine notebook and wrote in it at breakneck speed throughout this story. "Why do you still have day jobs?"

Solana radiated frost again. "Do you mean, because I should be able to get the spirits of those who've passed over to give me winning lottery numbers?"

Marion looked up. She didn't blush but she cleared her throat before answering. "Well, yes. Something like that."

The frost changed to condescension. "Those who've passed over use me as a conduit when needed. They are not puppies to be trained with a rolled-up newspaper to be obedient to my will."

Mac reentered the room as more thunder crashed. "All set?"

The power went out.

"Son of a gun. I'll check the circuit breakers."

Cedar pushed aside the drapes. "Power's out all along the lake. Electricity doesn't affect Solana's gift. I'll turn off all the light switches in the dining room and here so when the power returns it won't break her concentration." He took a step toward the dining room. "Would you like to sit in? I'll bring another chair."

Mac shook her head. "No, thanks. I'll call Penelec for a power restore time estimate. I'll stay away from these rooms so you won't be disturbed."

She retreated toward her office. Cedar herded everyone still standing to an empty seat around the coffee table.

Rain pounded the bay window. Thunder and lightning increased.

Giulia glanced at Frank and the same thought crossed their faces: What a Hollywood setting.

The glow of the candlesticks flanking the Ouija board brought out the warmth of the cherry wood. Giulia chose a chair at the end of the table from which she could watch the entire room. Frank took the couch cushion next to Solana. Giulia gave him an infinitesimal nod. Cedar, to her surprise, took the seat opposite Giulia. She'd been sure that he'd sit next to his wife to work the room from her verbal or nonverbal cues. Giulia might have an open mind about psychics because of the experiences of trusted friends, but not for half a minute did she believe in someone who relied on a toy manufacturer's gimmick.

"The planchette has room for Solana and four others to have their fingers touching it," Cedar said. "Those four have to sit on either side of Solana or directly opposite her. If you want to play musical chairs, now's the moment."

More thunder. Giulia held up her hands palm out, as did Gino. He and CeCe negotiated and CeCe switched seats with him and took the chair next to her husband. This configuration allowed Joel, CeCe, Anthony, Frank, and Solana to touch the planchette.

The sounds of the rain and their own breathing filled the room. Mac's footsteps crossed from her office to the kitchen.

A cell phone played the ESPN update, *da-da-da, da-da-da*. They all jumped.

"Sorry," Roy said. Every single person around the table except Cedar and Solana muted their phones.

Giulia turned on her voice memo function and set her phone face down on the rug to conceal the light.

When the rain and breathing were again the only noises in the room, Solana said in a quiet, even voice, "Those of you not touching the planchette do not need to hold hands. We're not in a direct-to-DVD movie. I ask only that you remain quiet. For the four of you who desire to touch it with me, the rules are simple. Do not attempt to move it on your own. Do not press down on it to try to prevent it moving. If the spirit of the weeping woman chooses to send us a message, it may startle you. Please do not jerk your hands away. That may alter the message or disturb the spirit. If you must break your contact, wait until the planchette has stopped moving and slowly raise your hands."

The party game atmosphere crumbled at her words. Marion and Anthony glanced at each other, Marion's business demeanor cracking. Joel squeezed Gino's hands and Gino held on a second longer when Joel tried to release them. CeCe crossed herself.

An imp on Giulia's shoulder tempted her to bring up Bach's *Toccata and Fugue in D Minor* on her phone. She flicked the imp into the fireplace with an imaginary finger.

Solana's breathing slowed. Her head tipped up toward the ceiling, eyes still closed. Her hands raised and her fingertips lightly came to rest on the wide edge of the planchette. Cedar motioned to Anthony, Frank, CeCe, and Joel to find room on it as well.

"Will you speak to us?" Solana's voice came out sweeter, coaxing. "We are ready to listen."

The candles burned straight and clear.

Gino's eyes widened and he clamped his face into the crook of his elbow. His body shook once. Again. The arm came down to reveal watering eyes that glared at the orange pillar candle on the end table next to him.

Pumpkin spice, he mouthed at Joel, who bit both lips but the smile still peeked through.

"Will you speak to us?" Solana said again.

Several long seconds later, she said the words a third time.

The planchette moved.

Twenty-Seven

Marion gasped. Gino's mouth dropped open. Joel and Frank eyed each other with suspicion.

CeCe stared them both down. Anthony started to take his hands away from the heart-shaped wood, but resettled himself instead.

"We are listening," Solana said, still in that soothing voice. "What do you want us to know?"

A pause. The shoulders of the four didn't relax.

The planchette moved again, kept moving in tiny jerks and scrapes until it stopped at the letter *S*.

"S," Cedar said, his voice all business.

The planchette scraped to its left.

"O."

"S."

"A."

"D."

"So sad," CeCe whispered. "Oh my God."

"Why are you sad?" Solana said.

"A."

"L."

"O."

"N."

"E."

"I'm going to need a nightlight tonight," Joel whispered.

Cedar pointed a finger at him and shook his head. Joel nodded and focused on the board again.

The candle flames flickered.

Giulia's ears caught a new sound. It faded as the planchette moved.

"W."

"H."

"Y."

Marion, seated kitty-corner to Giulia, muttered, "The messages take too long. Entertainment can't be boring."

Giulia put a finger to her lips. Marion returned to writing in her notebook. CeCe kept reading the message letters out loud.

"S."

"E."

Joel put it together first. "Why are you in my house?"

"Holy crap," Roy said in a loud and shaky voice.

"Shh!" from all sides.

When the room quieted, Solana said, "When guests are in your house, you aren't alone any longer."

The other sound returned. Now Giulia recognized it: Crying. Perhaps the same voice that woke her up at two in the morning. She couldn't tell yet.

Anthony and Frank had turned their faces away from the Ouija board, one looking at the mantelpiece, the other down the hall toward the lighthouse.

The planchette remained still. Solana repeated her statement. The room grew tense. All the fingers touching the planchette except Solana's trembled enough to rattle the wooden instrument.

Solana said: "How can we help you?"

"G."

"E."

"T."

"O."

The crying stopped when the letter game restarted. Giulia refused to believe that a hundred-plus-year-old ghost couldn't manipulate the Ouija board and make that echoey weeping sound at the same time. By this time the ghost ought to be able to give a TED talk on multitasking.

"Get out of my house," Frank said. "Not much of a host, is she?"

Giulia tried to send Frank a psychic "Play along" message of her own.

The planchette flew to the words "good" and "bye" at the bottom of the Ouija board. Back and forth, over and over, "good" "bye," "good" "bye," "good" "bye," "good" "bye."

Still in her non-threatening voice, Solana said, "Let us help you. We want to share this house with you. Talk to us."

Giulia expected more disembodied weeping and a quick séance wrap-up. The planchetters glanced at each other. The moment stretched.

A shuddering gasp broke it.

Solana's back arched and her eyes bulged.

Seven faces gawked at her. Marion pushed back in her chair like she was trying to escape, but the chair legs scraped the floor and Solana's head snapped down. Those distended eyes focused on Marion, who enacted a perfect imitation of a rabbit mesmerized by a snake.

"I protect this house." Solana's voice, but different. A higher register and a more formal syntax. One at a time, she pinned all seven of them with that gaze.

Out of the corner of her eye, Giulia caught movement from Gino but kept her attention on Solana.

"You are obliged to respect this house," Solana/not Solana said. "I am its warder. No one will remove the treasure from this family."

A quick intake of breath from somewhere else in the room.

Solana/not Solana's face looked past the table; Giulia glanced quickly in the same direction. Mac stood by the glassed-in bookcase, also performing the rabbit-versus-snake pantomime.

"Who are you?" Mac whispered.

Solana/not Solana took her left hand off the planchette and pointed at Mac. "Do not shirk your duty."

A flash from Gino's chair. At the same instant, the power came back on. Light from the hallway spilled over the coffee table. Solana/not Solana gave another huge, dragging gasp and collapsed against the back of the couch. The candle flames blew out.

Twenty-Eight

Cedar jumped out of his chair and shoved Frank aside.

"Solana. Solana, wake up." He patted her cheeks.

Joel, CeCe, and Anthony backed away from the planchette, rubbing their fingertips.

Before Giulia could offer to help with resuscitation, Solana opened her eyes. She raised her hands and inspected them, turning them front to back and rubbing the gold manicure.

"My hands look wrong." Solana's voice sounded like itself again. "Why do I have painted fingernails?"

"Solana?" her husband said.

She blinked several times, sat up, and looked around at the faces surrounding the table. "Who ended the Ouija session?"

Everyone started talking at once.

"It moved on its own. We didn't manipulate it. Did we?"

"Mac really has a ghost."

"Are you serious? The spirit spoke through me?"

"Oh, God, I'm not going to sleep for a week."

"We've got a bottle of Jameson in our room."

"I'll pay you for a shot."

Giulia scooped up her phone and stood. As though that movement broke a second trance, chairs were pushed back and the pacing started. Giulia aimed directly at Gino, who was speaking in a low voice with Joel.

"Let me see the picture, please?"

Gino gulped. "You saw my flash?"

Giulia bent her neck backwards to favor Gino with her patented Teacher Glare. "If no one else saw it, you can thank the well-timed return of electricity."

He hung his head. The touch came through for her yet again.

"Solana was freaking me out. I wanted to see if she'd, like, mass-hypnotized us or if a ghost really took over her body."

"And?" Giulia caught her hands clenching and unclenching.

"I haven't looked at it yet. I have no spine."

Joel tugged the phone out of his hand. "It's a good thing I know your password." He typed it and opened the photograph. "I'll be damned."

He turned the phone to show Gino, whose skin paled beneath his beard.

Then he handed it to Giulia.

Gino had snapped the photo at the moment Solana/not Solana pointed an admonishing finger at Mac. The bulging eyes had been real. So had the stern facial expression, unlike Solana's general air of competent serenity.

"You heard her voice change, right?" Joel said to both of them. "I didn't imagine it?"

"More important," Gino said, "is whether you four pushed that planchette around the board yourselves to mess with the rest of us."

"Swear to God, no," Joel said. "Frank," he raised his voice to cut across the babble, "tell me you didn't mess with that planchette."

"Swear to God," Frank said.

"Neither did I," Anthony said.

"Me neither," CeCe said.

Eight heads swiveled as one to Solana, still on the couch.

Cedar got to his feet, emanating righteous indignation. It transformed his five foot seven hippieness into Mighty Protector of His Woman.

"Solana has never manipulated a séance and never will."

"Sorry," Joel and Roy mumbled.

Solana held up a hand. "It's all right. They witnessed something extraordinary. The natural defensive human reaction is to protect the one-dimensional world they're used to seeing."

Giulia stepped forward, ingenuous mask in place. "Solana, tell us what we saw. You four who worked the planchette, what did you feel? Sorry, sorry, I meant you four who touched the planchette."

"I felt nothing at first," Joel said.

"Not for, like, five minutes," CeCe said. "Then it got warm. Didn't it?" She pointed her index finger at the three men.

Frank nodded. "First I felt warmth and then it started to vibrate."

Anthony said with a show of reluctance, "Yes, I felt the warmth, but the vibration could have been our unsteady fingers."

Joel said, "The temperature increase could have been body heat from our fingertips transferring to the wood."

"Those phenomena occur during all of my Ouija sessions," Solana said. "My website has many testimonials regarding them."

"If you're that skeptical," Cedar said, "examine the planchette for yourselves." He picked it up and held it out.

With an apologetic expression, Giulia took it. She made big motions of shaking it and trying to unscrew the little balls on the bottom for the four legs with her right hand. While doing that, her left fingertips searched for a minuscule switch or heat and vibration triggers.

Both hands came up empty.

"I can't find anything." She handed it back. "I apologize."

Color returned to Solana's face. "No apologies necessary. I'm glad you inspected the planchette. Cedar tells me that the Woman in White spoke through me."

"It was freaky," Joel said.

A benevolent smile touched Solana's lips. "Truthfully, such a connection has only happened once before. Back in college, wasn't it?" she said to her husband.

"Yeah, for that Day of the Dead festival." He didn't look pleased at the memory.

She nodded. "That spirit was powerful and unpleasant. I only expelled it with the help of my professor in Occult Studies."

"Well, butter my butt and call me a biscuit," CeCe said.

Startled laughter answered her.

"My grandmother used to say that," Joel said. "I grew up in Georgia."

"South Carolina," CeCe said. "What part?"

They moved away from Solana into the sunroom too quickly for a casual change of topic, talking Southern food and family in shaking voices. Gino and Roy followed at a pace an unkind observer might have called "scurrying."

Solana said, "I wish we had thought to bring the video equipment."

Giulia's hand went to her pocket, where her phone was probably recording the swish of cotton fabric against the speaker.

Cedar folded the Ouija board. "We couldn't use a video on the website without getting signed permission. Too awkward after the fact. I know you're for real and so do your followers."

Frank and Giulia held out their hands to Solana. "Thank you for a fascinating experience," Frank said.

Solana and Cedar shook hands. "It was our pleasure," she said.

Anthony and Marion said, "Yes, thank you," as they read through Marion's notebook.

As Solana passed Mac, she said to her, "I need to rest after a session, but I'll be happy to discuss any part of it with you tomorrow."

"Thank you." Mac's voice was brisk again. "I'll call you. That would be very interesting."

Mac turned away and began checking light switches in the living and dining rooms. Giulia waited until she returned to her office, then opened the glass front of the single bookcase in the living room.

"What's up?" Frank said.

She beckoned him next to her. "Did you hear that voice crying when the planchette wasn't moving?"

"I thought I did, but I wouldn't swear to it."

"You did. So did everyone else. At one point or another, everyone who wasn't touching that thing looked for the source. Mac wasn't in the room at first, then conveniently she was standing next to this when Solana became Mac's ancestor ghost."

"You believed that?"

"Of course not." She felt under the lip of the highest shelf. "You know that crying that woke me up in the middle of the night? I'm betting we missed a recording device on a timer hidden in here."

Frank started from the bottom. "That would mean she's definitely playing you."

"I know. I won't get angry unless we find something."

They found nothing on the undersides of the shelves. Giulia returned to the top shelf and tilted forward the first books on the left-hand side.

"These are half an inch farther forward than the ones on the next shelf." She bent over and pulled out some of those books. "The backing here is brown pressboard, but up at the top it's fake wood grain."

"Not for aesthetics?"

"I'll bet my next three cups of mint brownie coffee it isn't." She felt the backing with her right hand and stretched her left around to the back of the bookcase. "Aha." Abandoning the shelves, she pressed herself against the wall and squeezed her hand into the gap between the bookcase and the wallpaper. "We have the tip of a standard toggle switch back here."

"No shit."

"Just enough sticks out for my little fingernail to flip it on and off. I bet it's painted black to match the back of the pressboard, too." She took out her phone and hit the flashlight app. "I win."

Twenty-Nine

They escaped to their room to avoid meeting Mac.

"I'm surprised," Frank said. "She didn't seem like the type to screw with you."

"I'm disappointed." Giulia poked at her phone. "I think the lure of more publicity seduced her. Think of the Trip Advisor and BedandBreakfast.com spotlight blurbs: A Real Detective Spent Four Days at Stone's Throw and Witnessed Irrefutable Evidence of the Stone's Throw Ghost."

Frank, checking his own phone, said without looking up, "I suggest hiding a ten percent exploitation fee in all the charges on her bill."

"It's a thought. Did you happen to be looking at Cedar when the candles blew out?"

"No, Solana's ghost possession had all my attention. Why?"

"He might have blown out the candles. There. Got it." She moved from the chair onto the bed next to Frank. "I recorded the séance."

He dropped his phone. "You are brilliant."

"True." She pressed play.

The séance played out as they'd experienced it, with added rustles and occasional sound obstructions from Giulia's feet brushing the throw rug.

Frank hit stop after the second letter-by-letter Ouija message. "Those pauses weren't as long as they felt, with us wondering whether that freaky piece of wood was going to drag us around the board again."

"What do you think moved it?"

"Who, not what. My money's on Solana."

"Alone?"

"I think so." His phone rang with the ESPN update sound. He ignored it. "Joel was too nervous to work with her and CeCe tensed up like the planchette was going to bite her."

Giulia got to her knees on the other side of the bed and closed one window. "That storm killed the beautiful warm night." Stretching to the limit of her reach, she closed the other. "Anthony was in the planchette group for research. Marion took notes up to the ghost possession moment. You know, would a haunting add to or subtract from the bottom line of the B&B they plan to open?"

Frank pulled her back against him. "Okay. Solana by herself. If Cedar planted magnets under the table to work the planchette, I didn't see them. Fishing line wouldn't have worked because you sat on the far end, not a plant of theirs to play tug-the-wood with."

Giulia reached over his chest and hit the play button on her recording. "I can't hear the crying. We found the switch. It must be a recording."

"It wasn't loud. The mic may not be sensitive enough to catch it."

She cranked the volume. They listened to more of Solana's cajoling.

"The big surprise should be right about now," Frank said. "Her hands got all stiff and jerked the planchette and then she did her impression of Whoopi Goldberg in *Ghost*."

"That sound is Marion pushing back her chair," Giulia said.

Solana/not Solana spoke her first sentence.

"Play it again," Frank said.

"Shh. She'll talk some more in a second."

On the recording, Solana/not Solana continued: "You are obliged to respect this house. I am its warder. No one will remove the treasure from this family."

Giulia stopped the playback. "If she's faking it, she's good. Change to a more formal style of speech, throw in an old-fashioned word, keep the pronouncements generic."

"Except for the treasure," Frank said.

"She was looking at Mac when she said that. Everyone and their pet goldfish knows the treasure story because of that newspaper article." Giulia scrolled the recording back and replayed the possession monologue. "Can my eyes bug out on command like hers did?" Giulia stretched her eyelids.

"You need more practice," Frank said. "Unless it's genetic, like being able to curl your tongue or wiggle your ears."

They finished the recording. The last part was useless after Giulia hid her phone in her pocket.

"Nothing but thumps and swishes," Giulia said, frowning. "I couldn't think of a good way to hide it and still record."

"You got the meat of it, for what it's worth. We can't prove or disprove anything on the recording alone. Or on our visuals."

"Joel's idea of hypnotism is out too, since she looked more or less the same in real life and in the picture he took." Giulia switched her phone for her iPad. "We've got a phony psychic and a client with a loose definition of honesty. Yippee."

"As long as she's honest enough to pay the bill." Frank listened. "It stopped raining, but I don't want to go out for food now. Any more ghost chasing planned for tonight?"

"I'm not chasing anything unless I hear that crying again." Giulia typed notes on the séance into a single document. "I need to make separate research pages for everyone here."

"But not 'til tomorrow morning, right?"

"Mm-hmm." Giulia stared into the blackness outside the window, trying to pin down a detail about Solana.

Frank headed to the bathroom. Giulia remembered the last bit and put the tablet away. She turned down the quilt and tossed her clothes in the bottom dresser drawer. No sound from the bathroom. Now. The silky crimson nightgown slid over her bare skin. It hugged all her curves. One side was slit up to her hip socket. The bodice was lace everywhere and the spaghetti straps were held in place by snaps covered with tiny crimson rosettes.

It was the most daring thing she'd ever worn, including the wedding nightgown she'd received from Laurel and Anya at her bridal shower.

Frank came out of the bathroom and stopped cold in front of the window. Giulia leaned against the bedpost, unsure if his reaction was negative or positive. After all, this was the man who was once too shy to talk to her because she used to be a nun.

He ended her uncertainty by wolf whistling as he stepped forward and wrapped his arms around her. As his hands stroked along the nightgown, he pulled just hard enough to pop one of the little rosette-covered snaps.

"Oh, really," he said, and maneuvered both of them onto the bed.

Giulia opened her eyes. The pale moon shone into the room. What was wrong with its light? What was wrong with her eyes? Some type of weblike pattern interfered with her vision. She reached out to wave whatever it was out of her face. Her hand wouldn't move. She twisted and blinked and tried to sit up. The canopy covered her face. She opened her mouth and sucked in a clump of lace. She arched her back and jerked her head from side to side.

"Frank," she tried to say, but a different name came out of her mouth.

Her eyes opened. The bright moon lit the room like a neon sign. The canopy hung in its proper place over the bed. Frank lay beside her, snoring.

Thirty

At eleven thirty-five Monday morning, Giulia pulled into the parking lot behind Driscoll Investigations' building in Cottonwood. She blamed her late arrival on lingering over another superb breakfast and the poor driving conditions from a persistent drizzle covering most of Pennsylvania. Luck or someone taking an early lunch got her an open spot in the corner. She climbed the stairs, hearing Zane's voice on the phone muffled by the door.

Sidney fumbled with her computer the moment Giulia entered the office. Solana's voice as she discovered the ethereal veil around Giulia's head blared from her speakers. Zane shot her a dirty look and she cut the voice off.

Giulia facepalmed.

Zane finished his phone call. "Your staff respectfully requests an explanation of that upload before any other news or work assignments."

"How did you find it?"

Sidney's face radiated delight. "Olivier's younger brothers. Their latest hobby is recreating every experiment from this one-hundred-year-old boy's adventure book they found at the back of their grandfather's bookshelf. I subscribe to their YouTube channel. They put out a call for ghost pranks to stage a haunting and when I ran a search, up popped The Veiled Woman."

Giulia knew her face registered an emotion in a whole different zip code from "delight."

"Solana, the woman who used me as her stage prop in that video, is Mac's hired entertainment."

"You're slipping to the bottom of the first page of results," Zane said.

"Thank God. More important than my lack of Net notoriety is the discovery that Solana and Lady Rowan know each other." She pointed kitty-corner across the street.

Zane said, "To be impartial, each of them could be keeping up with the competition rather than working a mark together."

Giulia made a wry face. "The latter was my initial thought."

Sidney said, "Mine too. This job is corrupting us."

"True. Speaking of the job, I'm here to use our excellent internet connection for research. Have there been any emergencies?"

"Not one. Life is boring and routine," Sidney said. "You picked a good time to ghost hunt."

"That's right," Zane said. "Is there a lighthouse ghost?"

"I don't think so."

"Giu-lia."

"Sidney, don't let your head explode," Giulia said. "Mac created an elaborate ancestral ghost complete with ancillary newspaper interview to pique local interest. We've had a few incidents so far." She summarized the arson, shower glop, and shattered brick missile in a few sentences.

Sidney's head still looked in danger of imminent detonation. "You've found rational explanations for all of it, right?"

"Well, not yet." Giulia didn't let the hint of a smile touch her mouth. "We did find one hidden switch in the living room after the séance and ghostly possession."

"The what?" her assistants said.

Giulia stood between their desks and described last night's entertainment in much more detail than the humdrum arson and robbery. She kept having to stop and laugh at their reactions.

Sidney's fingers drummed on her desk with more and more force throughout the story. At the end, she burst out with: "Pardon my language, but that is a big, stinking pile of crap. These types are nothing more than internet scams in human form."

"I don't disagree with you," Giulia said. "This is one reason I'm closing myself in my office for a few hours. Pretend I'm not here."

Giulia fired up her computer and dealt with email first. She forwarded another possible client on to Sidney and a Diocesan request for information to Zane. Then took the printouts from their envelope and opened up a new spreadsheet plus a search window.

Page one, Marion and Anthony. Page two, Joel and Gino. Page three, CeCe and Roy. Page four, Solana and Cedar. Page five, Lucy. Page six, Walter. Page seven, Mac.

She didn't create a sheet for Matthew the handyman. She typed out M-A-T-T, but erased it a moment later. He didn't have the right feel for the mastermind of fires and brick bombs and theft and hauntings. Thoroughness demanded his own sheet, though. She retyped his name and left that page to be filled in later.

First she plugged in Marion and Anthony's address. Two point three seconds later Google returned several hundred hits.

"How nice of you two to be so involved in photo-op projects." She mentally slapped herself. "Stop pegging them as Suspects Numbers One and Two. Impartial research begins right now."

On his own, Anthony Haswell chaired three different trusts and ran his city's school board. His condo development business profits had dipped in the early 2000s, but rebounded late in the decade.

Marion started an au pair business thirty years earlier. Today it was a thriving home-based company that placed hundreds of young women and men around the country each year.

Giulia copied and pasted several paragraphs for closer study tonight at Stone's Throw.

At the end of the third page of results she found a *Forbes* magazine article. The successful couple's "How We Did It" story and their bucket list.

His list included building condos adjacent to pro football stadiums, in the same way exclusive housing developments sprang

·

up next to golf courses. Hers was simpler: She designed her own hats as a hobby and wanted to grow that into a boutique business.

Their shared goal: Invest in the bed and breakfast business. To that end, they were making the rounds of all B&Bs with historical significance. A charming way to spend their semi-retirement.

The undercurrent in the news articles stank of ruthlessness. Miss Manners might approve their clothing, their upbringing, their business sense, and their place settings at dinner parties, but under all that perfection they clawed and scratched and stabbed with the worst.

"Nice to know my instincts are sound. Okay, you two, just because you have big red 'suspect' signs glowing over your heads doesn't mean you're actually trying to force Mac out of business. Onward."

If the internet could be relied on, Joel and Gino had been joined at the hip since the dawn of Google. Of course it could. If it was on the web, it must be true. Right.

They were in theater and soccer at the same high school. Theater and soccer at the same college. Business degrees. Opened their own coffee shop right after graduation. Expanded it to a bar with live music weekly and soccer on several TVs. Made their local TV news as the second couple in town married as soon as Pennsylvania legalized gay marriage.

If ever two people looked to be exactly the way they appeared, those two were exhibit A. Giulia read through their Facebook and Twitter feeds but nothing pinged. Still, a clean record wasn't a guarantee that they had no sinister plots in mind. If they wanted a ready-made bed and breakfast as a change from booze and sports, who would suspect Mac's "truant nephews?" Certainly not Mac.

Cedar's internet footprint was half as big as the Joel-Gino entity and one-quarter the size of Anthony's. Not even a Facebook page.

A photo with professional qualifications on the site of the accounting firm he worked for; a few mentions in the business section of the local paper. In his professional photographs he dressed like every other employee. Giulia wondered how far he took dress-down Fridays.

Solana made up for her husband's lack. Giulia found her credit counseling advertisements in local weeklies; she conducted regular seminars at the library and YMCA. Halfway down the first page of hits, Giulia clicked a link that looked out of place.

She got a website with soothing blues and pale greens undulating like fog around plain black type. "Lady Solana" glowed beneath the colored fog. The About tab started with "Lady Solana Bridges the Gap Between Worlds." The News tab: "Lady Solana Erases the Stigma of Ouija Boards." The Testimonials tab wept with love and ecstasy. Well, almost all the testimonials. The bottom third of the page sported this: "While we have no doubt Lady Solana contacted my grandfather, the Other Side has not lived up to my expectations. I had hoped that crossing over would have changed Granddad for the better. Even with Lady Solana channeling him, I recognized the miserable bastard's attitude immediately. I apologized to Lady Solana and she was most gracious."

She also sold Ouija boards of her own design. Smart of her not to alert Hasbro's legal team.

Giulia again took screenshots of all the elements on the page and pasted them into Solana's Excel sheet. What a draw Mac had discovered. Or Lady Rowan had recommended to Mac, knowing the deep trust Mac had in her. Why the title of "Lady" so often? Did it add a regal cachet for the desperate? She wondered if Mac's "Time to book your new vacation" emails were all about the family legend: A genuine psychic will attempt to contact the Stone's Throw ghost! Will it manifest? Will it speak? Special pricing for that week only!

The scenario fell into place with ease: Rowan sees the news article. Even though Mac was sure to have told her all about the family legends, perhaps Rowan never really believed the gold didn't exist. Rowan worries that a new crop of treasure hunters will claim jump. Enter Solana, Rowan's professional contact, or professional rival, and they declare a truce. Rowan offers to plant the idea in Mac's head about Solana as a surefire summer attraction, and bargains with Solana for a fifty-fifty split of the family fortune if Solana contacts the ghost who knows its location. Finders keepers and too bad for Mac losing her family fortune.

Once upon a time, Sister Mary Regina Coelis believed all people were good at heart. Giulia Driscoll, Private Investigator, stopped believing that right about the time a crazy Christian cult kidnapped her friends' baby.

She shoved it out of her head, typed up her theories, and moved on to Lucy the housekeeper. Thank you, social media. Lucy posted college photos with booze. With friends. With booze and friends. With a theater troupe of some kind. Puppets. No, not puppets...marionettes. That might have been why she wanted the marionette song Friday night. Reliving happy college days, perhaps.

Theater degrees were hard to translate into a job that paid the rent. Giulia knew that from Laurel and Anya. So Lucy had a BA or MFA and was cleaning toilets and serving food to make ends meet. Giulia also knew what that was like, after ten years teaching while a nun, yet with no official teaching degree to use in the outside world.

Lucy probably had massive student loan debt, thus her snatch at any job she could find. Would a theater major see the romance in a legendary gold cache, or just the halcyon prospect of a debt-free life? Possibly both.

Unfortunately, she had no criminal record, not even for weed possession or a DUI.

Unfortunately part two: All Giulia's current theories presumed the reality of a cache of stolen gold coins.

Fortunately part one: Mac's profitable B&B was real, and a couple or a hardworking solo entrepreneur could make Mac's profit their own.

That was the next research line to take. A plot to scare Mac into selling her business cheap, then flipping the property and retiring on the proceeds.

She searched for lakefront property values and then for B&B values. The traffic noises and Zane and Sidney's conversation faded as she dived deeper into the numbers.

The main office door slammed against the outer wall.
"Where are you, homewrecker?"

Thirty-One

Giulia leaped out of her chair, knocking it against the wall.

"I hear you in there!"

Zane's voice: "Don't go any farther."

A string of f-bombs. The printer or the coat rack crashed to the floor. Giulia opened her office door. She wasn't about to cower in here while her admin dealt with a drunken idiot.

Zane stood between her and Flynt the scumbag. Flynt reeked of beer and cigarettes. His smarmy good looks had deserted him: His jowls sagged, his eyes were bloodshot, and graying stubble covered his chin.

He spotted Giulia and charged. Zane put up both hands and exerted a gentle-looking shove.

Flynt stumbled backwards into the opposite wall. A few seconds later he lurched forward, his lips spraying spit and curses, and launched himself at Giulia again.

Zane slammed a fist into Flynt's gut. Flynt folded in half. Giulia stepped up next to Zane and landed a clean uppercut to Flynt's jaw. Flynt crashed to the floor.

Sidney's voice talking to the 911 operator got through to Giulia's ears.

Giulia and Zane grinned at each other. Giulia shook out her hand. "Idiot gave me brush burn."

Flynt moaned and writhed at their feet.

"Dude," Zane said, "don't blow chunks on our floor."

Sidney hung up. "Ew. I can handle Jessamine spitting up, but an adult full of beer? Double ew."

Flynt started to unknot. Giulia sat on the backs of his knees. Zane knelt and twisted his arms up under his lank hair. Flynt told Giulia what he was going to do to her to make her pay. Zane twisted his arms at a more extreme angle and Flynt shut up. The lovely wail of sirens came nearer and nearer.

"Four minutes flat," Sidney said. "Thanks for marrying a cop, Giulia."

Heavy feet pounded up the wooden stairs. Two uniformed officers Giulia didn't recognize ran in and stopped, each with a hand on his holstered gun. Seeing the Flynt-Zane-Giulia tableau. They kept coming.

"Whoa," the linebacker-sized one said. "He's been at the cheap beer."

Muffled profanity from Flynt.

"Oh, no, he's drooling on my hand-buffed floor," Giulia said.

The linebacker moved in. "We'll take over for you. What did he do?"

Zane and Giulia alternated the story as both cops hauled Flynt vertical. In the middle of Giulia's explanation of why Flynt disliked her, Flynt twisted out of one officer's grip and swung a fist wide in Giulia's direction. Both officers tackled him. While one cuffed him, the other read him his rights. Flynt kept shoving his sneakers against the floor, trying to get leverage, still threatening Giulia.

"If his language blisters our paint, we'll sue," Giulia said.

The cops laughed as well as they could while hustling Flynt out the door and down the stairs. The entire staff of Driscoll Investigations followed them.

All the building's tenants huddled on the sidewalk. The Common Grounds baristas and customers all squeezed against the large windows like puppies in a pet store.

The Scoop arrived.

The cameraman jumped out of their creeper van before the driver put it in park. Flynt was still shouting accusations and threats against Giulia, all flip-flopping between "You wrecked everything" and the unprintable things he was going to do to her before he wrung her expletive-laced neck. The camera caught it all.

Ken Kanning, the face of *The Scoop*, exited the van's driver's side with his mouth moving triple-time.

Giulia said to Sidney, "I'm so pleased at the cheap technology that allows anyone to afford a police scanner."

The police crammed Flynt into the back of their car. His mouth hadn't stopped moving, but the closed windows muffled his shouts.

No such impediment blocked Kanning's voice.

"Be glad you can't hear him, Scoopers! We'll have to edit the soundtrack or the FCC will be all over us. The language! The threats! If I were the owner of Driscoll Investigations, I'd be relieved to see this lowlife locked up."

The camera's spotlight hit Giulia directly in the eyes. Giulia pushed aside Kanning's foam-covered microphone and walked up to the linebacker. She did need to speak to him. Her movement wasn't only because she knew Kanning avoided police interaction at all costs.

Kanning shifted his microphone to Zane.

Giulia looked over her shoulder, caught Zane's eye, and nodded. They'd planned for future *Scoop* encounters with a stock of non-answers. In cases where Kanning could get details from the police or any number of bystanders eager for their moment on TV, Zane and Sidney had blanket authority to spin the incident any way they chose, as long as the spin didn't compromise a client or an open case.

Zane gave Kanning an anime-worthy account of the upstairs fight.

Giulia said to the linebacker, "I'll be asking for an Order of Protection against Flynt for myself and my staff."

"Good idea, Ms. D. Captain Reilly'll take care of you as soon as you're ready."

"Have we met before today?"

"Not in person, but your Sicilian pizza is the best I've ever eaten. Did the Captain talk you into cooking for this year's Fourth of July picnic too?"

"Oh, now I see. No. Sorry."

"Damn. Excuse me."

"No worries. Thank you for arriving so quickly."

"We were the closest. Just doing our job."

Flynt banged his shoulder against the car door, spit flying from his lips again. *The Scoop's* camera swung toward the police car and its spotlight glared on Flynt's face shoved into the window. The police took off.

Giulia threaded through the thinning crowd and escaped inside the stairwell. Sidney followed, Zane a second later, while *The Scoop* chased the police car.

Up in the office with the outer door closed and locked, Giulia said, "I'm sorry, guys. I'll stop at the precinct before I drive back to the lake."

"Don't be silly," Sidney said.

"No worries, Ms. D," Zane said. "This job gives me so many ways to impress my gamer gang. A lot of them are either the fat, pasty geek stereotype or the skeletal, pasty geek stereotype, with or without zits. I'm creating my own badass legend."

Giulia's neck muscles unclenched. "I'm so glad you can look at it that way."

"Really, Ms. D., we're fine. Chicks dig scars, not that drunk-and-stupid gave me a scar. But chicks dig true stories of danger, and I have a date tomorrow night. *The Scoop* promised to broadcast my interview at the halfway point of their show tomorrow afternoon."

Sidney added, "And I'll have a story to tell Olivier over supper."

"New rule for DI starting today," Giulia said. "No more divorce cases."

Thirty-Two

Back in her own office, the remaining Stone's Throw research had become much more attractive. Walter first. Giulia played the recording she'd made of Frank's report after his fishing trip while she searched for Walter's web history.

Sheesh. Even more drinking photos. Walter holding a trophy from a college fishing competition. Walter at one middle-management job after another. Fast food. Video store. Retail sales in computers, shoes, appliances, sporting goods. His smile grew more mechanical with each photograph. His eyes stared into the camera without expression.

"I'd have chucked it all and bought a tiny boat rental business on the lake too, Walter."

She browsed the boat rental website. The prices were reasonable for rentals and repairs of boats and fishing equipment. Reasonable plus small market on top of a seasonal-only business didn't make anyone rich.

"So, Walter: Did you want freedom from the grind or are you scoping out the legendary family gold?"

She rubbed her eyes. Many more of these questions and she'd be able to build her own private retreat with them and beat her head against their inflexible walls.

CeCe and Roy.

She got as far as the first of the million-plus results before her higher-level cognitive functions came back from sabbatical.

That CeCe and Roy. She should've recognized their names now that she'd acquired close to a dozen nieces and nephews.

The children's entertainers boasted eight moderately successful recording projects. Proprietary home-based DVDs for learning guitar, banjo, and keyboard. Voice-over credits in several video games.

Their public face on the Net showed evidence of careful crafting and monitoring. No drinking photos. No unguarded Tweets. Not an R-rated word from either. Smiles in all their pictures: Teaching, interviews, visits to children's hospitals.

Except in one: A long-distance paparazzi shot of a nurse wheeling CeCe out of a hospital, Roy at her side. No, not a hospital. Giulia zoomed in. A birthing center. Cece's arms were empty.

Giulia grabbed screenshots. What Frank used to call her "bleeding heart instincts" told her to cross this couple off her suspect list. Three years of detective experience made her override sympathy and slap them into the list. At the bottom.

Onward to MacAllister Stone.

No Facebook or Twitter accounts, but a boatload of professional accolades. Young Mac aged into older Mac with grace as her blonde hair turned silver and her smooth face gathered laugh lines and worry lines. Her offices, all of which looked like clones of each other, became crowded with more and more awards each year.

The inn's property survey and deed were easy to find. Mac had certainly bought the lighthouse at a bargain, but Giulia had been right about the obscene price of the renovations. "Gutted" would indeed have been the only way to begin.

Write-ups in historical and tourism magazines showcased the B&B at its opening and its five-year anniversary. A handful of ghost hunters and ghost debunkers published about it as well, all with conflicting information. No surprise there.

Giulia spent some time researching the Stone family ancestors and treasure hunting. Those were a pair of black holes to get lost in forever. Genealogy sites proved the existence of the stagecoach-robbing Stone. Also several succeeding generations of Stones, most with families large enough to populate two basketball teams, plus substitutes on the benches. The stagecoach robber starred in a few penny dreadfuls, as well as compilations of legends of the Wild West.

That led to the treasure hunters. The fervor of recent converts to Catholicism or the latest diet miracle was a guttering candle flame compared to the inferno in the hearts of True Believers in buried treasure. According to the many websites, Giulia was a fool if she didn't abandon DI and purchase a metal detector and equipment to create 3-D sonar images of mounds. If mounds weren't calling to her, then she must purchase maps and follow obscure diary entries from various criminals who'd secreted their loot and died before they could spend it. A fortune could be hers if only she put forth the effort.

The phone rang in the outer office. Her concentration broken, Giulia checked the clock in her taskbar. Four ten. She still needed to research further into Rowan, but if she wanted to talk to Jimmy and the district attorney, she had to haul it.

No choice. She'd have to suffer under Stone Throw's slug-paced Wi-Fi to dig deeper into Lady Rowan, friend of Mac, diviner of the future through the Tarot.

Several mouse clicks later, all her research was emailed to herself for retrieval on her iPad. She called the precinct and asked the Bond Girl-in-training receptionist to let Jimmy know she'd be over there by four thirty.

She turned everything off and opened her office door. "Look at these two hard workers. The totalitarian dictator in me is pleased."

Zane choked. Sidney turned big chocolate chip eyes on Giulia and said, "Your oppressive regime will topple in a cloud of hazelnut coffee-scented dust. *The Scoop* will broadcast exclusive reports of our bloodless coup."

Giulia laughed so hard she had to sit in Zane's client chair or fall down. "S-stop or I'll g-get the hiccups."

"Serves you right. I thought you'd given up the convent's tyrannical ways."

Giulia gasped several times and succeeded in cutting off her helpless laughter. "Who are you and what have you done with Sidney?"

"I've been reading the classics to Jessamine every night after supper. Dumas and Dickens rub off on you really quick."

"Jessamine will grow up to win the Pulitzer Prize in Literature."

"Or she'll breed a better, softer, woollier alpaca and make us all rich. Olivier would like the Pulitzer Prize. Mom and Dad would like the better alpaca." She glanced at her screen. "That's the thirty-seventh garbage email today. Zane's going to look into better anti-spam filters."

Zane said in his old, timid way, which didn't suit his Humphrey Bogart voice at all, "If that's okay with you, Ms. D."

Giulia refrained from lecturing him. "Of course it's okay. Why would I hire an MIT grad and not listen to him on technical issues?" She stood. "I'm off to hunt ghosts and vandals."

"Ghosts? More than one?" Zane said.

"If there is a ghost, singular, it's a Stone ancestor who fell off the lighthouse Widow's Walk when she saw her husband drown. Sidney, I heard that. An open mind is a desirable attribute in this profession."

Sidney cleared her throat. "Is any part of that true?"

"Well, there was a Dorothea who married Ephraim Stone and who both died on October ninth, 1918. But the rest of it? I couldn't discover any confirmation in my research today. There may be evidence of a rigged white nightgown which flies up the lighthouse stairs. I hope it's only used during Halloween week."

"A nightgown on wires is amateur," Zane said. "My fraternity knew how to scare people at Halloween. We set up a morgue one year and only half the bodies under sheets were fake. We dressed as zombies and hid in the bushes. We dressed as ghosts and hid in the bedrooms and waited for the horny couples to sneak off for a quickie. My senior year we turned the frat house into a fairy tale castle. The girls loved it until we ripped off the Prince Charming masks and splattered them with fake blood and realistic amputated body parts. We went through a lot of booze after that reveal."

Giulia's mouth was hanging open. She closed it, swallowed, and said, "Next week we're going to have a discussion about you going undercover." She picked up her purse. "Now I'm off to see the district attorney about a restraining order."

Sidney said, "You are? Thanks."

Giulia gave Sidney her "no one appreciates me" stare. "A client's crazy husband threatens and attacks us and you're surprised I'm taking action? Baby Brain is supposed to go away after you give birth."

Sidney giggled. "It has, I swear. If we catch *The Scoop* lurking, we'll run the other way."

"I'll be back in the office as soon as I solve this lighthouse mystery." She listened to herself. "I'm living in a *Scooby-Doo* episode."

"Ruh-roh!" Zane and Sidney said together.

Thirty-Three

Criminals must have taken the day off, because for the first time in months Giulia wasn't deafened by screaming lowlifes as soon as she entered the police station.

The Bond Girl was a vision in teal today, from eyeshadow to fingernails to form-fitting sundress. Giulia had no doubt her pedicure matched as well.

"Katelyn," Giulia said, "I keep expecting your lipstick to match no matter what."

The receptionist pouted. "It did before I left the house, Ms. Driscoll, but my fiancé said only clowns wear that color on their lips."

Giulia planted her elbows on the desk. "Did I hear the 'f' word?"

Katelyn's rose-tinted lips parted in a wide smile. She held up her left hand. The round diamond set in a circle of diminutive blue, pink, yellow, and green diamonds caught the fluorescent light like a laser show.

"I sort of keep staring at it and forgetting to work."

"It's gorgeous. Congratulations. When's the wedding?"

"Not 'til next summer. We have tons of family who have to make travel plans. I sent him out to find extra-strength condoms so we don't have even the slightest chance of me getting pregnant. I've got the clingiest gown picked out. His ex-girlfriends and my ex-boyfriends will die from envy." The smile turned a shade evil.

Giulia laughed. "Make sure your friends take pictures."

"I've already got my photo brigade on alert." She pressed a button on her multi-line phone. "Captain Reilly? Ms. Driscoll is here."

The young man and older woman in handcuffs at separate desks ignored Giulia as she passed them. The detectives all waved at her. Jimmy met her at the door of his office.

"Giulia, we finally have a quiet day for your visit."

She pecked his cheek. "I don't know how to handle it."

When he closed them into his office, he said, "That Jane you sent over for me to interview handled it like a pro. We had three meth-cooking morons in here when she came. The usual: Swearing, making threats, trying to get out of the cuffs to fight each other over whose fault the bust was. She never blinked. One of them made a crack about her hair and she came back with a putdown that actually shut the moron up."

"I told you she was good. If I didn't have Sidney I'd hire her, but no one can replace Sidney." She sat down.

Jimmy pulled out his chair. "She's not you, but she's got what it takes. I'm plowing through the mountain of paperwork the City requires. It'll be my last assistant-less act."

A single knock at the door and Jimmy opened it on a tall, thin, bald man with flappy ears.

"Ed, thanks for coming. This is Giulia Driscoll, head of Driscoll Investigations. Giulia, Ed Stanek, District Attorney."

Giulia shook his hand. "How are your youngest daughter's trumpet lessons progressing?"

Stanek winced. "She stays on key about half the time now. Marsha says if I buy earplugs I'll scar my daughter for life. Does my wife care about my protesting eardrums? No."

Jimmy glanced from one to the other. "Didn't know you'd met."

Giulia said, "Remember that baby kidnapping case a few years back? We worked out my testimony over lots of coffee and pie at his house. His wife makes a pear and cherry pie to die for."

"I'll pass on your compliment." Stanek cleared a dozen file folders off a third chair and sat. "Reilly says you want an order of protection."

Giulia summarized the Flynt investigation up to that morning's incident. Jimmy handed him a copy of the police report.

"I doubt he'll try anything at the office again," Giulia said. "Not after the way we took him down. But in case he does, I'd like legal ammunition. Zane and I can take care of ourselves, but Sidney can't, not so soon after having a baby."

Stanek scribbled on a legal pad. "This won't be a problem. I'll set up a date for you to appear before one of the judges to make it official. Monday's already shot, so..." He took a tablet out of his briefcase and opened a calendar program. "How's Wednesday afternoon look?"

Giulia made a face. "I'm up at Conneaut Lake on a case. Email me with a firm time so I can let my people know and we'll rearrange our schedules."

"Good. Expect something from me tomorrow morning." He dropped the papers, legal pad, and tablet into the briefcase and snapped it closed. "Too many assholes in the world. Speaking of, Reilly, can one of your men let me into the holding cells? A DUI with manslaughter wants to plead and his lawyer should already be back there."

"Works for me." Jimmy stood. "Giulia, always good to see you. Tell Frank I've piled so much work on his desk he won't be able to see it."

"With pleasure." She shook the D.A.'s hand. "Thanks for your help. Your daughter will become a better musician soon."

He winced again. "If only I could invent a way to speed up that process."

Giulia pecked Jimmy on the cheek. "I'll bring Frank back full of energy and ready to work."

"I'll try to have a nice, juicy homicide for him. Make him earn his keep."

Thirty-Four

Throughout supper at the Jimmy Buffet-themed bar and grill, Giulia threatened Frank with spicy pickle spears. She also caught him up on all her research and the Flynt incident.

She added flair to Zane's explanation of his new way to impress women, but when Frank didn't respond, she refocused. His "Hulk Smash" air stopped her.

"Honey?"

Frank's voice came out low and gravelly. "If I ever see Flynt in person, I will tear off his balls and shove them down his filthy throat."

Giulia waited several seconds for the goosebumps his voice raised to subside. "Yes. Well, it's unlikely he'll show his face at the office, and if he has the ambition to track me down at home we both have guns." She offered him the rest of her fries. "I'm satiated with pickles and red meat."

They returned to Stone's Throw in time for the evening's cookies and iced tea.

Frank chose a lemon cookie from the tray and dialed a number on his phone as he walked through the sunroom. "VanHorne? Driscoll. Got your email. What's up with..." His voice faded as he moved away from the house's open windows toward the beach.

Giulia poured herself an iced tea and looked through the collection of CDs beneath the cathedral radio/CD player. Marion and Anthony sat on the couch reading together from a tablet.

"What if we sell the second cottage?" Anthony said. "We haven't used it in two years."

"The kids used it...no, you're right. That was last year."

From the corner of her eye, Giulia watched Marion sip tea and poke the tablet screen.

"The cottage won't net enough. Look at the size of this place. We'll have to ask Mac what her monthly operating costs are."

Anthony glanced at Giulia, then said to Marion, "Do you think that's a good strategy?"

Marion's voice grew sly. "Darling, you should trust me when dealing with other women."

Giulia opened a CD case and pretended to read the song list, made a face, and put it back.

Marion continued, "What are the comparison numbers between one with a hook, like this one, and one that's simply another bed and breakfast?"

Giulia reshelved the CDs and clapped her hand to her pocket. She took out her phone, got up off her knees, and touched the screen as she walked slowly out of the living room.

Anthony said, "The numbers bear out my initial thought that a hook increases business by four to seven percent in any given month."

Giulia pretended to answer the email she hadn't received and continued into the sunroom. The soft lights in the room turned the world outside the windows solid black.

Marion and Anthony's voices floated through the open doorway, crunching numbers, debating lakeside property versus historically significant sites versus areas with a current high tourism rate.

Giulia opened mahjong on her phone and played a game as she listened without giving any real attention to the tiles.

"The costs decrease by forty-six percent if we purchase an existing one." Anthony ran through numbers. Marion interrupted him several times before the discussion changed to interest rates and depreciation.

After five solid minutes of this, Anthony cut his wife off in mid-sentence. "We're missing *CSI.*" Half a minute later, they disappeared upstairs, no doubt to stream the show on the tablet.

Giulia was about ready to find Frank and drag him onto the beach for a moonlit walk.

"Oh my God."

Mac's voice from the kitchen area.

Giulia shelved romantic walk plans and ran through the hall and old-fashioned kitchen into the working kitchen, a narrow space filled with modern chrome appliances. Mac stood before the open refrigerator, her expression shifting between anger and disgust.

Giulia came up next to her. "What's wrong? Oh, gross."

Every item in the packed refrigerator was spoiled. Furry mold coated strawberries, raspberries, kiwifruit, and starfruit. Curdled lumps sloshed in the milk. Green and blue splotches marred the bread and English muffins. Stringy things floated in the maple syrup. Four egg cartons leaked sulfurous goo. Mottled black and green oranges had exploded in their see-through drawer. In another drawer, the labels on packages of more white and green fur insisted they had once held Swiss cheese. Next to them, the visible surfaces of the ham and bacon shone like gasoline slicks on asphalt.

On the counter, a cloud of fruit flies feasted on two bunches of blackened, squashy bananas. A battalion of minuscule ants covered the butter.

Mac opened the pantry.

Hundreds of bugs wriggled through the flour. Larger ants infested the sugar. The stench from the rancid walnuts and almonds clashed with the equally rancid peanut and almond butters. The brown sugar had fossilized. The coffee beans smelled dusty underneath more stale oils. The tea leaves resembled fireplace ash.

"I restocked everything yesterday," Mac said, her voice unsteady. "All the produce, the berries, the milk and eggs. I opened that bag of coffee three days ago. I used the flour and sugar this morning." She slammed her fists on the counter. "This morning!"

Giulia went for the defuse tactic. "The biscuits and sausage gravy tasted fine. Besides, a little extra protein never hurt anyone."

Mac turned big eyes on Giulia; eyes like Sidney's back when she was a bundle of stress and hormones in the third trimester.

Giulia closed the fridge. "Let's work out the timeframe for this. What time did you go grocery shopping yesterday?"

No answer. Giulia grasped Mac's closed fist and shook it gently. "Mac. Grocery shopping. What time?" She unhooked the magic marker from the magnetic notepad on the fridge door.

Mac blinked and her eyes returned to normal. "Uh, eleven o'clock. Maybe eleven fifteen."

One bullet on the page. "I don't suppose you saved the list."

"I don't need to. The breakfast menu is the same every week in the summer." Mac opened her clenched hands. "I have to restock for tomorrow morning. The farmers' market won't be open again until next Sunday. What am I going to do? I only buy local."

"Who has access to the kitchen?" Giulia kept the question sharp to cut through Mac's dithering.

"Me. Lucy. Matthew to fix things or grab a drink on hot days."

"Good. Everything was fine for breakfast. What about leftovers?"

Mac's replies came faster now. "There weren't any. I don't make extra. It destroys the food budget."

"You didn't pour the leftover milk from the coffee tray back into the gallon container?"

"Not on warm days like this. Too big a risk to the rest of the milk."

Mac began offering information without prompts.

Giulia wrote bullet after bullet, tearing the four-by-six pages off one after the other.

"After we cleaned up from breakfast, Lucy went on her cleaning rounds and I went to the farmers' market. I got back here around quarter to one and loaded up the fridge. I went to my office. I wrote checks and answered email. After that, I played around with ideas for Labor Day weekend. Lucy picked up her check, I don't know, after three sometime. I went to the kitchen for lemonade after she left. Then I made a sweep of the place and played croquet against Gino. Then supper. I came back at seven to bake the cookies. I buy premade frozen cookies, so I only have to set them on the baking sheet and turn on the oven. The iced tea was already prepared and in the fridge."

Giulia ripped off another sheet. "So everything in the fridge was fine at seven o'clock?'

Mac's eyebrows met. "Yes...the cookies finished at seven twenty and I set up the iced tea tray while they cooled."

"Okay. What made you open the fridge just now?"

"Tomorrow's breakfast is cheddar potato waffles. I set up everything the night before so it's ready to go in case I'm a minute or two late in the morning." She leaned against the counter. "I walk the grounds every night after I set out the cookies and drinks. It's always beautiful under the trees and by the lake. When I came back inside to set up breakfast, I found this disaster." She stared at the clock over the sink. "Quarter to nine, I think." She turned on Giulia. "You were in the house. What time did you hear me discover it?"

Giulia raised her eyebrows. "I heard something wrong in your voice and followed it. I didn't check the time."

"No one's perfect."

She opened the side of the fridge without the notepad and reached for the milk.

"Stop." Giulia put out a hand. "Fingerprints."

Mac laughed, an unhappy sound. "Ghosts don't leave fingerprints."

Giulia snapped the pen back into its holder. "No ghost put that bag of slime in the shower in Marion's room. I'm investigating targeted, tangible vandalism by living people who leave fingerprints."

"How would a human get the level of the spoiled milk at the exact same place it was when fresh?"

Giulia made allowances for Mac's frustration. "Is the milk at the exact same level, down to a millimeter?"

Mac started to put her face up to the plastic gallon jug, but backed away a second later. Giulia didn't blame her. The combined odors were enough to knock over a dead opossum.

"Point to you. I don't know the exact level. All right. The fridge is yours to examine. I have to find fresh food."

"We might be able to help with that." Giulia texted Frank. "Where's the nearest supermarket? Not one in town. A nice, big, anonymous place. Maybe a Walmart."

"No, no, no. I never buy Stone's Throw food from anyplace other than the farmers' market."

Giulia made further allowances. "Tonight's the exception. You have no food for tomorrow morning. You don't want to create talk in town with an uncharacteristic produce-buying binge. Therefore, Walmart. Where's the nearest gigantic one?'

"Meadville, but I only buy local, sustainable food from area farmers."

Frank walked into the kitchen. "What's the matter? *Cait naofa.*"

Giulia turned on her sunniest smile. "'Holy cats' is right. Honey, we have an emergency. Every bit of food in the fridge is spoiled and Mac needs to replace it all. Would you be Superman and drive her to the Walmart in Meadville?"

Frank opened his mouth. Giulia kept the blinding smile trained on him. He visibly regrouped. "No problem. I'll get the car keys."

Thirty-Five

After Frank and Mac left, Giulia plunged into frantic research on her phone. Of all times not to be near a fingerprint kit. Although only a psychic might have thought to bring one. Where was Lady Rowan when Giulia could have used her?

Unfruitful train of thought. If Lady Rowan could have predicted the need for capturing fingerprints, Solana might have tuned into that same astral wave. Of course, if they were working together to scare Mac out of business...

Google came through for her before she got stuck on that particular hamster wheel. Giulia had access to all the ingredients in this simple emergency fingerprint how-to. She raided the kitchen's junk drawer for cellophane tape and the pantry for cornstarch. She breathed a quick prayer to Saint Jude that the saboteur hadn't included cornstarch in his or her list of necessary breakfast foods to destroy.

Untouched. Giulia breathed a sigh of relief and *poofed* up a cloud of the stuff. She screwed the lid back on an instant before she sneezed.

Okay. Fridge closed. Febreze sprayed with generosity in the narrow kitchen space. Giulia turned off the lights and walked upstairs to her room. No one else was on the first and second floors, so she didn't need to waste time pretending to be casual. She grabbed her makeup brush and ran downstairs, jumping over the creaky steps.

First floor still empty. She flicked the kitchen lights back on and searched for something dark to tape fingerprints to. Envelopes. Too bright. Empty orange juice carton, the same. Plastic grocery bag, too wrinkly. She opened a thin cabinet door tucked into the far corner and discovered a stash of paper grocery bags.

Girding her figurative loins, she opened the refrigerator again. The stench hit her like a semi at sixty-five miles per hour. She squeezed shut watering eyes and opened them five seconds later, ready to work.

The milk first. She found one more essential item not on the helpful website: Hot pads to protect the plastic from her own skin oils.

One: Dip brush in cornstarch.

Two: Dust cornstarch over all sides of plastic jug.

Three: Apply strip after strip of tape and pray to Saint...

Giulia had no idea which saint was the patron of clear fingerprint lifts.

Twelve minutes in and most of one roll of tape, Giulia got a clean print. Index or middle finger, it looked like. Energized, she peeled the tape off with the precision of a surgeon. At least of the surgeons she'd seen on primetime TV.

Four: Apply tape to brown grocery bag.

The internet didn't lie. She'd lifted a legible fingerprint.

Palpable stenches and all, Giulia stuck her head into the fridge for her next test object. Perhaps the fruit drawer. She brushed cornstarch on the top of the handle and tore off a strip of tape to fit its entire length.

Three...two...one...The tape popped like bubble wrap, cornstarch puffing in all directions.

Giulia almost cursed until she spotted the maple syrup bottle. Hot pads on; bottle to counter. The dangly green filaments sloshed against the white puffballs as the syrup settled. She'd never been so grateful for her cast-iron stomach.

Now. Smaller pieces of tape. She went with the obvious: A right-handed food-spoiler would pick up the handle of the heavy gallon jug with the right hand and balance it with the left. One cornstarch-loaded makeup brush later, she used up most of the tape in columns three inches on either side of where her own fingerprints would hit.

She repeated "Easy...easy" to herself as she peeled away each strip of tape. Another print appeared close to the top of the second column. She transferred it to the paper bag. Near the bottom, half a print.

That was the last of them, though. She tried the orange juice, the meat drawer, and the plastic wrap around the bacon and ham, but no luck. As a last resort, she pulled five whole and partial prints from the refrigerator door handles and taped them all to the bag.

Her nose thanked her for closing the refrigerator. Before she cleaned anything, she took several pictures of the fingerprints, making sure to steady her elbows on the counter to increase her chances of one sharp picture of each. Then she wiped down everything twice since cornstarch clung to surfaces almost as bad as baking cocoa did.

She was wringing out the dishcloth when Frank and Mac returned.

Frank carried two boxes labeled "Apples" and Mac carried one from a lettuce grower. All three of them set everything from the boxes on the counter and as one they took a deep breath and opened the fridge.

"It's worse than I remembered," Frank said.

Mac pulled out the fruit drawer in silence and dumped the oranges into the bag Giulia held out for her. One went *splat* and everyone cringed, but no juices fountained out.

Frank and Mac emptied everything into plastic trash bags. Giulia tied them up and set them in the back corner, away from the doorway leading to the big kitchen/reception area. While Mac washed out the flour and sugar jars and the butter dish, Giulia mixed vinegar and water and wiped down the refrigerator.

Mac's voice broke the silence. "Thank you both for helping with this."

Giulia exchanged relieved glances with Frank. "We're not exactly guests."

Mac banged the flour jar on the counter. "This ghost is costing me more money every week."

Giulia opened a bag of flour and poured it into the clean jar. "Ghosts don't leave fingerprints."

Frank gave her a thumbs-up.

Mac appeared to really see Giulia for the first time since they returned with fresh groceries. "You found fingerprints?"

Giulia pointed to the edge of the brown bag up on top of the refrigerator, out of the way. "Five complete prints and three partials, mostly from the door handle. Mine will be on the handle for sure, but they're already on file. So are yours now, from Saturday's robbery."

Mac set down the clean and dry sugar canister. "Lucy's will be on there too." She covered a fresh stick of butter and looked around the kitchen. "The only food or drink I want to pre-set tonight is a glass of wine in my own living room."

Giulia picked up the grocery bag with care. "I used up all your tape."

"I'll deduct it from your fee." Mac managed a feeble smile.

Thirty-Six

Up in their room, Giulia set the paper bag at the bottom of her suitcase and flopped across the bed. Frank came out of the bathroom drying his hands.

"You sure know how to show a guy a good time, lady."

"I bet you thought married life with a former nun would be all dull and pious."

"I did wonder if you might need to relearn how to have fun." He flopped next to her. "I'm even too tired to check my fantasy stats. By the way, where did you learn that fingerprint trick?"

She held up her phone. "Google is my friend."

"I could've used that a few times in my career." He yawned. "Want to crawl into bed smelling like vinegar and mold or shall we shower first?"

"When you put it that way, I vote shower."

Two in the morning. Again.

At least it wasn't the weeping ghost this time. Giulia lay in bed listening to moans and creaks until she was both wide awake and ticked off.

She tucked the covers around Frank and crawled out of bed. Easing open the dresser drawer, she put on the first t-shirt and shorts her hands touched. Then, phone in hand and flashlight app ready, she opened their room door.

The noises paused, then restarted. Upstairs. One of the empty rooms or the attic. She debated going to the kitchen for salt, but she'd spent last Halloween with her friend Sister Bart's family and they'd given her an education. Salt alone wasn't enough to banish a spirit. It had to be combined with certain herbs, and her middle-of-the-night brain wasn't giving up the information.

Fine. She'd sit down with this Stone family ghost and invite it to air its grievances. Ever since Giulia had put on the habit, people opened up to her like she was a confidential advice columnist. That hadn't changed post-convent. So if Giulia schooled her anger into quiescence, this ghost might talk to her.

She watched her certainty that a human agency was the cause of all the B&B's troubles waver and sputter. Two a.m. was not a propitious time for rational thought.

Then she climbed the stairs to the third floor. The moans got louder. The design of the hallways and stairwells confused the ears. Giulia tiptoed to the foot of the narrow attic stairs. Yes, the moans came from up there...wait...they came from behind her. To her left. Upstairs.

A hand grasped her shoulder. She jumped and ducked away and stifled a scream as she brought up her phone flashlight.

Frank flung his arm over his eyes.

"What's going on?" he whispered.

Giulia waved her arm all around her. "Don't you hear it?"

At that moment, the groans and creaks took on a definite, faster rhythm. From behind the closed door facing Giulia, a woman's voice gasped out obscene commands.

Frank put his arms around Giulia. "Let's get back to bed."

Angry and mortified, Giulia stalked down the stairs, halting Frank right before the step that cracked. Only when they reached the safety of the Sand Dollar room did she notice her icy feet and burning face.

Giulia stripped off her shorts and dived under the covers in her t-shirt. Frank climbed in wearing his sweatpants.

"What was that all about?" he said.

Giulia stared up at the lace canopy. "I thought the two a.m. ghost was back."

"If that's a pair of ghosts replaying their last moments on earth, they died happy. Besides, didn't you say your ghost was a weeper?"

"Yes, but I thought it was performing a new trick."

Frank put his arm over her midsection. "Wait. Now you think there really is a ghost?"

Giulia shoved her pillow over her face. "I don't know what to think." A moment later she slid it up over her head. "No. I take that back. I do know what to think: Somebody is trying to muddy the issue by cooking up a two a.m. haunting. If they're targeting me then I need a refresher class in going undercover. If it's one of the couples, I'm crossing off CeCe and Roy after tonight. If it's Walter, then he has more ambition than you gave him credit for." Giulia yawned. "How am I coherent at this hour? Who did I leave out?"

Frank yawned a second later. "If I was coherent, I'd suggest we make our own haunting like that couple upstairs." He yawned again. "How about tomorrow night?" He pulled her against him. A few seconds later, he was snoring.

The scream brought Giulia to her feet out of a restless sleep. She checked the clock: Three a.m. this time.

At least it wasn't her personal weeping ghost branching out into new scare tactics.

She stood barefoot on the wooden floor for a moment, then dragged her shorts back on and opened her door.

Marion opened her own door a second later. "Did you hear a scream?"

"Yes." Giulia wondered if her own bedhead was half as crazy as Marion's clown hair.

Roy and CeCe leaned over the banister. "Did anyone hear a scream?"

Giulia said, "Yes. I'll be right back. Just have to get shoes on."

She shoved her feet into sneakers and decided to let Frank sleep.

When she came out, Marion had smashed down her hair and put on sandals with her pajamas. Roy and CeCe joined them, wearing matching bathrobes and flip-flops.

"Where should we start?" CeCe said.

A different voice, half as loud as the first one, called "Help!"

"First floor," Giulia said.

Everyone clattered down, the squeaky step repeating like a car alarm. They stopped in a group in front of the antique doll carriage.

"There's a light at the foot of the lighthouse stairs," Giulia said, moving again.

Solana lay beneath Cedar at the base of the spiral staircase. His left leg was bent at an angle nature never intended the fibula to achieve. Her eyes were closed and her face was so white it looked like she'd applied stage makeup.

Giulia said, "I have some training. Let me look."

"So do I," Roy said.

He crouched next to Cedar's leg and Giulia knelt by Solana's head.

"I couldn't keep her awake after we fell," Cedar said. Roy touched Cedar's leg and he cursed in a voice far from his businesslike tone of yesterday.

Giulia patted her empty pocket. "Does anyone have their phone?"

CeCe handed hers over and Giulia opened the flashlight app, then one of Solana's eyes. The pupil stayed dilated. She checked the other eye: The same.

"My guess is concussion. I don't want to move her head."

"I'll call 911," Anthony said, moving out into the small foyer.

Marion was already back into the souvenir room. "I'll wake up Mac."

"Where did her head hit?" Giulia said to Cedar.

Another string of curses as Roy probed the break. "I'm not sure. The railing, I think. We kept bouncing off those damn winding stairs. Couldn't get a grip on anything. Dammit, you, stop touching my fucking leg!"

"You're moving it when you talk," Roy said. "I'm trying to keep it steady."

"I tried to get my arm between her head and the cement floor. That's how I got twisted up." Cedar closed his eyes and took a couple of short, sharp breaths. "Sorry, dude. Hurts like a sonofabitch."

Anthony returned. "EMTs and police on their way."

Solana moaned. Giulia braced the unconscious woman's head in a "boxing the ears" hold. "I'm not sure what to do with head and neck injuries, except to keep them steady."

CeCe ran into the dining room and returned with several linen napkins from the place settings. "If she vomits, I'll clear her mouth."

The bizarre tableau didn't move for a few moments.

"Why were you in the lighthouse in the middle of the night?" Giulia said.

Solana, eyes still closed, answered in a voice similar to the one she cajoled the ghost with during her séance.

"We followed the Woman in White."

All of them turned to Cedar.

"Sunday's session in the parlor was so unusual Solana wanted to try contacting the spirit again after dark. We don't live too far from here, so we drove over about two a.m. and set up the Ouija board."

Giulia wondered if CeCe and Roy's enthusiastic activity had interfered with Solana's concentration. She didn't say that out loud or treat Cedar to a well-deserved lecture about the error of treating Mac's property as though it were his own. "Mac locks the doors as soon as everyone's inside for the night."

He inhaled sharply and a small whimper escaped his lips. Then he took a slower breath and said, "A five-year-old with internet access could break into here. Small-town life makes people careless. We set up the board here at the foot of the stairs. She offered herself to the ghost again. We got a whole hour of nothing. Right when I was ready to give up for the night, she stiffened up like she did on the couch. Then she got up and started climbing the stairs."

The sounds of two different sirens penetrated the walls.

"Small town. Not far to drive," Roy said.

"Go on," Giulia said.

"Her lips were moving, but I couldn't hear her voice. Then I swear to the gods I saw a white dress floating up the stairs." He glared at their faces as though expecting them to laugh. When no one did, he went on. "Solana must have been following it all along and either her belief gave the spirit energy to manifest to me, or I tapped into Solana's sight. It's happened before. I heard a voice whisper about protecting the treasure, just like in the séance."

"But you didn't see anyone?" Giulia said. "Only the floating dress?"

He shook his head, grimaced, and said, "Only the dress, going up higher around those stairs until it disappeared. Then Solana reached up like she was trying to grab hold of something, or maybe someone's hands, and she overbalanced." His brow furrowed. "Yes, she did hit her head on the railing. I tried to catch her, but I was three steps below her. We rolled and bounced down those steps and I tried to twist to break her fall. Her eyes opened and that's the scream you heard, I guess." He took another short breath. "I picked the wrong day to quit heroin."

The house behind them filled with lights and noise and heavy footsteps. Mac ran in followed by two EMTs carrying emergency kits.

Giulia said, "Solana fell and hit her head on the railing." She gestured toward it with her own head. "We're not sure if she also hit it on the floor, so we've been keeping it immobile."

Roy said, "Broken leg here, also trying to keep it immobile."

The EMTs, both male, each took one patient. Giulia and Roy eased out of the way when the EMTs gave them the signal. The noise had brought Frank, Joel, and Gino downstairs. Anthony explained the situation to them, the police, and the EMTs as the latter worked.

Giulia stood against the wall closest to Cedar, waiting, callous as it was, for the pain of his broken leg to make him blurt out something useful.

Sure enough, when the EMT inflated an air cast around it, Cedar cursed the ghost. "You dead bitch! You lied to us!"

The EMTs glanced at each other, then at Mac.

Solana moaned again in that not-quite-here voice, "Where is the gold? You promised the hidden gold if we helped..." Her head tried to thrash in the neck stabilizer.

One of the EMTs put his hands on her shoulders. "Ma'am, please remain still."

"Ready?" the other EMT said.

The police officers positioned themselves at either end of Cedar's gurney. "We've got this one."

"Cool. Thanks. You want to head out first?"

The officer in the lead said to Mac, "We'll be back to take statements as soon as they're in the ambulance."

Cedar cursed in a different tone than before. "We landed on her grandmother's Ouija board. When Solana comes back she's going to have a shit hemorrhage."

"Comes back?" Giulia said.

She realized what he meant right as he gave her an "are you stupid" glare.

"After she realizes Dorothea's left her again, dummy. Ow! What the hell kind of techs are you? Stop banging me around."

Giulia gathered the three pieces of shattered wood and retrieved the planchette from under the staircase. Cedar accepted them with another grimace and folded his hands over the wreckage.

At this moment Giulia realized she was wearing an orange t-shirt over blue shorts, and her bright red sneakers didn't match either piece of clothing. Then again, the group of wide-awake guests in their ludicrous combination of bathrobes and beachwear resembled an explosion in a crayon factory.

Frank came to her side now that the space was free. "Treasure hunters?"

"Are you surprised?"

"Nope."

The police returned and Giulia stepped forward with Marion to tell about the scream that woke them up. Roy and CeCe gave their version. The officers split them into two groups and wrote out four accounts of what they'd seen and heard at the foot of the lighthouse stairs.

It was five thirty when the police left the lighthouse to Mac and the uninjured guests. The upper half of the foyer door began the change from black to gray. Giulia and CeCe shivered.

Mac said, "I'll make coffee."

Giulia said, "By any chance, do you have hot chocolate?"

Joel and CeCe said, "Oh, yes."

Anthony said, "Screw that. I've got Jameson in my room, remember? I'll bring it down for anyone else who could use a shot in their coffee."

"You win," Joel said. "We've got a stash of homemade chocolate chip cookies in our room."

They headed upstairs. CeCe replaced the napkins on the dining room table. Marion took out paper napkins from the credenza and set the coffee table. Gino and Roy transferred the coffee cups from the dining room into the living room. Mac and Giulia went into the kitchen.

When she and Mac were alone in the kitchen, Giulia said, "Did you lure those two into the lighthouse to shut them up?"

Thirty-Seven

Mac clutched the bag of coffee filters. "What?"

Giulia returned the can of coffee to the pantry. "I found the hidden speaker in the bookcase yesterday, after the séance."

"I—I—"

"Right about now, I'd say you've been playing me for publicity." Giulia opened the refrigerator and brought out one of the new gallons of milk. "A private investigator who found evidence of an actual Stone's Throw ghost would be great for business."

Mac dropped the coffee filters and clutched Giulia's hands. "No, no, it's not like that. I swear I had nothing to do with the possession or their accident." She glanced out toward the antique kitchen and pulled Giulia around the corner of the L, out of sight of the doorway. "I use the speaker on Halloween night when the costume party is in full swing. That's the only time, it really is. I promise." Her eyes shifted to the counter and the wall, but didn't meet Giulia's.

"And last night?"

"What do you mean?" More eye acrobatics.

"Mac, if you want to stick to that story, it's your choice. Driscoll Investigations doesn't work this way. We'll pack up and be out of here before breakfast."

Mac's hands clutched tighter. Giulia wished her nails weren't quite so long.

"No! Please don't leave. I need your help."

Giulia inclined her head toward the doorway and Mac lowered her voice.

"This is the truth, I promise. I did turn on the speaker last night. The opportunity dropped into my lap; how could I not use it? Solana with all her eerie atmospheric trappings was good, but I knew a little boost of weeping ghost would put it over the top." Mac's words tumbled over each other. "I had just turned the switch off when she pointed at me and spoke in that otherworldly voice." She finally looked Giulia in the eyes. "All the other séances this summer got us a big fat nothing. The guests got itchy after half an hour. I was thinking about dropping Solana's act, but I never told her. Never. Now all of a sudden, just when you're here, she goes full-on *Exorcist*. Rowan was right about you. The Veiled Woman brought the other world into contact with Solana. I admit it; the whole thing scared the shit out of me."

The perking noises from the coffeepot slowed to an occasional *blip*.

Giulia said, "And the white nightgown she said she followed?"

Mac released Giulia, whose willpower kept herself from rubbing the fingernail-shaped dents in her skin.

"That wasn't my doing, I swear. I have a gauze dress on wires in the attic that I use on Halloween, but it's up there now, all packed away. I'll show you. I don't know what Solana and Cedar expected to happen in my lighthouse in the middle of the night. Too many weed-laced brownies frying their essential brain cells would be my guess. But I swear on my great-great-great-grandfather's unhallowed grave that I was asleep in my bed when all this happened. Ask Marion. It took her pounding on my door and ringing my doorbell for more than a minute to wake me."

The desperation in her hazel eyes clung to Giulia like steam from the coffeepot. Giulia would get nothing useful from Mac in this state. "All right. When this impromptu breakfast breaks up, you and I will take a trip to the attic."

Mac plunged forward as though to kiss Giulia, but Giulia's body language must have conveyed "Don't go there," because Mac did a one-eighty and started a second pot of coffee. She picked up the first carafe. Giulia poured milk into a cow-shaped creamer and followed her out to the living room.

Not one person spoke until the coffee was poured and whiskey added and the first drinks taken. Giulia and Marion shivered. Gino and Roy sighed.

"That's better," Frank said.

Joel handed the cookies around. "All the guys at work who think B&Bs are girly vacation spots will eat their hearts out when I tell them this story."

"Ghoul," Gino said.

"What? Nobody's dead. Broken bones and crazy psychics do not a morbid story make."

"My grandfather used to add Black Velvet to his coffee," Mac said. "I tried it once when I was a teenager. This is much better."

"At least there are enough clouds to give us a really good sunrise," Marion said. "Look at those colors."

The men glanced out the bay window and returned to their coffee. CeCe snapped a picture with her phone. Giulia walked to the side of the couch and held the curtain aside to watch the brilliant oranges and reds unimpeded.

"Would anyone like more coffee?" Mac said.

"I would," Anthony said.

"Me too," Roy said.

"These are quite possibly the best cookies I've ever eaten," CeCe said.

"That's the sleep deprivation talking," Joel said, "but thank you."

Ten minutes later and without any further conversation, Giulia, Mac, and CeCe gathered cups and napkins. Joel swept up the cookie crumbs.

"I'll push breakfast back to eleven," Mac said.

"Works for us," Gino said.

Marion and Anthony returned to their room, followed up the stairs by the others in twos.

Giulia said to Mac, "Would you like help with the dishes before we head to the attic?"

"No, thanks," Mac said. "I'll load these into the dishwasher to give all of them time to get into their rooms."

A few minutes later, Giulia and Frank followed Mac upstairs, skipping the creaking and cracking steps. They all trod with care up the uncarpeted attic stairs at the end of the third floor so as not to alert CeCe and Roy. Mac unlocked the door.

The sun still lurked behind the pine trees across the lake, but it had risen enough to brighten the end of the attic with the cracked window.

Mac pulled a chain next to the stairs and a long fluorescent bulb lit the near side of the attic. Giulia went directly to the cracked window, kicking up dust that danced in the natural and artificial light.

"Does that say 'Mine'?" Frank said.

Giulia nodded. She brought her face right up to the glass, but didn't touch it. The sharp edges glittered in the morning sun. Her opinion remained the same: An artist had crafted this message. The lighthouse ghost was not real.

"I keep the Halloween props in this corner, out of direct sunlight," Mac said.

Giulia turned back, blinking to adjust to the dimmer light. Mac stood at a metal shelving unit behind one of the eaves. She pulled a long box off the bottom shelf and removed the lid.

"See? Everything's right where it should be."

She lifted a thin metal framework looped from end to end with fishing line.

An old-fashioned white nightgown hung from two ends of the fishing line. "The box is covered with dust because I don't touch this shelf until the last week of September. You see? I didn't have anything to do with Solana's dead of night excursion."

Giulia rubbed the material between her fingers and inspected the mechanism. This could have been the white gown she'd followed on her first night here. "How does it work?"

"See how one of the rods is painted to look like two bricks separated by mortar? I hook that one ten feet up on the lighthouse wall. The other end screws into the catwalk around the light itself." She lifted a remote switch out from under the folds of material. "I set up a small black light and use this switch to make the nightgown fly up the lighthouse stairs about an hour before midnight on Halloween, depending on how the party's going. Lucy dresses all in black and hides on the catwalk to roll the nightgown up right away. One or two guests always follow it partway up the stairs. Then I wait for a break between songs on the CD player and turn on the speaker." She turned the remote over in her hands. "It's harmless. Everyone always says how entertaining the week is. Then they recommend us to their friends."

Giulia replaced the dress and Mac fitted the rods and fishing line back into the box.

"What else is up here?" Giulia said, thinking of the footstep-like sounds she'd heard on her Friday exploration.

"Garlands of imitation fall leaves." Mac touched the boxes as she named their contents. "Victorian dolls in costumes, ghosts and witches, crêpe paper pumpkins, costumes for the cats and the dog."

Giulia walked through the attic, listening for creaking boards and assessing the shrouded furniture and shelves of seasonal decorations for noise potential. Mac followed her like a fretting shadow. Frank stayed out of the way by the staircase.

"Look," Mac said when Giulia ended her explorations at the splintered window. "Even if I have an ancestral ghost who carved this message and the scratches on the lighthouse wall, why would she play along with a stranger's games after all this time? Besides, Solana's 'possession' seems phonier the longer I think about it. I'd bet the utility money those two are complete frauds. I didn't need them to be genuine to be entertaining."

Giulia let the silence lengthen after Mac stopped talking. Not ten seconds later, Mac started again.

"It's all because of that newspaper article. I've been telling the story of my stagecoach-robbing ancestor for years. Suddenly my ghost is obsessed with the nonexistent Stone gold hoard? I don't believe it."

Giulia said, "If you have a ghost."

"It's easier to believe those two Ouija board performers have been secretly messing with my business all month. She changed her face so little during that séance, yet she looked like an entirely different person. She must have amateur theater experience. Plus it'd be easy to sneak in here at night or when I'm busy."

"Speaking of that, Cedar picked the lock on either the lake door or the porch door to get inside. I advise deadbolts on both doors."

"He what? Of course he did. I should've figured that out. Well, they're fired as of right now." Mac stomped toward the stairs. "Deadbolts won't blend with the restoration décor."

Giulia mimed swatting the back of Mac's head.

Thirty-Eight

When Frank came out of the shower a little before ten that same morning, Giulia had been waiting eight minutes for the first fingerprint picture to upload.

"What's that face for?" he said.

"The Wi-Fi here doesn't like photo attachments." She wriggled her mouth and nose. "My face is going to freeze in this expression if this blasted picture doesn't send. I have eleven more after that."

"Come with me, fair lady, and I will lead you to the promised land of stronger Wi-Fi signals."

Giulia hopped off the bed. "You're a lifesaver. Where?"

"There's a hot spot on the beach near the boat rental place. I figure it's the confluence of all the stores. Or something. Zane would probably know."

"Not probably. Definitely. Let's go."

They walked out through the sunroom onto the already populated beach.

When they got within twenty feet of the boat dock, all the bars on Giulia's phone lit. She plopped herself onto the nearest bench and opened her email. The first attached photo was in her sent folder at last.

"My hero." She kissed Frank and attached the next photo to a new email. Ten minutes later, all the fingerprint photos had finished sending and she called Zane.

"I sent you a dozen fingerprint pictures."

"The last upload is almost finished." Zane's voice sounded even more Bogart-esque with waves hitting sand in Giulia's other ear. "What did you use to lift them?"

"Cornstarch, thanks to the internet. Could you run those through our usual processing place as a rush with my apologies?"

"Will do. What if they want to charge extra because of the reverse image?"

"Agree to anything up to thirty percent more than their usual fee. Call me if they try to go higher." She thought a moment. "If you guys want to keep the door locked while you're there, do it. Tell Sidney I don't want her walking to the parking lot by herself even though it's still light out when she leaves."

"Yes, Mom." Sidney's voice from across the room.

Giulia made a face at the phone. "I'm serious. Can Olivier meet you or even drive you to work for the next week or two?"

Zane said, "Ms. D., I was thinking that if Sidney drives to my house in the morning, I can drive us both here and home again at night."

"Perfect. Sidney, you know better than to dismiss any threat offhand. Will you please change your schedule to make Zane's plan work?" Giulia sat up. "What about Jane?"

"Jane says," Jane's voice came from close to the phone, "that if pencil-dick comes in here again I'll shove his head so far up his ass he'll have to punch a hole in his navel to breathe."

"Awesome," Sidney said.

"You rule," Zane said.

"Jane, I applaud your attitude but do not under any circumstances put yourself in danger. If he shows up again, call 911. Remember, we should be getting the order of protection today or tomorrow."

Sidney said, "So if we can't punch his lights out the courts will."

"Bingo. Zane, email me when you have fingerprint answers. If we're lucky, they won't all be the owner's."

*   *   *

Breakfast didn't make it to the table until eleven fifteen, which wasn't a problem since no one came downstairs before eleven. Fruit-filled crêpes and bacon and egg popovers were a good excuse for lack of table conversation. Yawns and requests to pass the milk or sugar or whipped cream did not count in Miss Manners' rules as table conversation.

Cedar and Solana appeared in the dining room doorway when Mac began collecting plates an hour later. Frank and Joel grabbed chairs for them and helped them sit. Cedar's cast stretched from mid-thigh to ankle and he would've fallen over his crutches if Frank hadn't steadied him. Solana had no visible injuries.

"We checked ourselves out of the hospital," Cedar said. "They weren't happy. Like I care. I refused to let them put me under to set my leg. Don't trust any doctors anywhere. My leg's still numb from the Novocain or whatever they used. I quit counting at ten shots."

"What did the doctors say?" Mac said.

"My leg's broken in two places. Cast for six weeks; physical therapy for another six. They gave me a prescription for some controlled substance or other. Stupid drones. All-natural is the way to go." He winked at the room. "Solana makes these terrific brownies, you see."

Mac hid her hands beneath her gingham apron. "Solana, did you have a concussion?"

"Not at all." Her serene smile took in everyone around her. "Temporary inhabitation of the body by a spirit causes certain physical changes, one of which is dilated eyes."

"But we heard you scream when you fell," Giulia said.

"That wasn't me. It was Dorothea Stone reliving her fall from the Widow's Walk through me."

Mac said after a long silence, "I see."

Cedar said, "Any breakfast left?"

Mac returned to the kitchen. A minute later a microwave *beeped* and she returned with two full plates.

Lucy followed with coffee and orange juice.

They ate like two starving people forcing themselves to a sensible pace. Everyone watched. Marion brought out her moleskin notebook and began writing. Giulia sneaked a glimpse and caught the name "Dorothea." More fodder for their copycat haunted bed and breakfast, perhaps.

"You should've seen the glop they tried to feed us at the hospital," Cedar said around a mouthful of crêpe. "If that mound of yellow paste they called eggs had even one natural ingredient in it I'm Harry Houdini."

"Mac," Solana said after dabbing her mouth with a napkin, "your stress is filling the air with blacks and reds. We are not going to sue you. The accident in the lighthouse was my doing because I didn't properly integrate Dorothea's spirit into my own."

Cedar pushed away his empty plate. "That was delicious. We're heading home to a well-deserved nap."

Solana, still serene, smiled at Mac again. "You have to keep working on those colors. You have too many reds."

Giulia wondered if it really was serenity. Detachment, perhaps, from the head injury? From her own supply of pain pills? Probably not from weed-laced brownies if their stash was back home.

Solana floated to her feet. "Would you mind if I took a few photographs of the lighthouse? I'll send you a link to the story when I publish it on my website."

Mac turned on her business side. "Of course you may, and thank you. I'll be interested to read it. Cedar, could I see you in my office for a minute?"

Giulia rose from her chair. "Would you like me to go with you up the lighthouse stairs, Solana, in case you need help balancing?"

"That may be a good idea," Solana said. "We'll be back next week, Mac. We want to talk to you about keeping the sessions through the end of October."

Cedar hauled himself upright. "Damned cement shoe."

Solana crouched in front of the model in the souvenir room. "Yes...yes...up and down those winding stairs. Night after night, year after year. Circling the gallery and staring out at the lake. So many nights...they blend into each other after so long..."

Giulia wanted to kick her. This dreamy shtick was as bad as a cheesy Saturday night horror movie. Then Giulia wanted to kick herself. The detective business wreaked havoc on her Franciscan values of peace and forgiveness. She supposed there was a slim chance Solana wasn't showing off her Stanislavski acting skills.

Speaking of the Franciscan mindset, cynicism was not one of the attitudes to cultivate.

Solana patted the lighthouse model and stood. "I'm not wholly back in this century yet. Would you mind taking pictures for me as I point things out?"

"Not at all." Giulia gave her Bright Smile Number Two, reserved for medium-sized annoyances.

She followed Solana to the base of the spiral stairs and took photos at her direction. The stairs. The windows. The light. They climbed halfway up, Giulia behind Solana in case she got dizzy, and Giulia took the same photos from that angle. They climbed to the top and captured the Widow's Walk and the view out to the lake.

Giulia went first down the stairs to continue as dizziness fall blocker if needed. Solana didn't converse. Giulia's newfound cynic put the odds of Solana in deep thought at twenty percent, Solana communing with the spirits at ten percent, and Solana calculating her next move to fool the rubes at a solid seventy percent.

Giulia's conclusion: She herself needed a refresher course in how to compartmentalize work and spirituality.

Frank and Roy hovered outside Mac's office. Raised voices behind the closed door warned Giulia in time.

She led still-floating Solana past the office and out onto the porch, talking in her ear all the way about the experience of being inhabited by Dorothea Stone. Solana sat in the basket chair. Giulia hurried back into the house.

The voices grew loud enough for Giulia to hear the exit interview.

"You can't blame us for your lack of security," Cedar said.

"I can completely blame you for breaking and entering. Do you treat all your clients' property as your personal playground?"

"We did nothing of the sort." Cedar's voice cracked when he got defensive. "You hired us to contact your family ghost."

"Read your contract," Mac said. "I hired you to conduct a weekly séance to entertain my guests."

"Now you're objecting to our success?"

"What success? Your wife gave a convincing performance Sunday night. I admit that. Don't try to claim she contacted a ghost that doesn't exist."

"What?" His voice cracked again.

"Now you're claiming selective amnesia? I told you and your wife about my family legends so you could use them effectively in your performances. You—"

"You liar! Your friend Rowan told us you were a true believer. You sure believe everything she tells you. What's so different about us?"

"Rowan never broke into my house in the middle of the night. Lucy's inventorying the heirloom case as we speak."

Cedar abandoned complete sentences for disjointed excuses and profane accusations. Frank and Roy reached for the door handle at the same instant, but it opened before either of them touched it.

Mac held the door wide and pointed to the porch. "You're fired. Get out and don't come back."

Giulia opened the screen door. Cedar crutched out by himself. Tweedledum and Tweedledee eyed the crutches and flexed their claws. Roy, CeCe, Marion, and Anthony crowded onto the porch. Mac blocked the doorway.

Cedar gave the cats a threatening grimace and said to Mac. "Thanks for nothing. Let's go, Sol."

Solana had apparently heard none of the argument, since she and Mac air-kissed. She pressed Giulia's hands with deep sincerity, and Cedar hobbled down the porch with his wife at his side.

"He's not going to drive, is he?" Roy said in a stage whisper.

"I think she is," CeCe said in the same tone of voice.

"She told me in the lighthouse that she couldn't operate her camera phone because she wasn't fully in the twenty-first century yet," Giulia said.

"This won't end well," Frank said.

"Should we warn the police?" Marion said.

Anthony shrugged. "What would we say?"

"A psychic channeling a nineteenth-century ghost is driving a Prius down South Lake Road. The ghost does not have a valid driver's license." Frank chuckled. "They'll tell us to stop drinking at breakfast."

The group watched the slate blue car navigate the oval driveway.

"She avoided the grass."

"Good thing the gate is still open."

"She's turning without a signal."

"Holy cripes, she almost sideswiped that garbage truck."

No one moved until the Prius was out of sight. As they filed inside, Giulia's ears were anticipating the *screech-crash* of Solana/Dorothea's inattention, but only the usual traffic noises reached them.

Thirty-Nine

Giulia slipped away from the porch and tugged Mac back into her office.

"I only caught bits and pieces. What happened?"

Mac's neck and ears still burned a blotched crimson. "He actually tried to blame me for their break-in because my locks were so easy to pick. I don't know what Rowan was thinking when she recommended them to me."

"Perhaps Rowan didn't suspect a legitimate supernatural contact would alter their moral compass."

Mac's righteous anger drained away. "Once I knew they broke in, I assumed the whole possession scene was an act. Do you think it could have been real? I thought you were anti-ghost."

"I'm open to all possibilities until the case is solved." Giulia expected a trapdoor to open at her feet and drop her straight down to Hell for the unending series of lies she'd told since entering Stone's Throw. "Is Lucy really checking for stolen valuables?"

Back to mottled anger. "No. But she will." Mac opened the door and shouted Lucy's name.

Giulia climbed up to the Sand Dollar room for more research, which lasted until the district attorney called seven minutes later.

A three thirty slot had opened in his favorite judge's schedule and could she please drive back to Cottonwood immediately?

Giulia primed herself with two cans of Coke and hit the road. Jane, Sidney, and Zane met her at the courthouse and the entire order of protection process wrapped up in twenty-three minutes. In the parking lot afterwards, she gave them a theatrical rendition of the three a.m. break-in and shouting match of dismissal.

"You might as well be living in a bad episode of Beach Bum Ghost Hunters," Sidney said.

"Is that really a TV show?" Jane said.

"No, but it could be." Sidney unlocked her phone. "Jessamine rode on Belle's back with a lot of help yesterday. I have adorable pictures."

Sidney moved into the shadow of the courthouse wall to avoid glare from the sun on the screen. Giulia and Jane "aww"-ed.

"I notice Olivier out of spitting distance," Giulia said.

"He takes no chances now."

Jane said to Giulia, "When are you coming back for real?"

"I'm not sure. If the psychics were behind the plot to get hold of the B&B, then it all should stop and we'll work up a case for the owner to nail them. I'm banking on definitive fingerprint results from the fridge containers. Zane, anything yet?"

Zane looked up from his phone. "I left a message before we headed here. The minute I get the results I'll email them to you."

"Okay. Anything else I should know about?"

Three headshakes.

"You are model employees. I'd better head back while I'm still on a caffeine and sugar high."

Giulia stopped at the Jimmy Buffett burger place a few minutes before six to pick up the order Frank had called in. The low sun shone on the packed outdoor bar but the restaurant inside held all the takeout orders, so she got in and out in ten minutes.

He'd set up beer and napkins on the patio table. She fell onto a chair and raised her face to the sun.

"I am the walking dead."

"I could've ordered the burgers rare for you. You know, in place of fresh human meat?"

She made a face. "I don't like my meat talking back when I bite into it."

They made dents in their food while Giulia told Frank about the court appointment.

"The lawyer for Flynt's wife was there too."

"Same reason?"

"Yup. She left his clothes in the driveway, changed the locks, and installed a security system, which he tripped trying to break in the back door after he posted bail. All caught on video." She dragged several fries through a mountain of ketchup. "These are possibly the best fries I've eaten in a month. Crêpes and fancy breakfast muffins are not enough to last the day."

Frank opened a second beer. "I was not idle while you were gone. A new couple checked into the empty room on the third floor. I have their names and address. After which I too did not sun myself like a lizard on the beach. Walter and I discussed the manly sport of catching and gutting fish, and I regaled him with an unembellished account of the séance and its three a.m. sequel. The sirens woke up half the town."

Giulia plucked Frank's spicy dill spear from his takeout container and chewed it with extra relish. Frank rewarded her with a shudder. Life was back to normal.

"He reciprocated with some interesting rumors about Auntie Mac and the family legend."

Giulia leaned across the narrow table and kissed him. "You are a better Watson than Jude Law. Handsomer, too, although I'd like to perform an in-person appraisal to make sure."

Frank assumed a lofty, certain-of-his-superior-claims air and continued. "That local news article about the lighthouse and the family history generated a lot more interest than Mac thinks. Ghosts are one thing, but buried gold? Little Walter has rented three times as much scuba equipment this month, all to the locals."

Giulia drank the last of her beer. "I doubt Mac knows that."

"Walter didn't tell her. He pointed out again that he's not too fond of his sweet old auntie."

"Define 'not too fond.'"

"If you're thinking he's been sneaking up here to put gunk in showerheads and make a nightgown flap like a ghost, I don't buy it. From what I've seen, he's one hundred percent into doing the least amount of actual work it takes to get by."

Giulia wrinkled her nose. "Boo. A convenient criminal would have meant we get home sooner. Is there any more beer? No, I take it back. I'm too whipped to process more alcohol. I'll be right back." She ran inside, rinsed the beer bottle three times, and refilled it with cold water. When she returned to her chair, she said, "So the neighbors are treasure hunting. Since nobody's found anything, I presume Mac's story was true about the hidden treasure being nothing more than a legend."

"It's too bad," Frank said. "A stash of real gold coins would be a sight."

"Feel free to rent scuba gear from Walter." Giulia snapped shut her Styrofoam takeout container.

"No thanks. I'd have to listen to him whine some more about the Stone family's unwillingness to support him. I asked him why he wasn't working here with Mac, making it a true family business, and his fangs came out. He called Mac a cheap bitch who holds grudges. Seems he made a few duty visits to Mac's father and tried to stab everyone else in the back for a bigger share of the family fortune. Unfortunately for him, Mac and her surviving sister scooped the lot, which wasn't a pile of money by any stretch. Everyone else got pocket change. Walter claimed his share was a six-pack's worth." He picked up both containers and headed inside.

The first thing Giulia checked up in their room was work email.

"Zane came through." She opened the fingerprint report and read it through once, then once more. "Is Mercury in retrograde?"

"What?"

"The fingerprints on the milk and maple syrup containers are all Mac's. The ones on the refrigerator door handle are—wait for it—mine and Mac's."

"Let me see." He picked up the tablet and skimmed the report. "So we've got two choices."

Giulia rubbed her face with her hands. "Either Mac is one of the best liars I've ever met or mournful dead Dorothea objects to breakfast food." She managed a smile. "Or I saw that article online and decided to toss away my conscience and cheat a complete stranger out of her rightful inheritance."

Frank handed her back the iPad. "Must be choice number three. That's so you."

She drummed her fingers on the quilt. "Wasn't it Sherlock Holmes who complained that criminals knew too much about fingerprints?"

"It's a hazard of the profession. Would you like to listen to my dissertation on the evils of Go Phones and criminals' affinity for them?" He yawned and leaned across Giulia to see the digital clock. "It's only eight o'clock. In my dissolute youth I'd be good for another six hours."

"In your dissolute youth you weren't up at three a.m. because of treasure-hunting psychics." She yawned in turn. "Or if you were, your grandmother has been holding out on me. She tells me all the best stories of your childhood."

"I call no fair. You had to go and jump the wall and make all your relatives stop speaking to you. I know I'm being deprived of juicy and embarrassing stories from your supposed dissolute youth."

Giulia favored him with a beatific smile.

Forty

"Wake up." Frank's voice.

Giulia opened one eye and at the same moment heard the knocking on their door.

"I'll get it." She padded to the door and opened it enough to stick her head around the edge.

Mac stood at the crack, fear and exhaustion in her face. "Can you come?"

"Two minutes."

Giulia closed the door and opened the closet. "Something's spooked Mac."

Frank threw off the quilt and grabbed the pants Giulia tossed to him. After pulling on her jeans, she hooked her bra and found a t-shirt. She picked up her phone and stepped into her sneakers as Frank opened the door.

Mac beckoned and they followed. A different quiet filled the house at six thirty in the morning than at three thirty. Of course, that quiet had been broken by multiple screams.

Rays of morning sun lasered through the pine trees on the other end of the lake.

Wavelets lapped the beach and seagulls fought for pieces of leftover food half-visible in the sand.

In a perfect world, Giulia would make enough through Driscoll Investigations to afford a house on this lake. And while she was wishing, she might as well put in an order for a unicorn to ride to work. With sparkling rainbows flowing from its mane as she cantered along the streets of Cottonwood.

They followed Mac past the knight into the lighthouse. Lines of red paint dripped down the wall next to the first narrow window. Giulia raised her phone and took several pictures in a row before the letters became illegible.

Someone had drawn a lopsided square on the wall and within it written in capital letters, "PLEASE FORGIVE ME."

"I don't usually come in here before the daily tour," Mac said. "Lately, though, I've been doing a quick walk-through of the first floor."

Giulia climbed the stairs and took more pictures. "It's still wet."

"Is it paint?" Frank said.

She leaned across the gap between the stairs and braced her hand against the wall. "I'm not sure..." She sniffed and recoiled. "Good Heavens, it's blood."

Mac fell against the wall. "No, no, no." Her head swung back and forth. "No, no, no."

Giulia got a grip on herself. "Honey, I need something to scoop this into for a test."

"Be right back." Frank ran into the house proper and returned in less than a minute with a butter knife and a small glass. "Mac, I borrowed these from the kitchen." He climbed to Giulia and held her waist while she reached out to scrape as many of the thicker dribbles as she could.

"Okay, pull me back." When she was steady on her feet she wiped the flat of the knife against the edge of the glass. "I need plastic wrap."

She carried down the glass in one hand and the knife in the other. Mac had stopped repeating "no" but the lines in her face were carved even deeper now. From her posture, it looked like the wall was the only thing holding her up.

Frank said, "I can drive it to the lab this morning. All we want is confirmation, not DNA matches, right?"

"Well...No, because when we catch whoever's behind this we might have to look for a murder victim."

Mac made a strangled sound and slid to the floor. Frank's and Giulia's heads snapped around, but Mac was conscious. She'd buried her head in her hands as she rocked back and forth.

Frank said to Giulia, "Good point. I wasn't thinking. Okay, I'll shower and hit the road. I'll stop at the precinct to catch up on things afterward, so I won't be back 'til this afternoon sometime." He raised his voice. "Mac, where's the plastic wrap?"

No response. The rocking continued.

"Mac. Mac."

Giulia crouched next to the old woman and put both hands on her shoulders. "Mac, cut it out. You have a business to run." She gave the bony shoulders a sharp shake. "Wake up."

The gray head rose, the hazel eyes round and rimmed with white. "I'm cursed."

"Bullshit," Frank said. "You're letting this get to you."

"If it was your business, wouldn't it get to you?" Mac's mouth snapped shut and she glared at him.

"That's better." Giulia held out a hand to help Mac up.

"Thank you. I was rattled. What did you need, Frank?"

"Plastic wrap."

"First drawer on the right side of the refrigerator."

He kissed Giulia on the cheek. "I'll call you."

Giulia said to Mac, "I don't want to scrub this off. Is there a painting large enough to cover it anywhere in the house?"

Mac turned her back to the gory message. "In the library. No, no. There are a few old landscapes in the attic." She took a step toward the house.

"Wait." Giulia slapped the brick wall. "We'll need a drill and two screws."

"Right. Those are in the cellar. Come with me into the office."

Mac took a keyring from one of the cubbyholes in her roll top desk and detached one key. "The paintings are under a tarp on the opposite side from the Halloween shelf. I'll bring the drill."

All was silent behind the bedroom doors as Giulia passed them. She didn't stop to listen for phantom footsteps from the attic. Enough weirdness for one day. She hoped. The fluorescent light illuminated the correct side of the attic for her needs, and she spotted the tarp right away.

Months or years of dust exploded from it when she flipped it back. She buried her face in her t-shirt and coughed so hard her stomach muscles protested. Finally she wiped her eyes and ventured back into the air.

An amateur beachscape met her gaze. Extremely amateur. Those orange beachgoers should've stayed away from the cheap spray tan. Those seagulls had flown too near a nuke plant. The style looked familiar. She knelt to tip it forward and caught the signature: MacAllister Stone, age 10.

All thoughts about the beachscape deleted from her brain and tongue, she tilted the painting against her chest and inspected the next one. A mother-daughter portrait in dark oils. No. The next: An early American style horse and buggy in winter. Next: A ship of some kind with multiple sails riding high waves on a stormy night. This artist had talent. Everything seemed to be in the correct perspective. The few seagulls had the correct number of wings and eyes.

Best of all, the dimensions of the painting and its frame were enough to cover the entire bloody message on the lighthouse wall.

Giulia slid it out of the stack and leaned the rest of the paintings against each other, then against the wall again. She restrained her energy when replacing the tarp.

This time she didn't choke. The painting wasn't heavy but it was unwieldy. It took her twice as long to return to the lighthouse because she spent all her time not banging the frame into the walls or banisters or tables.

Mac was pacing from the history room past the suit of armor to the base of the spiral stairs and back again. She didn't appear to see Giulia lugging the oversized gilded frame until Giulia blocked her path.

"Where have you been? It's almost seven thirty. What if one of the guests gets up for an early walk on the beach and sees the message?"

Giulia counted to ten in Latin, because her Latin wasn't as good as it used to be and the effort always distracted her from whatever was annoying her. "If you have the drill, let's get this hung up."

Mac ran into the lighthouse and picked up the drill from a toolbox on the floor. Giulia hefted the painting up the stairs and positioned it.

Her eyeballing had been correct: It covered the entire drippy mess with room to spare.

"Got the positioning?" Giulia's voice was thin from the strained angle of her body.

"Yes. You can move back."

Giulia rocked herself back against the opposite railing and Mac stepped into place. The drill whined and crunched as it created two holes. Mac switched drill bits and drove two three-inch screws into the wall.

"All right. You can hang it up."

Giulia's smile was crooked. "Actually, I can't. I'm not tall enough."

Machine Mac shifted gears and looked at Giulia like she was a faulty cog. "Yes, you are short. I didn't notice it before. Here. Give that to me."

She took the painting, eased the picture wire away from the back a little farther, and hung it on the screws. Giulia climbed up two more steps.

"A little to the left. More. Now it's tipping too much. Back to the right. Good."

She followed Mac down the stairs. When Mac had packed up the drill, Giulia said, "Let me put it away for you."

A tight shake of the head. "No. I need to regain control of my morning. This will be away before Lucy arrives to help with breakfast."

"Okay." Giulia returned to her empty room and picked up the clothes Frank had tossed on the bed. A long, hot shower eased some of her tension. Afterward, she wrapped her hair in one towel and her body in another and sat on the bed with a plain legal pad and pen.

The bloody message cleared almost no one.

- Cedar: Out because of his leg.
- Solana: In because of...everything. Suspect Number One, supplanting Marion and Anthony.
- Anthony and Marion: In because of their B&B plans.
   - o Marion's freak-out over the shower gunk could have been an act.
   - o A really good act.
   - o She'd started her own successful business. She might come across all snooty and better than "the help," but when she wants something enough will she regress to her working roots?
   - o Anthony. Never trust the quiet ones? Willing to get Marion whatever she wants?
- Joel and Gino: In because...Nope. Still no reason to suspect them. They're way into Mac's Halloween Week, but so what?
- Roy and CeCe: Out...ish.
   - o Their website showed a full list of gigs, albeit at grade school after grade school. They don't appear to need the money (but everyone could use a pile of gold) and don't have the time to run a B&B, let alone work multi-level hauntings.
   - o They might want to turn the B&B into a permanent studio.
   - o They're clever enough to stage the hauntings, but are they creepy enough to write messages in blood and ruthless enough to scare Solana into a potentially fatal fall?

- Walter: Suspect Number Two, knocking Marion and Anthony farther down the list.
  - It's easy to fake laziness and dissatisfaction.
  - If he's faking those, what else could he be faking?
  - Based on Frank's reports, he's not faking the dissatisfaction. Scratch that part.
  - If he's only pretending to be lazy, then all the B&B incidents could lead back to him.
  - Is his girlfriend, whom neither I nor Frank have yet seen, prodding him like Mary Todd Lincoln with the White House in her sights?
- Lucy: Dissatisfied, therefore Suspect Number Three.
  - Is she fed up with trying to use her MFA and will settle for owning her own B&B?
  - Does she hate Mac enough to try and kill a guest?
  - Has this year or two or three of taking orders become a Last Straw?
  - She works the nightgown trick on Halloween, therefore...
- Mac: No. Once and for all. If Mac is manipulating DI, then I need to turn in my membership card for the "Ability to Read People" club.
- Rowan.

Time to research Rowan.

She set her tablet on top of the legal pad. The search results page loaded without much delay, but Rowan's GIF-heavy website took six minutes and twenty-seven seconds.

What, did WordPress market an "occult" template? Rowan's pulsating fog of purple and green was less soothing than Solana's, but the tabs were much of a muchness. About, Testimonials, Services, News, Tarot decks for sale instead of Ouija boards.

Giulia flexed her fingers. Now that Mac had fired Solana, Mac might cling tighter to Rowan. Good luck prying apart two old friends. Rowan would have to show up on Mac's porch with a revelation beyond weak enough for Giulia to be able to disprove in such a way to raise the hired PI's merits above Rowan's.

Maybe Rowan would arrive with a personal message from Dorothea Stone about installing deadbolts.

She started a third page.

<u>Proof that Every Guest This Week is Part of a Conspiracy to Steal the Legendary Gold.</u>

- Solana and Cedar convinced one of their spirit friends to write the message in the glass on the attic window.
- Joel and Gino cozied up to Whining Walter and paid him to start the fire and steal Mac's purse.
- Anthony and Marion bribed the handyman to plant that bag of yuck in their shower pipe.

She let her pen take over, but not like Solana's Ouija board. No bug-eyed possession here. Pens didn't have eyes to bug out anyway.

- Joel and Gino are actually Mafia, and the Stone stagecoach robber cheated an early American branch of the Mafia out of its share of the loot. The newspaper article helped them track down this long-overdue payment.
- Anthony and Marion have access to a wormhole universe populated by invisible subservient worker bees who are perpetrating all the damage plus the ghost noises.
- Solana convinced either Dorothea or a different spirit to scratch the lighthouse wall above the stairs higher than humans could reach. And a third spirit to write this morning's bloody message. Even though Mac did have an ancestor with that name, did her Dorothea really die in a fall over the gallery railing?

Nitpick: Where did a spirit get that much blood?
Nitpick number two: Where did anyone get that much blood?

Nitpick number three: This job wasn't supposed to include a possible murder investigation.

The door flew open and Mac's hand caught it right before it slammed into the wall.

"Again, please. The third floor."

Forty-One

Giulia grabbed clean clothes and shed the towels in the bathroom. A minute later she pushed her phone into her jeans pocket. "Ready."

Without a word, Mac led her upstairs to the empty bedroom and closed the door.

"They went for a walk before breakfast after they called me up here. Lucy's downstairs making the bacon and asparagus frittatas for me. It's in the bathroom."

Prepared for almost anything, the black shoe prints on the bathroom wall were something of a letdown.

"They dirtied the wall and wanted to apologize in person?"

"No. They said that a series of muffled thumps woke them in the middle of the night, but they went back to sleep. This morning, they found these prints on the wall."

Thanks to no deadbolts on the first floor doors, all suspects remained on the table. Giulia wanted to smash the delicate bud vase on the windowsill.

"You're thinking ghosts?" she said.

"Of course I am." Mac's voice slashed across the *g*-word. "You need to read this." She fished a pamphlet out of her apron pocket and shoved it at Giulia. "I didn't give you the history of the land because I thought it had no bearing on my family haunting. I was wrong." She grabbed two handfuls of gray hair and yanked. "You've got to stop this. Please. You're clergy. Can't you exorcise it?"

Giulia didn't have the hour it would take to explain. She said, "We will stop it," and led the way out of the bedroom. Mac headed downstairs but Giulia turned around and took photos of the shoeprints, which were on the wall facing the toilet. She sat on the toilet lid and tried to reach the wall.

Her feet fell short by a few inches, but anyone five foot nine or so could have made it. Last, she dragged two fingers over the corner of one of the marks.

She sniffed the dark residue and rubbed her fingers together. Shoe polish. Two years polishing the retired nuns' shoes had ingrained that smell and feel into her mind for life.

Nine o'clock. The aroma of brewing coffee reached this floor. CeCe said from behind her door, "Come on, honey. It's our favorite vacation breakfast."

Giulia sprinted downstairs.

Joel looked next to and around and behind Giulia. "Where's Frank?"

"Network crash. He's driving to the rescue as we speak."

Gino raised his coffee cup in a salute. "More bacon for me."

"All bacon is shared between us," Joel said. To Giulia, he added, "We wrote it into our marriage vows."

Giulia sipped the thin coffee. "That might be the most sensible marriage vow I've ever heard."

Mac and Lucy served frittatas with a side of hash browns and a lemon-blueberry muffin.

Giulia said to CeCe, "Every breakfast I make after this will be completely inadequate."

"I know, right?" CeCe elbowed her husband. "This one makes up a grocery list every year for when we get home. So every year I tell him I look forward to seeing him in the kitchen."

Giulia made polite conversation with the new arrivals in between vying with Joel and Gino for the most extravagant frittata compliment. Mac's hostessing was so professional that Giulia began studying her expressions and mannerisms to use the next time she needed a poker face.

As Mac returned post-dishes to begin her welcome and history speech, Marion and Anthony excused themselves.

"It's our annual antiquing excursion," Marion said, the most excited Giulia had seen her all week.

Giulia detected a lack of enthusiasm on Anthony's part.

She tagged along on the lighthouse tour with the new couple. Mac's speeches varied little. The suit of armor was admired, as was the new painting. Mac ad-libbed a story about it involving her great-grandfather and a record fish that got away.

They spread out along the Widow's Walk. On this textbook June day, a handful of cotton ball clouds speckled the blue sky. Sailboats with glowing white sails skimmed across the lake. Like every other morning, kids laughed and squealed and splashed in the water to either side of the lighthouse grounds. A fresh breeze caught Giulia's hair and clothes.

Mac leaned back against the wooden railing. "The original cap to the lighthouse was one of my great-grandfather's frivolous touches. In keeping with the legend of the family's black sheep, he had a weathervane cast in the image of a horse-drawn stagecoach." She bent farther back and pointed. "If you lean back out just a little, you can see the wind blowing it in—"

With a loud *crack* the railing split apart and Mac fell.

Forty-Two

Giulia lunged and grabbed Mac's wrists. Mac slammed against the bricks as Giulia crashed onto the gallery face first. For a second she couldn't breathe. The next second her shoulders announced they were being ripped from their sockets. The second after that, two hysterical female voices assaulted her ears. Behind her, the new guest vented one breathy shriek after another. Below her, Mac screamed for help.

Two knees invaded her line of sight and a pair of longer arms reached down and larger hands took hold of Mac's forearms.

"Together," the new guy said.

"Mac, stop kicking," Giulia said, her own voice strained. "Ready," she said over her shoulder.

"On three. One. Two. Three."

They pulled. Mac yelled like she'd been shot. They pulled again, and Mac's fingernails appeared above the platform. Behind them, the breathy screams had stopped and a normal-ish voice spoke to the 911 operator.

They pulled again. Mac shut up and planted her sneakered toes onto the bricks.

Again, and Mac's top half showed. With the fourth pull, Mac's knees hit the gallery but her rescuers didn't let go until her entire body overbalanced and she landed on top of Giulia.

Mac switched to a string of curses. One curse, to be specific, repeated over and over and over.

If Giulia's shoulders weren't quivering like Jell-O, she would've laughed. "Mac, please get off me."

"I can't." A different curse this time. "My wrists are broken."

Giulia's rescue partner stepped in. "Mine aren't." He hauled Mac up by her armpits.

Mac sat next to Giulia, wrists flopped on the wooden walkway. "What the hell just happened?"

"The railing broke." Giulia leveraged herself into a sitting position, her shoulders protesting at every inch.

"Impossible. Matthew was up here two weeks ago to replace a split board. He said everything was good and solid."

Giulia pointed to the fresh gap with a grimace. Mac turned her head and cursed again.

An ambulance siren came nearer. They all stopped trying to talk until the driver pressed the off switch. Giulia got to her feet, checked a part of the railing closer to the house and leaned over.

"We're at the top of the lighthouse!"

A deep male voice said, "Hello?"

Giulia, Mac, and the other couple all yelled, "We're at the top of the lighthouse!"

Equipment rattling and footsteps on the asphalt, then just the rattling as two EMTs ran across the grass.

"We're at the top of the lighthouse," Giulia called a third time.

They looked up, looked at each other, looked up again. "Please tell us you don't need a stretcher up there."

Giulia looked at Mac, who shook her head.

"No," Giulia said. "We think it's broken wrists."

"Coming up." They vanished through the lake-facing door and the sound of their boots echoed up the spiral stairs.

The new guests waited for the EMTs to squeeze onto the gallery. "We'll get out of your way," they said and crowded through the opening and downstairs.

"Mac, you're giving us a lot of business lately," the EMT with the deep voice said. "What happened now?"

Mac and Giulia took turns telling the story.

The first EMT took charge of Mac. The other EMT inspected Giulia's shoulders.

"They're not dislocated. You work out, I can tell. You strained pretty much every muscle and tendon you own, though. Let me see your ribs." He pulled up Giulia's shirt and palpated her flesh while she tried not to yelp. "No splinters. Some abrasion. You're going to want to get checked at the ER. Nothing's broken, but I'm feeling a couple of bruised ribs."

His partner said, "We hit the dislocation lottery over here. Left shoulder and wrist. Abrasions on the ribs and legs, but they can wait 'til we get on solid ground."

Mac's EMT helped her stand and fit through the opening to the catwalk. Giulia stood with a little help and followed.

The trip downstairs was a slow one. The EMTs sighed in unison when they stepped off the final stair.

"Oh, solid ground, how I love you," Giulia's EMT said.

"Thank you for coming up to help us," Giulia said. "We're not at our most flexible this morning."

"Neither rain nor snow nor heights which rightfully belong to the birds can keep us from rescuing damsels in distress."

Giulia laughed and clutched her side. "Ow."

"Into the ambulance with you."

"I think you're right."

Giulia climbed into the idling vehicle next to Mac, who was on a gurney with her EMT checking her blood pressure. The ambulance started with a jerk and the siren cranked up a moment later. Mac and Giulia cringed.

Mac's EMT banged on the partition. "Turn it off, Jim."

Silence followed a few seconds later.

"Thanks," Giulia said.

Small town emergency rooms had that generic hospital smell of disinfectant and body fluids and cheap cafeteria food, but they also had one thing over ERs in bigger towns: No crowds. Giulia made it through intake, treatment, and release in a little over an hour. Armed with hospital packets of ibuprofen and a bottle of water, she chose one of the identical uncomfortable plastic waiting room chairs.

No sign of Mac, but over the tinny paging system calls someone was yelling behind the treatment hallway's double doors. Giulia didn't dwell on the treatment for dislocated shoulders and broken wrists.

A perky morning show blathered on the wall-mounted TV. Giulia didn't want to text Frank and worry him, so she reached for her phone to write a memo about this incident and figure out the possibility of everyone's involvement. It took a lot of hate or greed or both to craft a fatal "accident" like that.

Her pants pocket crackled. Right.

The pamphlet Mac had given her. She pulled it out and tried to smooth it against her thigh.

Haunted Conneaut Lake.

Not more hauntings. For the first time in her life, Giulia considered boycotting Halloween.

To block out the endless *pings* preceding "Doctor Whatsyourname, please call extension one-oh-one," she opened to the table of contents of the sixteen-page stapled booklet.

Page 1: The Conneaut Lake Monster
Page 3: Natalie Hopewell and Her Poisoned Pecan Pie
Page 7: The Crows in the Church Tower
Page 10: The Three Brothers of Silas Fisher
Page 13: Widow Burke's Revolutionary War Battle

Given the titles, she went with the penultimate story.

"In 1819, Silas Fisher built a sprawling house on the shore of Conneaut Lake for himself, his wife, their seven children, two pointers, and two retrievers. The family lived by hunting and fishing, and prospered until Silas' three elder brothers arrived without warning in December of 1822.

"Luke, the eldest, kept a sight too coy about their appearance for Silas' liking. But family was family, and Silas wouldn't turn a dog out of doors with winter settling in for a four-month stay."

No artist herself, Giulia tried to admire the woodcut-style illustration of a large family reading from a Bible around a huge fireplace. But no humans really had bulbous heads with solid demon eyes. When she counted three feet on one of the men and multiple arms on two of the children, she repressed a desire to watch the perky talk show and continued to read.

Blah, blah, blah, evil brothers, bored wife, scared children. Scared dogs. That was new. She found herself hoping for the timely appearance of that Conneaut Lake version of Nessie.

"The showdown happened in the early hours of the morning of February third. Silas' oldest daughter, Charity, ran barefoot and in her nightdress through a quarter-mile of snowdrifts to one neighbor's house. She carried her youngest sister in her arms. At the same time, the middle brother, John, carried his two youngest brothers to the neighbors on the opposite side, half a mile away. All the children were in nightclothes and weeping in terror."

Giulia gave a fifty percent chance to Silas murdering his brothers with the help of the oldest boys, thirty percent to Silas catching his wife Lusilla in bed with one of the brothers and shooting both, ten percent to the three brothers murdering Silas and his wife, and ten percent to the murder of Silas alone and Lusilla casting her lot with one of the brothers.

Great. Now she was thinking in phrases as cliché as the tripe in her hands.

A soap opera had replaced the perky morning show. Giulia kept with the booklet as the lesser of two evils.

Blah, blah, blah, dead bodies everywhere. She flipped the page, but that turned out to be the first page of the final story. Flipping back, she read on until she reached the important element:

"In a wooden chair pushed up against the wall sat Lusilla with open eyes, blue lips, and protruding tongue, a twisted hemp cord around her neck. Mud stains from the soles of her shoes marked the wall. The middle son lay on the stair, another cord around his thin neck, marks from his shoes on the side of the packed dirt stairwell."

Giulia flung the booklet at the wall.

She was not buying this. Mac expected her to read this and believe some poor man who went insane and murdered his family two hundred years ago was replaying his last hours with such force that his dead and gone victims still left marks on the Stone's Throw bathroom walls?

She retrieved the wrinkled booklet from the floor and read the story's last paragraphs. Oh. One of the surviving daughters married a Stone. No denying every generation of Stones had plenty of eligible sons and daughters to go around.

Her shoulder registered a delayed protest at the fling. Guess she'd better not put off taking the ibuprofen any longer.

A nurse wheeled Mac through the double doors as Giulia screwed the cap back onto the water bottle. The nurse parked Mac at the front desk and brought papers on a clipboard over to her. Mac signed them with her right hand. As Giulia came nearer, she saw the dark blue sling around her left arm and the Ace bandage on that same wrist.

"Hey, Mac. Would you like me to call for a taxi?"

Mac handed all the papers back to the nurse. "I've already called Lucy. She should be here in a few minutes. Help me out of this contraption, please."

"Ms. Stone," the nurse said, "the hospital has a policy."

"Bullcrap," Mac said. "I haven't been admitted and I've signed myself out. You have no say over what I do."

Giulia took her imperious upraised arm and helped her stand. The nurse backed the wheelchair out of range.

Mac took a second to adjust the sling, pointing a warning finger at the nurse who advanced to help.

"There. Stupid contraption. I apologize for all the yelling back there. You people did a great job getting me to a state where I can still run my business."

The nurse who had wheeled her into the emergency waiting area returned with a bag of supplies. "Use these, Ms. Stone, or you'll end up back here needing surgery. This is a snap-and-go ice pack. Use one twenty minutes on, twenty minutes off for the rest of the day on both injuries. Tomorrow you can go a little longer between icings, but use your judgment if the swelling gets too much. There's also ibuprofen for the pain and swelling. Keep your shoulder and wrist as motionless as possible. The more you follow these rules, the quicker you'll get out of the sling. Don't forget to follow up with your primary physician in a week."

"Yes, yes, yes. I've taken care of myself for most of my seventy-four years. I can handle this too."

The nurse dropped her professional smile as soon as Mac turned away. Giulia winked at the nurse and followed Mac to the sliding doors.

"Nothing's broken after all?" Giulia said, breathing air free of disinfectant.

"No, thank God. I don't know how you managed it, but only my left wrist and shoulder are dislocated. Guess that side took the brunt of your grab."

Giulia counted to ten in Latin again. "You're welcome."

"Here's Lucy." Mac stepped toward a rusted Volkswagen Rabbit.

But it was Walter behind the wheel.

Forty-Three

"Hey," Walter said when Giulia opened the passenger door for Mac. "Luce asked me to pick you up in case you needed help and stuff."

"Thank you." Mac eased into the passenger seat, banging her wrist on the doorframe. "Dammit. I already hate this sling."

Giulia climbed into the backseat.

"Sorry it smells like bait in here, ladies. I was restocking when Luce called me." He zoomed through the parking lot and into the street. "So what happened?"

Mac produced a light laugh. "I'm getting old, Walter. Slipped off the gallery while I was showing the new guests the weathervane."

Giulia stared holes into the back of Mac's head. Walter ran a yellow and drove onto a side street.

"Water on the boards or something? You really ought to watch your feet up there, Auntie."

"You're right."

Walter rolled through a stop sign and turned right. "Did you catch yourself on the railing?"

"With one hand. Ms. Driscoll grabbed the other one. Together we hauled my old bones back onto the gallery." She turned her head to look straight at Walter. "Without her, you and Cousin Connie would've been running Stone's Throw tonight."

A pause from Walter, which could've been put down to waiting for cross traffic on Water Street. "Don't talk like that, Auntie," he said after completing a left turn. "You'll be telling the family stories for a long time yet. Besides, I've got my boats and Connie's who the hell knows where. Last I heard she was in Japan writing a history of this tribe of women who dive for pearls half-naked."

The conversation turned to the pursuits of more distant relatives until the car parked in front of the B&B's white porch. Walter helped Mac out of the car. Giulia got herself out.

"Thank you for picking us up." She didn't trust herself to say anything further.

"No problem. Thanks for helping out Aunt Mac."

They smiled fake smiles at each other.

"Thank you, Walter." Mac pecked his cheek. "If you're here, who's watching the boat shop?"

"Lucy. I'll send her back as soon as I park the car." He buckled his seatbelt and waved. "See ya. Watch out for ledges."

Mac and Giulia walked up the steps. Giulia rubbed the beagle's ears till they flopped over each other. The calicos projected masterful indifference.

"Mac, we should call the police about the railing."

"No." Short and sharp.

"What if one of the guests had leaned on that part of the railing instead of you?"

"No one ever leans on the railings but me." Mac faced the Welcome sign but her eyes weren't focused on it. "I also told the hospital staff that I slipped on the gallery and fell through the railing gap."

Giulia transferred her attentions to the cats, who deigned to purr. "Despite your assertion, you have a houseful of guests and an enticing view from the gallery. What if one of the guests had fallen at the same time you did? What if one of them had fallen instead of you? You panicked when the brick injured me." She lowered her voice. "If Marion or Anthony had been injured, how fast do you think their lawyer would show up here?"

Still facing the sign, Mac said, "You're dancing around the real question. That isn't like you."

Giulia avoided synchronized swipes from Tweedledum and Tweedledee. Petting interlude over, Giulia stood. "You lied to the doctors. You're forcing me to lie by omission unless I choose to go to the police with the actual story." She stepped to Mac's side and lowered her voice further. "Everyone in this town may know you and like you, but the statement of a professional private investigator will carry enough weight to make the police question your original story. Give me a reason not to turn around and walk straight to the police station."

Mac started to gesture with her left arm and stopped with a grunt. "Are you sure you want the police interfering around here? They'll ask all kinds of questions and upset the guests so they stop talking to you at all."

Giulia shook her head. "If that was a threat, it failed. I get along quite well with the police. Do you think that other couple has kept quiet about what happened this morning? Your guests are already upset. I guarantee it."

"I'm telling you, no one goes up there unless I'm leading a tour, and no one's ever leaned on the railing besides me. I'll announce that all lighthouse tours are canceled until I get a new, stronger railing built." Mac looked at Giulia at last. "You heard my speech twice about caution on the Widow's Walk. My guests aren't going to talk to the police. They'll assume I've already done that. I'll downplay my fall and spin the whole thing into a new Dorothea story. Joel and Gino will take my spin and run with it. Tomorrow morning everyone will be looking forward to Solana's next séance." She made a rueful face. "I'll have to ask Rowan if she's willing to sit in next Sunday."

"I forget that you spent decades managing multiple hotel staffs." Tweedledum rubbed his head against Giulia's leg. *Fickle beast*, she mouthed at him.

The screen door opened and Joel ran onto the porch. "Mac, you're okay! Gino, Anthony, they're back."

A sea of arms swept them inside. Mac flipped a switch Giulia hadn't yet seen and became Scarlett O'Hara. The men fawned over her, led her to the sunroom, offered to get her a beer, commiserated about her sling and Ace bandage. Giulia wouldn't have been surprised to see her pull a fan out of nowhere and flutter it coquettishly before her face.

Giulia took advantage of her sole superpower, invisibility at will, and stopped just outside the sunroom doorway. Mac kept to her plan, announcing a temporary hold on lighthouse tours. Anthony wanted to know if she planned to replace the wooden railing with cast iron. Gino offered to fetch and carry breakfast the next morning. Mac talked up the way her feet slipped and how she'd bounced against a previously unknown weak point in the railing. In the midst of this, Lucy came through the sunroom door.

Kind concern replaced her usual resigned-yet-aggravated expression. She didn't fawn with the others. Rather, she morphed into a sympathetic friend.

Okay, that was ascribing motives where none may exist. Lucy could well like Mac while despising her job.

Or Lucy could also be one of the best actors Giulia had ever seen.

When the house became quiet, Giulia sneaked up the lighthouse's spiral stairs. So much for Mac's insistence that no one ever went up there without her. It was past noon by now and the sun's heat sucked the air out of the brick cylinder. At the height of the catwalk, the temperature increased by at least twenty degrees. Outside on the gallery the unshaded sun jumped the temperature another ten degrees at least on this windless day.

The railing bowed out over the patio like an open door. Giulia knelt next to the broken piece to take close-up pictures. The two-inch diameter wooden railing was sawn almost all the way through. Anyone leaning against it would have snapped apart what was left. Giulia took more pictures of the jagged point on the outward-bending piece and the gap on the tiny piece still attached to the upright.

If Giulia thought for one moment bringing the local police into this case would solve it faster, she would've walked out of Stone's Throw directly to their station.

Instead, she walked the gallery's circumference, shaking each joint of the railing. Three more of the eight intersections where the vertical-turned wood beams met the horizontal ones were held together only by a splinter.

She called down several Biblical curses on the perpetrator and took more pictures before she descended the stairs without a sound. Only Anthony was still in the sunroom, on his phone. Giulia caught his attention and mouthed *Mac?* with questioning hand gestures. Anthony cupped one hand over the phone and pointed with the other toward the driveway. *Carriage house,* he mouthed.

Giulia walked straight through the house, ignored the porch animals, and up to the front door of the carriage house. It was unlocked. She closed it behind her.

"Mac? It's Giulia."

No response. Giulia walked down the entrance hall into the living room. Mac lay on the long side of the pale green couch, her head on a seashell pillow. Giulia sat on the edge of the coral chair near Mac's head. Mac's eyes opened and she yawned.

"Giulia...They gave me a shot of something before they worked on my shoulder. Just want to sleep..."

Giulia locked away every iota of Franciscan kindness and empathy. In the voice she used to read her nieces and nephews to sleep when they stayed overnight, she said, "Tell me the story of the Stone gold."

Mac smiled. "Everyone loves to hear that one." She repeated pretty much the same story used in the newspaper article, her voice running down like an old-fashioned wind-up toy.

Giulia didn't let one strike stop her. "Is the gold hidden in Stone's Throw?"

Mac's eyelids dragged open, but she looked past Giulia toward a high window. "No..." Her eyes closed and she emitted a delicate snore.

Giulia followed Mac's gaze. That particular window framed the top of the lighthouse. All right then. She took two single-use ice packs out of the hospital supply bag next to the couch and snapped them active. When she was certain they worked, she draped one over Mac's left shoulder and the other over her wrapped wrist.

Frank drove up as Giulia closed the carriage house door. She waited for him. He locked the car and gave her a one-arm shoulder squeeze. "What did I miss?"

"Ow, ow, ow." Giulia pushed him away.

Frank became half cop and half concerned husband. "What happened?"

Giulia rotated her shoulders to work through the end of the pain. "Someone sawed through half of the railing joins on the Widow's Walk. Mac fell. I caught her. Mac has a dislocated shoulder and wrist. I'm just sore."

Frank's expression made Giulia think he was counting to ten in Irish.

"I don't like censored stories. Let's find some lunch and you can tell me all the gory details. I could eat liver and onions, I'm so hungry."

Forty-Four

Frank choked on a steamed clam.

"You pumped a drugged old lady for information?"

Giulia held out his bottled water and he glugged it down. The Beach Boys-loving outdoor bar was only half-full and they had the corner seats to themselves.

The music feed chugged through every album in order of release, as far as she could tell.

The bartender informed them they were listening to *Wild Honey* since it was one o'clock.

Giulia added more tartar sauce to her fish sandwich. "All this rich food. My workout schedule will need extra sessions when we get back. Yes, I pumped her. She's a duplicitous old lady. I have no regrets." She held out her hand. "Pickle, please."

"A handful of fries in trade, please."

The bargain transacted, Giulia said, "I want to go up in the lighthouse with you and search for this legendary gold."

Frank swallowed another clam. "You're sure she's been lying to you all along?"

"Not exactly lying. I think she's been waiting to tell us various parts of the truth until the revelation served her purpose." Giulia ate the generic kosher dill with more enjoyment than it deserved to watch Frank make his "pickles are horrifying" face. "We need to know if this gold is for real, and now. There are way too many unanswered questions."

"I'm all for wrapping this one up." Frank dispatched the last of his clams. "I couldn't find my desk under the paperwork. By the way, the lab says they should be able to give me basic blood test results by three."

"Excellent."

After lunch they walked back along the beach. June's weather had performed a complete one-eighty and decided to mimic late July, which would've been fine if Giulia had been wearing her bathing suit. The beach was packed like opening day at the State Fair, complete with several different kinds of blasting music and people who had no qualms about elbowing anyone out of their way.

The grass on the B&B's patio became an Eden.

"I like people, don't I?" Giulia said.

"Only in small doses." Frank opened the door to the lighthouse vestibule.

They started where the brick walls connected to the cement floor. First they tapped and checked for loose bricks. Next they tried the stairs, but the solid wood steps held no secrets.

On to the deep window recesses. The hurricane lamp in the lower one didn't even have oil in it, let alone gold coins. The vase in the upper one surprised Frank with a spider the size of his thumb. He didn't quite scream like a girl, but he did drop the vase, which bounced and rolled against the thick pane of glass. The spider scrambled into a hole between two of the bricks.

"Plastic," Frank said. "No one cares about authenticity anymore."

Giulia was laughing too hard to reply.

"I am heading up to the catwalk," Frank said in a huffy voice. "One of us should take this seriously."

Still chuckling, Giulia followed him. Because her shoulders weren't happy with the idea of stretching, Frank climbed the short ladder and felt underneath the light and its combination stand and socket.

"A whole lot of nothing." He backed onto his knees, then got to his feet. "Maybe she didn't lie about the treasure being a myth."

"Why look up at the light when she was loopy from painkillers or muscle relaxers or whatever?" Giulia tapped her foot on the step. "I am so frustrated. She's blocking me right as the danger goes to Red Alert. All I can think of is she's working from misguided loyalty."

Frank sat next to her. "To whom, specifically?"

"Walter or Rowan. I'm not sure which. Even though Walter is less than optimal, he's still family."

"I asked around discreetly. Walter was either working on the boats or in one of the bars every night something happened here."

Giulia's chin hit her chest. "You're not helping."

"Hey, I can't make him appear in two places at once." Frank wiggled Giulia's elbow. "Picture Conneaut Lake with two Walters. Small children would be afraid to go fishing but bars would make a killing."

"Maybe after Dorothea sobs through the halls at two a.m. she visits Mac for some family time."

"And they've bonded over old family photos while doing their nails." In response to Giulia's "huh?" look, he said, "Isn't that what women of all ages do for girl time?"

"Is anyone up there?"

They both jumped at Lucy's voice.

"Yes, it's the Driscolls," Giulia said.

"Oh, Ms. Driscoll, I guess you didn't hear that Mac closed the lighthouse until the outside railing gets fixed."

"Thanks, Lucy. We'll be right down." Giulia gave a panicked look at Frank.

He shrugged his shoulders. They descended, but Lucy was no longer there.

"We should've lowered our voices up there. They must have carried," Giulia said.

"Nothing we can do about it now, except brace a chair under our bedroom door at night."

Another voice warbled from the antique kitchen. "Mac, darling, where are you?"

Giulia stopped cold in the hall doorway. Lady Rowan, in many-colored layers of paisley and tulle on top of black palazzo pants, stood by the trestle table rearranging the fresh carnations in the vase.

Her nephew Jasper stood half a step behind, arms ready to help her balance.

She turned toward Giulia with a blue-tinted carnation in her left hand. Her right index finger pointed at Giulia. "Your ethereal veil surrounds you like a cloud of witnesses. You must tell me what's happened. When I read the cards this morning I saw danger in the past and in the present. I knew I had to be here to support Mac."

Jasper waved at Giulia until Giulia dragged her attention away from his aunt.

"Ms. Driscoll, we're not making this up. Aunt Rowan had me cancel three appointments and close the store to drive her here."

Rowan's fingernail changed its target. "You, hiding in the dining room. Turn off that phone. I did not give you permission to record me."

CeCe stepped into the doorway kitty-corner from Giulia, who closed her eyes and gathered strength. Not more YouTube videos.

Rowan tilted her head and became a multicolored bird with flowing wings. "My grandchildren play your dinosaur songs constantly."

"Thank you." CeCe's voice was more subdued than Giulia had yet heard.

Rowan tilted her head the opposite way. "I have no patience with all the fussbudget doctors we have these days, but you really should stop drinking tequila."

CeCe bristled. "Who are you to tell me how to live my private life? I was recording you because you're colorful and entertaining."

Rowan dismissed her with a wave of one many-ringed hand. "Go pee on a stick."

CeCe stood motionless for a long moment. Then she ran past them all, the screen door banging in her wake.

Rowan's finger aimed at Giulia again. "What happened to Mac?"

Despite being fed up to her eyebrows with people ordering her around, Giulia gave her a brief explanation of that morning's accident. When she finished, Rowan turned on one heel, allowed Jasper to steady her, and headed out the screen door.

Mac appeared in the carriage house doorway. "Rowan?" Her voice and eyes drooped. "What are you doing here?"

"MacAllister Stone, your aura is the color of a swamp in winter."

Mac held onto the doorframe with her good hand. "It's the pain meds."

Rowan beckoned to Jasper. "Help me down the stairs, dear. We have to work on Mac. Ms. Driscoll, I expect you to use the power I see in that veil aura to stop Mac's troubles immediately."

Giulia stalked through the house and out to the patio, where she picked up a bocce ball and smashed it into the grouping at the far end of the court. Three large balls flew into the air and landed on the grass.

Her right shoulder and back screeched at her like nails on a chalkboard. She crouched on the grass, breathing through the pain. Stupid her. Stupid Rowan. Stupid ghost.

Frank sat next to her. "If I mention the Veiled Woman, you won't be able to chuck the next ball at my head, right?" He massaged her shoulders with a light touch.

Giulia clenched both fists. If Rowan could see her aura now...

And then she let it go. A deep breath. Another. A long look at the lake shimmering in the sun. A smile for three preschool kids building a My Little Pony out of sand.

She sat up, rotated her shoulders and back, and nodded at Frank. "Thanks. Because my throwing arm is on the injured reserve list, it would be unsportsmanlike of you to mention that particular entity."

"Fine. I'll play fair." Frank retrieved the three balls and set them in the court. "Between possessed psychics, bloody writing on the walls, and this ongoing game of pin the tail on the ghost, I want to install a deadbolt on our door." He tossed a fourth ball into the grouping. "Oh, right. Locked doors won't stop a ghost."

"But they'll stop a living human. I vote for a chair shoved under the doorknob."

Frank's phone rang. "Driscoll. Yeah, Owen, what's the word?...What? Are you serious?...Come on, you know I'm not dissing your skills...All right. Thanks for letting me cut the line. The rest of the tests will be ready when?...Sounds good. I owe you." He returned the phone to his pocket. "It was duck blood."

"What?" She made a noise of pure frustration. Then, "Thank God it wasn't human."

Frank kicked the *pallino* to the opposite end of the court. "A nice, juicy murder would be just the thing to wrap this mess up fast."

"You are a sick individual. You're also missing the good news here: Who has easy access to ducks? The guy who spends ten hours a day at the dock."

Frank made a rude gesture at a seagull diving on something in the grass. "Get out of my face, useless bird. I have only a minor problem picturing Whining Walter slashing a duck's throat and draining its blood."

"Hold it." Giulia whipped through her mental catalog of facts for this case. "Drat and drat. He can't stand blood. You said so yourself."

Frank stared with blank eyes at the bocce court. "You're right."

"However, I have no problem picturing Walter sawing through the gallery railings so Aunt Mac will fall to her death on the patio stones. I have less of a problem picturing Solana or Cedar or Rowan or Jasper doing the same." Giulia studied the seagull with more intensity than it deserved "Well, not Jasper, really. But that would mean Rowan's feeble old lady shtick is as put on as her community theater outfits." She worked her shoulders some more. "About the mysterious bloody message. Let me see if I can turn Rowan's theatrics to our advantage."

Forty-Five

Frank went for a walk along the beach to that bench in the center of the rapid Wi-Fi triangle. Giulia headed inside for water and to formulate a Rowan attack strategy.

A metallic crash came from the kitchen as Giulia passed the doll carriage.

She ran into the narrow room. Lucy, on her knees, was picking up little frozen cookie half-dollars. An upside-down cookie sheet lay on the floor behind her.

"Can I help?" Giulia said.

Lucy looked up. "Oh, Ms. Driscoll. Are you sure you wouldn't mind? Mac's in the carriage house with her crazy friend and she can't lift anything anyway, and I wanted to get tonight's cookies baked now because I've still got cleaning to finish and those stupid cats are trying to kill me."

Giulia joined her on the floor and together they found all the cookie bits. "Shall I get more from the freezer?"

"Two dozen, please, thanks. Tonight is sugar cookies with M&Ms. All the boxes are labeled." She soaped a dishcloth and wiped up the smears and crumbs from the floor while Giulia set the cookie sheet on the counter and counted out twenty-four frozen cookie buttons.

Lucy slid the tray into the oven and brought out iced tea mix. "I've only heard bits and pieces about this morning. What exactly happened up on the Widow's Walk?"

Giulia retold the story, downplaying her own part in the rescue, while Lucy filled the glass dispenser with water and ice and added the powdered mix.

"Wow," she said when Giulia finished. "I thought those railings were sturdy as iron. Mac spent so much on the restoration. Wonder why she cheaped out on that one thing."

Giulia gave her a neutral reply. She wasn't falling for this passive, sweet Lucy, not when she'd seen angry, frustrated, sneering Lucy so many times these past days. Granted, she'd been looking for discontent, but why be surprised it existed? She ought to give herself more credit for detecting essential clues.

The oven timer buzzed. Lucy took a hot pad out of one of the drawers and set the cookie sheet on top of the oven. Giulia, being an adult and all, did not snatch a hot, fragrant, chocolate-studded delight the instant Lucy turned away to get a spatula.

"What else can I do to help?" Giulia said.

"Oh, no, really, I've got it from here. Tea in the fridge, cookies in a basket with the red cloth, set them both out at seven." She looked at the oven clock. "Oh, geez, it's twenty to five and I haven't set the table for tomorrow's breakfast."

"I'll get out of your way, then."

"Thanks a bunch, Ms. Driscoll. Some of these guests don't see me at all."

Giulia allowed herself a moment of grunt-to-grunt empathy. "Like you're furniture. I know."

Lucy set the tea in the refrigerator and studied Giulia. "You do know, don't you? Dishwasher?"

"Also laundry and housekeeper."

Lucy held out her fist and Giulia bumped it. "You're a guest, so please don't offer to help with breakfast. Mac will be in here directing everything." Her smile turned sarcastic. "Some people don't think it counts as work if your clothes aren't covered with oil and fish scales by the end of the day. It's a good thing I know how to use a hammer and saw and manly tools like that, right?"

"Testosterone kills too many brain cells."

"That and booze." With a muttered, "Men," she ran water into the sink and added dish soap.

Giulia tossed the rules of polite society into the trash and walked across the parking lot to the carriage house. "Mac? I'm coming in." She opened the door and entered without an invitation.

Rowan's purples and greens complemented the seafoam couch like she'd planned it. Maybe she'd given Mac feng shui advice for her personal space. Jasper stood at one of the windows looking out at the lake. Mac sat in one of the coral chairs, her arm on a seashell pillow and her face less gray, but with tiny pain lines at the corners of her eyes.

"What do you want?" she said in a faded voice.

Rowan jumped into the conversation. "She has waves of determination pouring off her. I do believe she suspects me of playing a part in your troubles."

Polite Smile Number One appeared. "I think we all agree that the situation has escalated from vandalism to life-threatening."

"Oh, very well." Rowan patted Mac's uninjured hand. "You leave this to me. The pain pill should kick in anytime now. Jasper, come help me with the stairs. Ms. Driscoll, come along."

Giulia walked behind Rowan and Jasper, every shred of willpower focused on letting the scene play out rather than shouting, "Stop leading me around like a dog on a leash."

Rowan paused when she reached the inn's living room. "I sense residue of a strong spiritual contact." She looked over her shoulder at Giulia.

"Solana held her weekly séance on that couch. This past Sunday, her Ouija board spelled out several messages and at the end she appeared to be possessed by a ghost who claimed to be Mac's ancestor."

Rowan's hands stroked the air, the couch, the coffee table, and the mantelpiece as she stuck her tongue out like a snake sensing what it couldn't see.

"Let's get to the lighthouse now." She held out an arm for Jasper.

Giulia kept behind them so she could drop Polite Smile Number One. When they passed the sunroom, Joel and Gino were pressing their faces against the windows. They came inside a moment later.

"What's up, Giulia?" Joel said.

Rowan butted in again. "'I'm here to help Mac and attune myself to the spirits in her house."

Gino coughed. Joel turned and took the stairs two at a time, returning with CeCe, Marion, and Anthony.

Rowan moved into the lighthouse tower and paid no attention to anyone living except Jasper. She touched the painting on the wall. Giulia held her breath, but Rowan passed it by and ascended the first few steps. Jasper kept one step below her, but Rowan remained steady. Her hands came up again, palpating the air.

"Dorothea Stone, why are you making trouble?"

Silence.

Rowan's voice scolded. "Dorothea Stone, you come out this minute and talk to me."

Silence from the heights of the lighthouse. At its base, feet shuffled and voices whispered. Jasper turned his head and made a shushing motion.

"I protect this house."

Everyone jumped. Giulia crowded next to Jasper and twisted her head to see up the spiral stairs. Hot breath tickled her neck. She elbowed backwards and Joel's voice whispered, "Sorry."

Rowan recovered the next moment. "We are not here to harm this house."

"You come to defraud and despoil."

Rowan *tsk*ed. "You mustn't paint us all with the same brush, Dorothea."

"Leave this house. Leave it. Leave it." The hollow voice came nearer with each repetition. A bare foot appeared at the third turn above Giulia's head. A long white skirt followed, then a vintage Van Halen concert t-shirt.

Forty-Six

Marion tittered.

"A ghost with modern taste in music," Gino said. "That's a new one."

Another step and Solana's head topped off the incongruous clothing.

Rowan's voice didn't alter. "Dorothea, your host knows me. Allow her to speak to you. She will tell you my purpose here."

Solana/Dorothea stopped her descent. Her face turned to the group at the foot of the stairs.

Her arm rose slowly, slowly, until one finger pointed at Giulia. "The Veiled Woman must..." Her voice faded and her eyes rolled completely back into her head.

"Gross," Joel whispered.

Solana/Dorothea's legs buckled. She fell against Rowan. Jasper caught them both, staggered, and his heel slipped on the step below.

Giulia, Joel, and Gino made themselves into a buttress and tried to break the fall of the three psychics. Instead, all six hit the floor.

Frank walked in from the souvenir room. "Giulia? I thought you'd be..." He gaped. "What did I miss?"

CeCe's phone emitted a single high *beep*. Giulia knew that sound: The end of an iPhone recording. Oh, joy, more YouTube hits in her future. She sighed. Nothing she could do about it.

"Jasper, you're squashing my legs." She didn't mention what the triple catch had aggravated in her already-strained arms from yesterday's rescue.

"Sorry, Ms. Driscoll. Aunt Rowan, can you get up?"

"If someone removes Solana's elbows from my ribs."

Frank took Solana by the upper arms and heaved.

Rowan huffed and puffed. "Much better. You. The rich one. Help me up, please."

Anthony's head swiveled left and right. When no one else moved, he stepped in front of the stairs and pulled up Rowan by her hands.

Jasper jumped up and helped Giulia. Gino and Joel got to their feet and backed away from the psychic trio.

Frank still held Solana in a vertical position. Rowan patted the unconscious woman's cheeks.

"Solana, you showoff, wake up."

Solana inhaled and opened her eyes.

Gino whispered, "At least they're not all white and demonic anymore."

"You watch too many horror movies," Joel whispered.

"Rowan." Solana's voice cracked. She cleared her throat. "I thought I heard you."

"What are you doing?" Rowan said.

"Dorothea had a message for me. I tried to contact her at home, but she's tied to this place. The Stones have a strong sense of family."

"Don't I know it. But Mac told you not to come back. You can't be arrested for trespassing. It's the wrong kind of publicity."

"You don't understand. Dorothea lived in this house long before Mac. The needs of our ancestors supersede our petty mortal desires."

"Good point. Did you receive her message?"

Solana's eyes tried to retreat, but they gave it up halfway and returned to normal. "I think so. I don't remember anything after climbing up to the Widow's Walk to speak to her."

Rowan put an arm around her. "Let's go apologize to Mac, if she hasn't fallen asleep from the painkillers. Then I'll guide you through a meditation to help you remember."

Jasper took Rowan's other arm and they left through the lakefront door.

"That old woman treats the inn like she owns it," Marion said.

Gino said, "What's up with this 'veiled woman' thing?"

Giulia didn't have to counterfeit frustration. "The next time someone points a fingernail at me, they will be in serious danger of getting it slapped down."

"As long as CeCe's there to record it," Joel said. He joined Gino, Marion, and CeCe around CeCe's phone.

Giulia dragged Frank out into the sunshine. "If I hear 'The Veiled Woman' one more time, I am going to say something regrettable."

Frank kissed the top of her head. "If you do, I'll be the one capturing it on my phone."

Giulia shot such a dirty look at Frank he took a step back. She walked to the edge of the grass and let the beautiful, mundane beach and lake noises slough her clean.

Frank came over to stand with her. "Allow me to inform you of two momentous events. One, I now sit atop the fantasy leaderboard. Two, Walter owns more than one tool capable of sawing through the gallery railing."

She took his right arm and put it around her waist. He pulled her against his side.

"So, Veiled Woman, what news from the Other Side?"

She pummeled his chest until he wormed a finger into that ticklish spot on her ribs.

She squealed and gasped and flailed until he stopped, which also made her shoulders happy.

"Cheater," she said when her voice settled. "Rowan arrived in a purple version of Cedar's airy layered tunics and took over the world. I barged into the carriage house and allowed her to reach the conclusion that I suspected her to be in league with Solana. She paraded me to the lighthouse, picking up all those guests on the way, and tried to contact Dorothea herself."

"And got our friend Solana instead?"

"No, she got a two for one. Dorothea proclaimed vague warnings from beyond and Solana's eyes did their disappearing trick again. That has to hurt."

"I miss all the fun."

She wrinkled her nose at him. "If Rowan was trying to prove their innocence, Solana missed a voicemail. Today's show makes me suspect them even more."

"Mac too?"

Her lips twisted in several different directions. "No. I waffled about her before today, but she's not the villain of this melodrama. Here's what I'm thinking now: What if Solana and Cedar sawed through those railings Sunday afternoon when Mac didn't expect her to be here? The Dorothea act could be a convenient excuse to wander the inn at will and paint bloody messages and grimy footprints on the walls."

"And spoil an entire fridge full of food?"

Giulia hung her head. "Stop ruining my beautiful theories."

"I apologize. We have too many suspects for my taste." He took out his phone.

"Understatement of the day. I need some serious extra research time tonight."

Without a word, Frank turned his screen to Giulia. Today's Rowan/Solana/Dorothea video already had eighty-four views.

Forty-Seven

At nine o'clock Giulia gave up on the Stone's Throw Wi-Fi and walked to the local coffee shop. Frank, Joel, Gino, and Roy were in the middle of a beer pong version of croquet, lit by the floodlights on the second floor overhang of the B&B.

With a mocha smoothie at her elbow and excellent Wi-Fi feeding her tablet, Giulia started with Solana.

Twenty minutes later, she followed an odd comment in an old LiveJournal discussion down a wandering path to a small town paper's police blotter. Busted for weed possession: Elaine Solana Appleton.

Giulia got so excited she slurped the smoothie, causing giggles in a five-year-old at the next table. Giulia stuck out the tip of her tongue and the little girl mimicked her, then giggled some more.

With Solana's full legal name in Giulia's possession, she traced the psychic's career from a second bust to three months' probation. After that she hid her weed better, got an accounting degree, married Cedar, and created Lady Solana. The blonde, overweight, nearsighted high school senior in the first mugshot bore zero resemblance to the skinny, businesslike woman with dark, asymmetrical hair using a Ouija board to channel dead Stones.

Giulia rubbed her hands together à la Simon Bar Sinister and went after Cedar.

His family rejoiced in unusual first names. He'd been a model student and continued to be a model employee. Boring, even. A real-life illustration of the Monty Python sketch about charted accountancy. She refused to give him props for hiding his weed and heroin habits better than his wife. All that meant was he had the smarts to make sure all spotlights focused on Lady Solana.

She finished the smoothie without further slurps. Therefore: Solana and Cedar could be behind everything for the money. Heroin and weed weren't cheap. Also for the boost to her authenticity. Sucker in more rubes and fatten the drug budget.

Onward to Rowan. Giulia reread Zane's initial research results. Divorce fees. Steep ones. Did her Tarot income cover her mortgage and store rents, plural, with a cushion, or were she and her younger husband living on ramen?

She sidetracked to dig on the husband and nephew. The facts of their military service were easily located, but specifics ended there. She quit that diversion. She had no desire to ping Homeland Security's radar.

Back to Rowan's college years. A helpful sorority sister of Mac and Rowan's had scanned and uploaded whole chunks of their yearbook for their fiftieth class reunion. Many candid activity photos, music recitals, theater performances.

Mac and Rowan on the track team. Mac playing oboe in the symphony orchestra. Rowan winning a dance marathon. Mac and Rowan in the school's productions of *Peter Pan*, *The Wizard of Oz*, and *A Midsummer Night's Dream*. They'd alternated as cast members and stage crew.

Both an embarrassment of riches.

Rowan and Solana possessed the skills to pull off all the Stone's Throw "accidents." Both of them could qualify for the "land grab" column and the "family gold" column. Giulia wished for a touch of poverty in these "suspects" columns. She needed a hard target, fast.

Last, a dive into Ancestry.com. The way this research was going, she wouldn't be surprised if every single guest this week turned out to be related to one of the gazillion Stones. Including herself and Frank. It'd be a family gold free-for-all.

But first a quick break to clear her brain. She closed her tablet and went outside for a walk on the beach before the genealogy session.

A small, moving light appeared in the top of the lighthouse. She ran.

The light was gone when she reached the lakeside door. She begrudged the minute it took her to slow her breathing so she could climb after whoever it was without gasping. She opened the door and turned the handle so it closed without a *click*. A dark corner of the vestibule hid her tablet so her arms were free to nab this "ghost." The suit of armor didn't even register on her consciousness. No light was visible in the almost total blackness of the lighthouse. Maybe the circular stairs blocked it. She didn't use her flashlight app to climb; she had the railing to guide her. She slowed her pace after she passed the second window. Who would she surprise? Jasper and Rowan? Walter? Had Solana sneaked back again? She set one foot on the top step.

A phosphorescent clown swooped into her face out of the empty blackness, green-glowing arms reaching for her eyes. In the same instant she gasped and stepped backward onto nothing.

She couldn't get breath to cry out. She stumbled down one step. Her toe missed the second.

As she fell, her right hand caught the wooden railing. Her body swung around and her back slammed into the railing as her left hand latched onto the wood.

When her shoulders stopped screaming at her, she looked up into the dark apex of the lighthouse.

The clown doll had vanished.

Her entire body shaking, Giulia texted Frank. An eternity later—only a minute by her phone's clock, but what did it know—Frank pounded up the stairs to her.

"What happened?"

She raised a still-shaking, but not as bad as before, hand and whispered, "A glowing clown doll loomed out at me. I almost fell, but caught myself on the railing."

Frank switched to Irish curses. Giulia put her fingers on his lips. "Help me up so we can look for wires."

He put his hands under her elbows, stopped moving when she gasped, and switched his hands to her waist. After a second to get steady, she led the way up, both of them using their flashlight apps.

They scoured the catwalk. The ceiling. The ladder. The opening to the gallery. The light itself and its gel color-changers. No wires. No hooks. No drips of glowing paint. Nothing.

"Now I'm angry," Giulia said, the adrenaline rush gone.

"I'm going to make him regret this."

Giulia kissed him. "Or her. You're sweet. Come on, I want to check something."

She led the way into Mac's office and took the attic door key from the niche in the roll top desk. They slipped into the stairwell leading to the attic without anyone seeing them and opened the door with minimal noise.

"It should be on the shelf with the Victorian dolls, if Mac didn't lie about this too." Giulia used her flashlight and kept it shielded so the light wouldn't show through the window. She knelt on the floor and took down square boxes, rectangular boxes, narrow boxes, opening the first few until she saw the labels on the ends. Bride. Groom. Witch. Three trick-or-treaters. Five Christmas Carolers. It had to be here. She was not seeing ghosts.

"Here's a trunk labeled 'To Be Repaired.'" Frank lifted the lid. "Lots more boxes."

Giulia came over to him. "You take the left side and I'll take the right?"

"Vase."

"Picture Frame."

"Lampshade."

"Did I tell you how tempted I was to surprise you for your birthday with a tasseled lamp like the ones in the hallways?" Giulia lifted out the next box. "Clown doll."

"Those lamps are something out of a reality show nightmare. Well? Open the box."

Giulia clenched her teeth and removed the lid. Empty. No, not quite. She shone her flashlight into the tissue paper. A hand with painted fingernails, broken off at the wrist.

Frank picked it up. "Did the one you saw have only one hand?"

Giulia closed her eyes, but opened them a moment later. "I don't remember. All I can see is its glowing face and sunken eyes."

He replaced the hand. "A restoration nut like Mac wouldn't keep a hand without the doll."

"That doesn't mean the horrible thing wasn't possessed by a vengeful ghost." Giulia sat on her heels. "What am I saying?"

"This place is getting to you." He replaced the clown doll box.

"You think?" Giulia handed each of the boxes on the floor to him and he repacked the trunk. "I need to find out if Solana and Rowan went home. Their information's in my iPad. A couple of phone calls should do it."

Solana answered her phone and Giulia listened to her rhapsodize about her new ability to contact spirits. Frank heard most of it from his side of the bed. She finally put her free hand over his face because his expressions were making her laugh.

Too late, she realized Solana on her phone meant nothing, since Giulia didn't know if the number she had was for a cell or a landline. Drat. She had to rule out Cedar because of his cast. That set her back to Walter, Rowan, and Mac. Possibly Jasper as Rowan's young and limber assistant, although the possibility depressed Giulia. If you can't trust a war hero...

"I'm setting my alarm for seven a.m. Will you come up to the lighthouse in daylight so we can snoop again?"

Frank groaned. "Vacation is over."

If the sobbing ghost roamed the halls that night, Giulia slept through it. Likewise the strangling dream. If she'd possessed a hammer, the alarm clock might not have survived the morning.

"Ow."

Frank raised his head. "What?"

"I have discovered new upper arm muscles and they hurt. Will you check my back?"

Her husband pulled up her nightgown and whistled. "You have a railing-shaped bruise running diagonally from your right shoulder blade down to your waist."

"Wonderful. Let's go exploring first so I can soak in the shower afterward."

"It's all about you, isn't it?" He stretched.

"When I'm on a case, you bet it is." She tickled that one spot behind his left knee. "Up, you slug."

He leaped away using only his butt muscles and flailed bare arms and legs on the edge of the bed. One foot on the floor saved the rest of him from following.

"Now that you're up..." Giulia got out of bed and threw on yesterday's clothes.

The lighthouse in morning sunshine smiled on their efforts. Giulia found a shred of clear fishing line caught on the metal frame of one of the colored lighting gels. She followed its possible trajectory to a centimeter-sized hole in the wooden roof, visible only because she pointed out the general area to Frank and his extra height brought him close enough to spot it.

"Found another one a foot to the right."

Giulia handed up her phone and he took pictures. She was embarrassed at her relief. No possessed dolls. No ghosts. Regular antique dolls hooked up to nearly invisible strings to scare her into falling down these stairs and breaking her neck.

Her or Mac.

Forty-Eight

Breakfast made it to the table only twelve minutes late. Rowan and Jasper squeezed into spare chairs in between Gino and Frank.

"We slept in Mac's spare room," Rowan said. "That is, I did. Poor Jasper got the couch, but his joints don't go snap-crackle-pop in the morning."

Lucy carried in the dishes and Mac followed with more coffee and other one-handed extras.

"I don't know what this is called," Giulia said after a couple of bites of sausage, gravy, and biscuit, "but I taste coffee, which makes it the perfect breakfast food."

Joel said, "You've never had Red-Eye Gravy? How have you lived?"

Mac said, "Don't compliment me, compliment Lucy. She did ninety percent of the kitchen work this morning."

Praise from everyone except CeCe, who traded her plate for her husband's fruit and poached egg. All through the meal, she kept looking sideways at Rowan, who preened.

Everyone pitched in after breakfast and brought dishes into the kitchen. Giulia walked Mac to the far end of the narrow space.

"I need to show you something."

Lucy took charge of the dishes. "I've got it, Mac; you know you can't wash or dry with your arm like that."

Giulia and Mac walked through the house. Joel and Gino came downstairs a few minutes later in swim trunks and carrying towels.

Frank followed them, also in swim trunks. Marion and Anthony didn't reappear.

Roy and CeCe passed Giulia carrying a camera with a lens bag, an easel and a paint tote. "It's art day."

The new couple was the last to leave. She carried a homemade shopping tote with "All your kitsch are belong to us" silkscreened onto both sides.

"Marion and Anthony will be packing," Mac said as she and Giulia climbed the spiral stairs. "Lucy mentioned she heard you and Frank talking up here yesterday."

"We were looking at the railings. Four more of them are sawed most of the way through." Giulia waited for a reply. Waited some more. Mac didn't say anything until they reached the catwalk around the light.

"What did you want to show me?"

"Last night I saw a small light moving around up here. I snuck up the stairs to see who it was. When I got to the top step, a glow-in-the-dark clown doll flew into my face. The only reason I'm not dead is because I managed to catch myself on the railing as I fell backwards."

Mac didn't reply. Giulia wondered if her pain meds had kicked in and she wasn't in the here and now anymore.

"Frank and I came up here early this morning to search. We found this." She led Mac to the shred of fishing line. "And those." She pointed to the holes in the roof.

Mac blinked, confirming Giulia's impression that the meds had flicked the slow-motion switch on Mac's world.

"Do you suspect anyone?"

"Yes, but we need hard evidence."

Another blink. Then a head shake like a dog drying itself off after getting caught in the rain. "Damn these muscle relaxers. They're relaxing my brain cells. You have a suspect but not enough evidence? That's good. How much longer..." A wide-mouthed yawn.

"How long will it take?" Giulia made an open-handed gesture. "We hope to find what we need soon. We can't promise anything."

A slow nod. "All right. Thank you. I think I need to lie down for a while."

"Let me go first." Giulia stepped down one tread. "You can put your hands on my shoulders if you need a little steadying."

They created a lopsided procession. The more than six-inch difference in their heights wasn't designed for taller Mac to lean on shorter Giulia during a descent. When Giulia's feet touched the floor, Mac sat on the third step from the bottom and leaned her head against the balusters.

Giulia crouched in front of her. "Would you like me to help you back to the carriage house?"

The silver head lifted slowly. "I think that'd be a good idea."

Mac leaned on Giulia's shoulder and they started out. By the time they reached the porch, Mac's dead weight made Giulia appreciate all her circuit training at the gym. When she knocked on the door, Rowan and Jasper took charge of Mac like they were her nurses or bodyguards.

Giulia headed for the island between the divided driveway and collapsed on the grass. Cool, comforting. No ants that she could feel. Now for the research last night's clown doll attack prevented her from finishing. She called work.

"Zane, it's Ms. Driscoll. I need to hijack you and our fast internet connection."

"Sure thing, Ms. D. My fingers are at your command."

"You know that super-secret credit report backdoor you discovered last month? Can you look up Rowan Fortin, Elaine Solana Johnsen, maiden name Appleton, and Walter Stetler?" She spelled out everything.

"On it." Tapping.

Giulia tried a few gentle stretches with her right arm. Ow.

"In order," Zane said. "Rowan Fortin pays rent on the Tarot business. No late payments in the last two years. Scrolling...All those divorce lawyer debts are here. She's been late on each one of them within the last year. The bankruptcy is still on here. No credit cards or red flags."

"Not what I hoped to hear. Moving on."

Tapping. "Elaine Solana Johnsen or Appleton has a mortgage and a car loan jointly with Cedar Johnsen. All payments on time and up to date. Two credit cards, both maxed out. The first late payments were last month."

"So things are tight."

"It would appear." Tapping. "I could say I expect the car loan to be late next and the mortgage last, but I'm not psychic."

"Ba-dum ching." Every time Zane loosened up enough to make a joke, Giulia wanted to high-five him.

"The third report." Tapping. "Whoa."

If Giulia were superstitious, she would've crossed her fingers. "What?"

"If their algorithms used negative numbers, Walter wouldn't be able to buy a pack of cigarettes on credit. He contacted one of those debt consolidation places last month, but never followed up."

"Wait. What debt consolidation place?"

"Just a sec." Clicking. "New Growth."

Giulia smiled for the first time in days. "If that was a blind choice from a late-night infomercial, I'll open a psychic hotline next week."

The tapping stopped. "Why?"

"Solana owns a credit counseling service, whose name is..."

"New Growth?"

"You said the magic words."

Sidney's voice came through too muffled to understand.

Zane said, "Sidney says I have to put you on speaker."

"Giulia." Sidney's voice, much clearer. "Jane said she remembered Lady Rowan's face from somewhere and she found it last night. Did you know Rowan was part of an avant-garde theater company and Mac was one of its financial backers?"

Giulia trapped the phone between her shoulder and ear and opened up her case files. "No. Keep talking."

"Olivier says avant-garde theater is a sign of deep-seated insecurities and a desire to sneer at the rest of the world."

Giulia scrolled with her left hand and tried bicep curls with her right arm. Her arm registered an official protest. "Are those terms in the approved psychologist diagnosis manual?"

"Well, some of them are. Anyway, the theater group had its own Facebook page, which is gone now, but Zane found all these cached pages. A bunch of angry people posted nasty stuff on them."

Giulia switched the phone to her left shoulder and used her right hand to search faster. "Please give examples of nasty."

"The blame game. Lots of fingers pointing at everyone in charge. The treasurer didn't watch the budget. The art director picked bad plays. The actors were hacks. The set designer built artsy sets their audiences couldn't relate to. The backers took the operating committee to Small Claims Court, saying that they mishandled the funds and should pay all the members back out of their own pockets."

Giulia whistled. "Did they win?"

"Yes. The judge lectured everyone about not having enough business sense and not knowing their audience. They did something called *Rhinoceros* with puppets. Jane says it's like the poster child for French avant-garde. Nazi rhinos, for real. She said her ex started snoring during the second act when she took him to see it."

"Wait a second, Sidney," Zane said. "Ms. D., there's an item on Walter's credit report about a theater. I'm reading...Mac is MacAllister Stone, right?"

"Yes."

"Then Walter was involved with that same theater group. It doesn't say how, but maybe he's an actor?"

Giulia gripped the phone with her good hand and held her breath as though breathing would jinx whatever this was. "I can't picture him on a stage. He used to be middle management at sales places, so maybe he did their advertising and marketing."

"Sure. Either way, because Mac and the other backers won their claim, she's listed as one of his creditors."

"That must make Thanksgiving dinners awkward."

Sidney said, "Wait, they're related? Does that make this Walter guy the fake ghost?"

"An hour ago, I would've said he didn't have the skill or the determination, but now that I know he's been in contact with Lady Solana of the Ouija board, I'm revising my opinion. Thanks, guys."

She ran around the house out to the patio and saw Frank's ginger head emerge from the water. She put two fingers into the corners of her mouth and whistled.

Ten heads turned in her direction, including Frank's. He waved and swam in.

When he reached her, toweling his chest as he walked, she said, "If you drown from cramps because you went swimming right after breakfast, Saint Peter will clock you over the head with the Book of Life."

"And you'll be an eligible widow." He kissed her cheek.

"Thank you, no. I'd like to enjoy marriage for a few decades. Listen to what my exceptional staff found out." She told Frank about the credit reports, the defunct theater company, and the connection between Solana and Walter.

"Jesus, Mary, and Joseph, it's like a soap opera."

"Come down to the boat dock with me, please? I'm not sure yet what to say to Walter, but something will ping in my head to make him spill."

"I repeat: A confident woman is incredibly sexy." He avoided her butt swat. "Give me a few minutes to get dressed."

Giulia didn't have to think of the perfect leading question after all. When they reached the boat dock, all the windows were boarded up. Two sets of adults and five kids were clustered around the door, chattering.

A printed notice in big black letters on white paper was stapled to the door.

"BANK-OWNED PROPERTY," it read, followed by a long paragraph about foreclosure citing several laws and subsections of laws, and at the bottom, "KEEP OUT." An industrial-sized padlock secured the door to the doorjamb.

"Dad, I wanna go fishing," a young boy said.

"Ma, me too," a young girl said, pulling on a brunette's skirted bathing suit. "Dad promised."

Giulia tapped the shoulder of a woman in shorts and a tank top. "Does anyone know what happened?"

"It was cool," an older boy said. "This black Lincoln drove up and two guys in suits got out. They knocked on the door and the boat guy opened it looking seriously shit-faced."

"Edward, language," the brunette said.

Edward ignored her. "They said he had fifteen minutes to get out and that they would inspect anything he took with him." A delighted grin appeared on Edward's face. "He cursed them out like he was on an HBO special."

A girl with short blonde braids and a fluorescent bikini said, "The guy in the black suit held up his watch so the boat guy could see it and the boat guy slammed the door in their faces. Then we heard banging and slamming and the boat guy and his girlfriend yelling at each other. The guy in the blue suit went back to their car and came back with a toolbox. Ma said their suits were, like, super cheap ones, didn't you, Ma? And the blue suit guy took out a drill and started drilling holes in the wall next to the door."

Edward said over her last words, "When the drill guy finished, the other guy yelled up into the open window there, 'You've got five minutes.'" He pointed to the upper floor of the shop.

"No he didn't," Blonde Braids said. "He was, like, super polite. He said, 'Five minutes left, Mr. Sattling,' or Saddler, or whatever."

"Who cares?" Edward said. "The blue suit guy brought out that gonzo padlock right when the boat guy and his girlfriend came out with two big suitcases. The boat guy tried to shove the suit guys out of his way, but they grabbed the suitcases and opened them up right here on the dock. We saw his girlfriend's underwear and everything."

"Guys are so gross," Blonde Braids said. "I think it's sad they had to pack up all their stuff so fast. What if they forgot something important?"

The tall man next to Edward said, "Then they should have saved their money and paid their bills on time. Remember that the next time you whine about mowing the lawn for five bucks." He poked Edward's arm.

Edward rolled his eyes at Giulia. "So anyway, the suit guys dumped the suitcases on the dock and shook out everything, even the underwear. Then they told the boat guy he could pack it all up and made him hand over his keys. Man, I was sure he was gonna deck both of the suit guys."

A younger boy said, "I heard one of the suit guys talking into his phone to somebody about getting ready to call the police. But nothing happened."

Disappointment filled his voice and face.

Blonde Braids said, "So the boat guy's girlfriend shoved everything back into the suitcases and they walked toward the street." She pointed. "People just stopped everything and watched them fight. She yelled at him about the mess he made of her clothes and he told her to shut the—" She glanced over at the woman in the tank top and revised. "He told her to shut up and get back to washing dishes because it's all she's good for. She heaved the suitcase right at his head. It was epic. It busted open and her stuff fell out and she turned her back on him and walked that way." She pointed back the way Giulia and Frank had come. "She left all her stuff there, right in the middle of the sidewalk."

"He picked it up for her," Edward said in a superior voice. "I bet his girlfriend dumps him because they've got no place to live. Who cares about her old stuff? Girls are so stupid about clothes."

"Boys are stupid about everything." Blonde Braids stuck out her tongue.

"You're just a dumb—"

Edward's father cuffed the back of his head. "I don't care what you heard today, young man. You will not repeat any of it."

The woman in the tank top took the hand of a small girl in a bright pink one-piece and beckoned to Blonde Braids. "We'll go back to the hotel and ask if there are other places to rent boats."

Edward stopped trying to surreptitiously rub his head. "Can we do that too, Dad? Can we?"

"Sure. Let's go exploring." He walked away, followed by Edward, the younger boy, and a teenage girl who'd been texting during the entire conversation.

Giulia stared out at the water for maybe half a minute. When she turned back toward land and Frank, she was already moving.

"You go look for Walter, okay? Are any bars open at this hour? No, of course not. The library or a coffee shop, then. Any place that will have a newspaper or tabloid with apartment listings for the customers to read. I'm heading back to Stone's Throw to talk to Lucy."

Frank followed her for a few steps. "Why her?"

"Washing dishes."

Frank kept after her. "I'm not stupid, but what connection did you make? Lots of places have dishwashers."

"Not dishwashers who worked in theater and are the housekeeper for one of their boyfriend's creditors. Go, Frank."

Forty-Nine

The house was empty of guests. Even the animals weren't in their usual spots on the porch. Giulia knocked on the carriage house door, but it was locked.

Neither Mac nor Rowan nor Jasper answered the doorbell or her repeated calls up to the open window. She backed up far enough to see the entire parking area. A Jeep was missing. Rowan and Jasper must've returned to Cottonwood after breakfast to run their own business.

She ran back up the porch steps. There were the cats, pretzeled together under one of the wicker chairs. Tweedledee hissed at her.

No Mac in the office; no one in the kitchen. No Lucy in the second- or third-floor bedrooms. Giulia stopped at the top of the first flight of stairs to catch her breath and strategize.

A whimper. Faint. Giulia leaped down the stairs and used the newel at the bottom as leverage to careen around the corner toward the lighthouse.

But it wasn't Mac fallen at the foot of the stairs. Jabberwocky the beagle lay there in a crumpled heap, blood matting his brown and white coat. He looked up at her with watery eyes and whimpered again.

"What happened to you, boy? Never mind; you can't answer me. Listen, Jabber, I have to find Mac. She'll know the vet's number."

The beagle's tail gave a weak thump.

"The fucking bank foreclosed on us this morning. They took everything, and it's all your fault." Lucy's voice above her, but muted. Out on the Widow's Walk; must be.

Giulia ducked under the spiral staircase and peered up through its central opening.

Nothing, again.

This "nothing" business was getting on her nerves. She put a foot on the bottom step and climbed as silently as though she was sneaking up on that phosphorescent clown doll.

"We want what's coming to us, dear Auntie."

Clearer now. Even angry, Lucy supported her voice with her diaphragm like a well-trained actor.

"It's not my fault Walter can't keep to a budget or retain customers." Her sentence ended in a sharp cry.

"Why didn't you take the easy way out, you old bitch? You're so into that psychic crap you should've turned tail and ran a week ago."

Giulia reached the catwalk around the light. She raised the top of her head and peeked over the edge with one eye.

Lucy kept ranting, her thin legs pacing two steps left, two steps right and back again. "The gas leak and the fire would've scared off anyone with half a brain. But no, I had to keep playing the supernatural game and put up with spoiled food in our apartment for two whole weeks. After I moved it into your fridge even that damn fish air smelled good."

Another set of legs was visible on the gallery outside, the feet in deck shoes without socks. That meant Walter was up there too, and Mac was probably cornered against the railing. The mostly sawed-through railing. And Giulia had sent Frank away on a useless hunt.

"Shut up, Luce." Walter, whining. "Tell us where you hid the gold, Aunt Mac."

Mac's voice came steady, but weaker than usual. "There is no gold. Great-Grandpa made up that story to entertain us kids."

"No!" A thump and another cry from Mac.

"Walter, you useless turd." Lucy's voice, speaking the way Giulia expected her to sound when she dropped her helpful face. "Your idea of supernatural terror wouldn't scare a roomful of brats at a Chuck E. Cheese's. I should've ignored everything you said to try. My old theater company would've haunted this place empty in a week and MacAllister Stone the Great Hotel Keeper would have had to bring out the gold to keep the bank from foreclosing. Just like you should've been able to do if you were a real man."

Giulia slid onto the catwalk butt-first to avoid anything like the sound of a footstep. From that angle she could see Mac's legs. Lucy and Walter were between Giulia and Mac, but they weren't blocking the doorway to the gallery.

Okay. She could slip sideways through the opening behind those two. The odds of achieving that without Walter or Lucy hearing her: Slim to none.

The odds didn't matter. She started creeping around the catwalk to the right, as Lucy and Walter were both angled slightly to the left.

"This is how it is, Mac," Lucy said. "Marrying your nephew might have been one of my stupider decisions, but I'm going to drag him up with me, not the other way around. No self-important bank manager is going to take my things ever again. Since you didn't die like you were supposed to three damn times already and leave your family treasure to us, you're going to tell us where you hid it. My ball and chain here is going to get his feeble hands dirty digging it up, and then we're taking it. I suggest you play nice, or I won't stop him from bashing in your turkey-wattled throat."

Giulia reached the doorway. Walter and Lucy faced three-quarters away from her.

Mac faced her full-on. A dark bruise discolored Mac's left cheek. Blood dripped from her swollen mouth.

She looked alert and furious, but not frightened. Impressive, since Walter hefted some kind of wrench discolored with blood. From the size of the wrench, Giulia expected Mac's teeth to be embedded in it.

Walter moved closer to Mac. "Don't be stupid. Tell us where you hid the gold."

Mac opened her swollen mouth and winced, but that was all. "Walter, for the last time, there is no secret pile of stolen gold coins."

"Bullshit. Great-uncle Luke showed me a piece of it when I was ten."

Mac shook her head and regretted it, from the look on her face. "He showed it to me too. He got it at an antique shop. I found the receipt."

"You lying bitch!" Walter swung the wrench, but Lucy blocked it.

"Sweetheart, you're not thinking." Her voice dripped corroded honey. "Auntie Mac is playing a long game. She's hoping someone will hear us talking and come see who's up here. She forgot that she told her guests the lighthouse was off-limits. All those lazy morons are off playing tourist. It's just Auntie Mac and her loving niece and nephew. And her loving niece has a year of menial labor to pay her back for."

Giulia got to her feet during this speech, moving in slow motion. When she finished, she stood in the open doorway an arm's length away from Walter and Lucy.

"You're freaky, Luce."

"You're not used to women with brains, Walter. I sure as hell wouldn't have screwed up the boat business and lost everything."

Walter gripped the wrench tighter. "You're a ball-buster, too."

"I'm confident. There's a difference. I want a real home and no debts and my very own children's theater, and I'm going to do it with your family's lovely gold. You'd know that if you'd ever listened to me instead of treating me like your other bimbos."

"Christ, shut up."

Lucy shook her head. "Someday I'll figure out what I saw in you." Her voice was rueful. "Oh, I remember. You told me about the Stone family gold when you got drunk on our first date. Which reminds me—" She grabbed Mac's dislocated arm and yanked her up so they were face to face. Over Mac's cry of pain, Lucy said, "Tell me where you hid it. Now."

Giulia lunged out of the door and grabbed the wrench from Walter's hand. Walter said "Hey!" and tried to grab it back. Lucy dropped Mac's arm and dived at Giulia. Mac stumbled out of the way. Giulia dodged Lucy's attack and tripped Walter as he made another snatch at the wrench. Walter fell against Lucy. Lucy overbalanced and crashed into one of the sawed-through railings. The railing cracked apart. Lucy's momentum took her through the broken wood and off the Widow's Walk. At the same moment, Frank leaped through the opening and tackled Walter. A wet *thud* cut off Lucy's scream.

"Lucy! Lucy!" Walter shouted his wife's name over and over.

Giulia dropped the wrench and went to help Mac. Frank dragged Walter back through the opening and onto the catwalk. Giulia got Mac onto her feet and blocked her view of the patio as she walked her through the doorway to the catwalk.

Frank wrestled Walter down the spiral stairs, Walter sobbing and struggling and running through a limited repertoire of curses. They banged and crashed all the way down.

Mac didn't say a word as Giulia eased her downstairs. Mac's good arm supported her dislocated one, but she winced with every step. When they reached the bottom, Giulia took out her phone to call 911, but heard the first siren before she input her password.

"Come on, Mac. We have to go out to the patio. The police are coming."

Mac said nothing, but didn't resist Giulia as she led her past the suit of armor and outside. Several adults in bathing suits crowded together on the grass at the far edge of the patio. Two more adults herded a handful of children away from the scene. The siren got louder. Another siren joined it.

Five feet away from the crowd, Gino lost his breakfast on the grass. Joel knelt next to him, pale and with closed eyes. Marion pushed through the crowd. When she reached the front of it she fainted in the best Method Acting tradition. A woman in madras plaid shorts and a tank top stepped over her for a better look at Lucy's body.

Walter sagged in Frank's hold, alternately sobbing and whimpering Lucy's name. The sirens cut off. Two more young women ran to the front of the crowd and screamed in tandem. The same two EMTs as before ran across the lighthouse's lawn. Two police officers came around from the opposite side of the patio and ran across the flagstones. The EMTs and the police skidded to a stop.

Only for a moment. Then one police officer herded the crowd back while the other stepped over a splash pattern of blood and brain matter.

One EMT felt Lucy's wrist and set it down, then all three backed out between the rivulets of blood.

Swimmers abandoned the water to follow the line of people climbing the slope to the patio.

"You killed her, Mac," Walter said, still blubbering. "If you'd lent me the money we wouldn't have had to scare it out of you." He tried to go to Lucy's body, but Frank held him back. "You killed her, you cheap bitch. You killed her."

More beachgoers ran onto the grass. So many camera phones *clicked* it sounded like hail hitting the patio stones. Anthony and Joel carried the groggy Marion off to one side. The texting teenage girl from earlier at the boat dock looked to be taking panoramic video until her mother snatched the phone out of her hands.

The older police officer walked over to Mac and Giulia. "Ms. Stone? What happened here?"

At that moment Solana appeared on the doorstep, still in the white skirt and Van Halen t-shirt. She raised her right arm, pointed to the top of the lighthouse, and intoned, "Dorothea Stone is avenged."

Everyone shut up. Mac lost her stupefied expression and glared at Solana. The police officers glanced at each other. Someone in the crowd giggled.

Solana stalked toward Lucy's body, one bright gold fingernail aimed at it. "The spirits will not be mocked. Their power courses through me. They demand to be heard."

The younger police officer left the EMTs and stopped Solana outside the perimeter of blood splatters.

"Ma'am, do you have information about what happened here?"

Solana didn't even glance at him. "The spirit of Dorothea Stone protects this place. Those who disregard her warnings will suffer her fate."

A dozen phones recorded everything. Joel held his own and Frank's; Giulia recognized the Pittsburgh Pirates case.

"This will be on YouTube as soon as she stops talking," Frank said.

Mac's re-injured arm combined with Solana's dramatics appeared to have cured Mac's stupor. "That woman is a menace."

"Think of the publicity," Giulia said.

"What? 'Come to Stone's Throw, home of the murderous ghost?' My email will be filled with canceled reservations. I'll be bankrupt in a month."

Solana capped Mac's prophecy. "Heed this warning, all you who do not respect the Stone legacy."

A teenage boy imitated Solana's sepulchral voice: "You're all doomed."

The three boys with him snickered.

"I will tell you of Dorothea Stone and her eternal watchings in the night." Solana swept her sunken-eyed gaze over the crowd. "Listen well, and keep in mind the fate of scoffers." The gold fingernail aimed at Lucy's body.

Giulia caught the eye of one of the EMTs and beckoned him over. "Mac's arm was re-injured in the situation up there."

The younger police officer joined them. "Coroner and backup coming down the driveway. Mac, as soon as you're patched up I'll need a statement."

Giulia stepped forward. "I'm a private investigator here at Mac's request."

He took out a notepad and pen. "I'm ready when you are."

Giulia told him about the vandalism and the apparent hauntings that started after the article in the local paper. While she talked, Solana shouted down the hecklers, her hair breaking its bonds of obedience and flying around her head like Medusa's snakes. The coroner and extra police took over the crime scene, herding the crowd away, taking pictures, marking the outline of the body. At least three teenagers climbed on their friends' shoulders to keep their videos going.

Frank was already giving his story to the older police officer. Walter had at last stopped whining and switched to blaming Mac for every job he'd failed at because she wouldn't give him his share of her inheritance. The officer cautioned him twice but Walter kept right on venting.

Giulia repeated everything Walter and Lucy had said and done to Mac up on the gallery.

The EMTs brought out the gurney.

"I am not a helpless old woman," Mac said. "My legs work fine. It's my arm and my face that need fixing up. For that I'll need my dentist and my regular doctor, not another trip to the emergency room."

The buzzcut EMT said, "Mac, you really should have your face and arm x-rayed."

The droopy mustache EMT said, "The insurance companies pay claims faster when they get information directly following an incident."

"I want that woman off my property." Mac pointed to Solana.

Giulia said to the police officer, "One second, please," before she turned to Mac. "All those people are getting this mess on video. If you have the police drag Solana away, you could look like the bad guy suppressing great spiritual truths."

Mac groaned.

"But," Giulia said, "if you let her ramble until she winds down, all those videos will load to YouTube and link to Twitter with hashtags for Stone's Throw."

"Oh, yeah, Mac," the mustached EMT said. "My sister in Altoona is into spiritualism big time. She called me to tell me about the two videos with your psychic friends already on YouTube. If she watches this performance she'll drag my brother-in-law here for their next vacation."

"See?" Giulia said. "You're worried about losing clientele, but have you considered a subtle shift in the year-round focus of Stone's Throw? The only Bed & Breakfast with a family ghost. Something like that."

Mac appeared to study the bricks of the lighthouse. "That's an idea."

The younger police officer came over to them. "Mac, I have the statement of the private investigator you hired. Can you tell me what happened in your own words?"

Mac's expression sharpened. "It's simple. My housekeeper Lucy and my nephew Walter, who are married to each other, decided the legend of the family gold was real and tried to kill me to get their hands on it. Ms. Driscoll here saved my life today by surprising them where they'd trapped me up on the Widow's Walk. When Lucy tried to attack Ms. Driscoll, she—Lucy—fell through the railing which either Lucy or my nephew had deliberately damaged earlier." She glanced at the patio, where the coroner's staff was bagging up the body.

"See the reward of those who refuse to believe!" Solana said from her new position atop the glass coffee table in front of the patio couch.

"That woman is standing on my furniture." Mac took a step toward her, but stopped when Giulia put a hand on her good arm. "All right. Let's go get x-rays. Giulia, I'll be back in a couple of hours."

The older officer said to Frank and Giulia, "Statements now?"

"Sure," Frank said. "We'll follow you there."

Giulia said, "With Mac gone, there isn't anyone to watch the house. Could someone in authority stay here until she gets back? All these gawkers could mean trouble."

"Sure thing. Hey, Chris, can you hang here for a while in case the audience decides to grab souvenirs?"

The younger officer gave him a thumbs-up.

The backup police officers handcuffed Walter and got him into the back of their patrol car. The EMTs wheeled the gurney with the body bag out to the ambulance. Solana appeared to be winding down. Chris stationed himself at the door leading into the lighthouse. Two of the teenagers who weren't recording Solana took a few steps toward the lighthouse, saw Chris, and found something interesting back toward the beach. A small group of adults and children wandered the grounds, taking pictures of everything. A seagull landed near the discolored patio stones and a woman shooed it away.

Frank and Giulia followed the EMTs out to the parking lot.

"I would like nothing but background check cases for the next two months," Giulia said. "Maybe I'll allow an asset search or two."

Frank buckled himself in. "Those are the most boring jobs we ever had."

"Bingo."

Fifty-One

Mac returned after four o'clock. Giulia and Frank had picked up a pizza on the way back from giving their statements to the police. Mac brought out a bottle of local red wine and the three of them sat at the trestle table in the antique kitchen.

"This is all going to hit me soon," Mac said. "Lucy was a sweetheart. Always smiling, always full of energy. We used to talk about her plans for the future and ways to get Walter off his lazy butt. I had no idea...about any of this." She drank her wineglass dry.

Frank refilled everyone's glasses.

"I don't understand people who sit and wait for success and good fortune to rain down on them." Giulia slid another piece of pizza onto all their plates.

"The idea of a mountain of gold is too much like a fairy tale to resist for some," Frank said.

"About that." Mac's puffy lips made a hint of a grimace. "I lied to you."

Giulia batted her eyes at Mac.

"I know. I'm sorry. You know what possessing a mountain of fairy tale gold does? It makes you distrust everyone." She adjusted her dislocated arm, now in a soft cast. "How am I going to handle breakfast tomorrow?"

"I'll help," Giulia said. "So about this non-mythical gold?"

"I should be paying you. Oh, wait. I am." Mac's lips approximated a smile. "To be honest, truly and finally, nothing held back, most of the story I tell everyone is true. We did have an outlaw ancestor who robbed stagecoaches. He was caught and hanged, and he did tell his wife where he hid everything he stole. This is where it changes. She found it and used a very little of it to survive. Her eldest son did the same, and on down the generations."

"By the time your turn came?" Frank said.

Mac tried for another wry smile. Her lips refused to cooperate. "I did rent scuba equipment and explore the caves. I found a small box with twenty coins. Better than a poke in the eye with a sharp stick, I thought. I'd brought a bag with me to collect shells and the like to decorate the house with."

"And as camouflage just in case you found something valuable?" Giulia said.

"Well, yes. When I cleaned and dried the box, I found a set of directions scratched on the inside, like a puzzle. A few words in each group, all over the inside like a crazy quilt. It took me a couple of weeks to piece them together." She drank a little more wine.

Giulia leaned forward. "This is as good as the story you tell the newbies."

Half of Mac's mouth smiled. "People say I have a knack for storytelling. The directions led me to my great-grandfather's grave. Seriously. He'd ordered one of those tombstones with a round glass inset for a photograph of himself. The frame of the glass was a different kind of puzzle. When I got it open, a key fell out." She paused. "That's where the exciting mystery ends. The key belonged to a safe deposit box in his and my names. I'd completely forgotten that for my eighteenth birthday he opened the box with me and placed eighteen silver dollars in it for me. When I opened it again after finding the key, it was packed to the gills with five-dollar coins from the late 1880s."

"Quite a nest egg," Frank said.

"I used a few to help finance the restoration, but I haven't touched them since. I wanted to make a go of Stone's Throw on my own."

Giulia said, "Coming clean to your private investigator helps her get results faster."

"I know, I know. But I was sure the whole purpose of the scheme was to force me out and take over my successful business." She eased in the last bite of her pizza via the undamaged side of her mouth. "Walter couldn't turn a profit with a lemonade stand during a heat wave. I loaned him money to pay off his student loans and he never paid me back. He's hated me since I bought the lighthouse. Great-Grandpa's legacy to him was a series of books on how to be successful."

"That's why you thought he was behind the haunting."

Mac stared at Giulia, her eyes surrounded by dark circles. "How did you know?"

Giulia didn't reveal how she'd been ready to accuse Mac's best friend. Happy clients paid their bills faster. "Walter plus Lucy, to be precise. Lucy for all the hard work and the constant goad of her half-life over the boat shop."

That didn't seem to register on Mac's consciousness. "Lucy and Walter trying to kill me up on the gallery proves the haunting was phony, doesn't it? I mean, that means they've been behind everything." She closed her eyes but opened them right away. "I mean, it all means Solana's a fraud and a basket case. Right?"

Mac probably shouldn't be drinking wine on top of whatever the ER shot her up with, but Giulia wasn't about to preach teetotaling to someone who'd escaped death twice in two days. She put on her best reassurance face. "Solana is...enthusiastic. She's like those ghost hunting TV shows that crank up the sensitivity meters on their instruments so every click and creak sounds like contact from beyond the grave. The only person haunting Stone's Throw was Lucy and her puppet theater skills."

Mac deflated. "I'm so glad. Not that Lucy died like that, even though she wanted me to end up the same way. I'm glad there isn't really a Stone family ghost. I never liked horror movies."

Fifty-Two

The following Saturday the doorbell rang and a minute later Frank called up to Giulia, "Package for you. I signed for it."

"Be right there." Giulia checked the timer on her phone and came downstairs. An extra-large FedEx box lay on the kitchen table.

"Who's it from? Oh, Mac. We didn't leave anything there, did we?"

Frank handed her the kitchen scissors. "Not that I know of. Maybe she's giving us one of the gloomy paintings in the dining room."

Giulia hefted the box. "Too heavy for that. Maybe it's the evil antique clown doll."

"If it is, I vote we take it outside and burn it."

"Agreed." Giulia sawed open the end of the box and pulled out a thick wad of bubble wrap. "It's not the doll."

"I can't see what's inside. This is fun."

"It's a book on ghost hunting."

"It's an invitation to Solana's new séance gig."

"How about it's a check for our fee?" Giulia peeled two pieces of tape from one side of the puffy square.

Frank patted the table. "Come on, come on."

"For a detective, you sure don't like mysteries." She unrolled the bubble wrap a little slower.

"You are a tease, woman." He feinted a snatch at it.

She slid to the opposite end of the table. "Patience is a virtue...oh, all right." She flopped the dwindling package over and over until the last of the bubble wrap fell away.

"A tube of Earl Grey loose leaf tea?" Frank's voice changed from puzzled to disappointed.

"It's too heavy for that."

Giulia popped open the lid and poured a stack of gold coins into her hand. Her voice failed her.

"*Cait naofa,*" Frank said.

The coins spilled from Giulia's palm onto the bubble wrap. "Three—seven—ten—twelve. 'Holy cats' is right. What are these worth? She must have sent an explanation."

Frank took the empty cylinder from Giulia's hand. "Nothing else in here." He tried the lid. "Aha." He pried a folded piece of paper from the inside.

"'Dear Giulia and Frank,'" he read, "'I received your invoice and wrote a check for the total. When I realized you didn't include a line item for saving my life twice in one week I tore up the check. What you have here are twelve Liberty five-dollar coins from my great-great-great-grandfather's stash. They were all minted between 1877 and 1883. I haven't valued the entire collection, but my educated guess is these coins are each worth between,'" Frank's voice failed, but he shook it off and continued, "'between eighteen hundred and twenty-one hundred dollars.'"

Giulia gasped.

Frank continued, "'If you'll take the advice of an old woman who successfully expanded a hotel chain into the entire northeast, you'll get yourselves a safe deposit box and pretend these don't exist. Hard work will bring you success, but it's nice to know you have something to fall back on just in case. With my thanks, Mac.'"

Giulia said in a shaky voice, "Twenty-one thousand dollars at a minimum."

"*Cait naofa.*"

"We can't accept this."

"The hell we can't."

"Frank." Giulia made an effort of strength and looked away from the coins. "This is incredible."

"Mac's right. You saved her life twice. You saved her business. It's a generous and extravagant and perfectly correct gesture." He poured the coins through his hands. "Now I know why misers fondle their hoard."

Giulia's phone buzzed against her hip. She had no idea how long it had been buzzing. Without a word, she ran upstairs into the bathroom and straight to the sink. Her hand trembled the least bit as she picked up the home pregnancy test to see if the window showed one pink line or two.

Alice Loweecey

Baker of brownies and tormenter of characters, Alice Loweecey recently celebrated her thirtieth year outside the convent. She grew up watching Hammer horror films and Scooby-Doo mysteries, which explains a whole lot. When she's not creating trouble for Giulia Driscoll, she can be found growing her own vegetables (in summer) and cooking with them (the rest of the year).

In case you missed the 1st in the series

NUN TOO SOON
Alice Loweecey

A Giulia Driscoll Mystery (#1)

Giulia Driscoll has just taken on her first impossible client: The Silk
Tie Killer. He's hired Driscoll Investigations to prove his innocence
and they have only thirteen days to accomplish it. Talk about being
tried in the media. Everyone in town is sure Roger Fitch strangled
his girlfriend with one of his silk neckties. And then there's the local
TMZ wannabes stalking Giulia and her client for sleazy sound bites.

On top of all that, her assistant's first baby is due any second, her
scary smart admin still doesn't relate well to humans, and her
police detective husband insists her client is guilty. About this
marriage thing—it's unknown territory, but it sure beats ten years
of living with 150 nuns.

Giulia's ownership of Driscoll Investigations hasn't changed her
passion for justice from her convent years. But the more dirt she
digs up, the more she's worried her efforts will help a murderer
escape. As the client accuses DI of dragging its heels on purpose,
Giulia thinks The Silk Tie Killer might be choosing one of his ties
for her own neck.

Available at booksellers nationwide and online

Visit www.henerypress.com for details

Henery Press Mystery Books

And finally, before you go...
Here are a few other mysteries
you might enjoy:

THE DEEP END

Julie Mulhern

A Country Club Murders Mystery

Swimming into the lifeless body of her husband's mistress tends to ruin a woman's day, but becoming a murder suspect can ruin her whole life.

It's 1974 and Ellison Russell's life revolves around her daughter and her art. She's long since stopped caring about her cheating husband, Henry, and the women with whom he entertains himself. That is, until she becomes a suspect in Madeline Harper's death. The murder forces Ellison to confront her husband's proclivities and his crimes—kinky sex, petty cruelties and blackmail.

As the body count approaches par on the seventh hole, Ellison knows she has to catch a killer. But with an interfering mother, an adoring father, a teenage daughter, and a cadre of well-meaning friends demanding her attention, can Ellison find the killer before he finds her?

Available at booksellers nationwide and online

Visit www.henerypress.com for details

PILLOW STALK

Diane Vallere

A Madison Night Mystery (#1)

Interior Decorator Madison Night might look like a throwback to the sixties, but as business owner and landlord, she proves that independent women can have it all. But when a killer targets women dressed in her signature style—estate sale vintage to play up her resemblance to fave actress Doris Day—what makes her unique might make her dead.

The local detective connects the new crime to a twenty-year old cold case, and Madison's long-trusted contractor emerges as the leading suspect. As the body count piles up, Madison uncovers a Soviet spy, a campaign to destroy all Doris Day movies, and six minutes of film that will change her life forever.

Available at booksellers nationwide and online

Visit www.henerypress.com for details

FRONT PAGE FATALITY

LynDee Walker

A Headlines in High Heels Mystery (#1)

Crime reporter Nichelle Clarke's days can flip from macabre to comical with a beep of her police scanner. Then an ordinary accident story turns extraordinary when evidence goes missing, a prosecutor vanishes, and a sexy Mafia boss shows up with the headline tip of a lifetime.

As Nichelle gets closer to the truth, her story gets more dangerous. Armed with a notebook, a hunch, and her favorite stilettos, Nichelle races to splash these shady dealings across the front page before this deadline becomes her last.

Available at booksellers nationwide and online

Visit www.henerypress.com for details

FINDING SKY

Susan O'Brien

A Nicki Valentine Mystery

Suburban widow and P.I. in training Nicki Valentine can barely keep track of her two kids, never mind anyone else. But when her best friend's adoption plan is jeopardized by the young birth mother's disappearance, Nicki is persuaded to help. Nearly everyone else believes the teenager ran away, but Nicki trusts her BFF's judgment, and the feeling is mutual.

The case leads where few moms go (teen parties, gang shootings) and places they can't avoid (preschool parties, OB-GYNs' offices). Nicki has everything to lose and much to gain — including the attention of her unnervingly hot P.I. instructor. Thankfully, Nicki is armed with her pesky conscience, occasional babysitters, a fully stocked minivan, and nature's best defense system: women's intuition.

Available at booksellers nationwide and online

Visit www.henerypress.com for details

PRACTICAL SINS
FOR COLD CLIMATES
Shelley Costa

A Mystery

When Val Cameron, a Senior Editor with a New York publishing company, is sent to the Canadian Northwoods to sign a reclusive bestselling author to a contract, she soon discovers she is definitely out of her element. Val is convinced she can persuade the author of that blockbuster, The Nebula Covenant, to sign with her, but first she has to find him.

Aided by a float plane pilot whose wife was murdered two years ago in a case gone cold, Val's hunt for the recluse takes on new meaning: can she clear him of suspicion in that murder before she links her own professional fortunes to the publication of his new book?

When she finds herself thrown into a wilderness lake community where livelihoods collide, Val wonders whether the prospect of running into a bear might be the least of her problems.

Available at booksellers nationwide and online

Visit www.henerypress.com for details